A DRAGON'S QUEST

BOOK THREE OF THE REMEMBERED WAR

ROBERT VANE

Copyright © 2021

All rights reserved.

No part of this book may be reproduced in any form or by any electronic or mechanical means, including information storage and retrieval systems, without written permission from the author, except for the use of brief quotations in a book review.

Cover by ebooklaunch

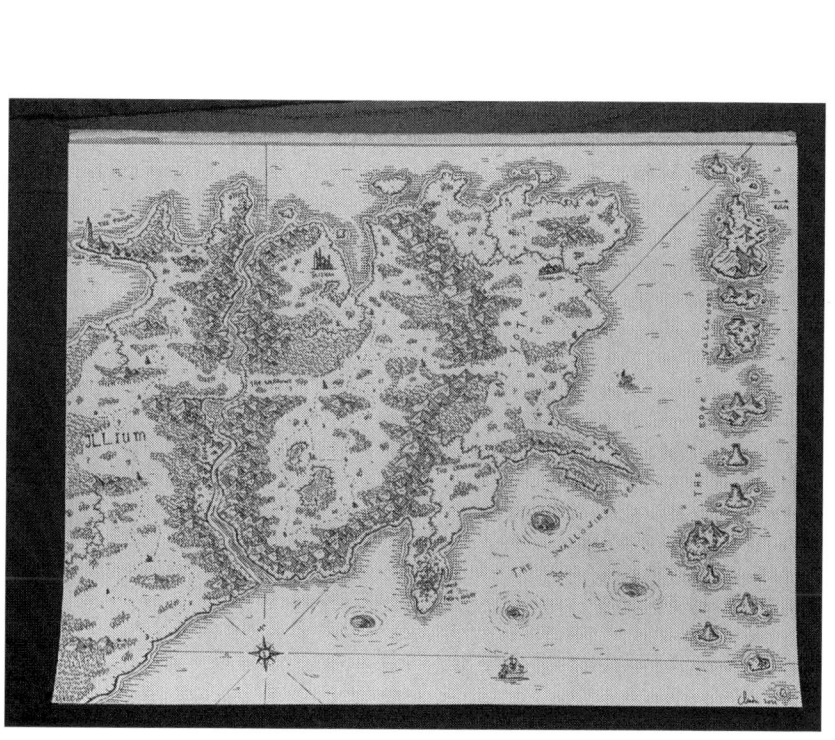

ONE

I killed the Skyking of Ni-Yota.

It was a quick death, and I'd done it at Aragor's behest. His killing had been an act of mercy—it had saved Aragor from losing himself, from becoming that which he had fought against. Thanks to me, Aragor, the self-proclaimed Skyking of Ni-Yota, would never succumb to the rust that had claimed the lands of Illium. Nor had I just casually decided to kill him. Before I had slain the king, I had tried to heal him. Unfortunately, my untrained power had not been equal to such a task. Even if I had understood the magic that my kind was apparently born to wield, I doubted I could have saved him from this particular doom. Whatever had infected him was far more than a mere wound, more than any plague. Death was Aragor's only escape from his fate, and he knew it. I did what had to be done. I hoped others understood this truth.

Beneath me lay a bloody mess.

The blood raptors that had ravaged the occupants of the great hall in aid of the traitorous dragon, Betal, seemed to recognize the death of their adversary. After Aragor's eyes shut, they halted their incessant attacks. The swarm swirled about the great hall, a wave of black twirling like a tornado. When Aragor's lifeforce departed, so did the birds, their black wings carrying them through the breach that Betal had made in the ceiling, their mission apparently complete. I watched the dark-winged vermin fly west, a pulsing cloud moving against the wind, back toward River Tayo and the hollowing horde beyond.

The great hall fell silent as the last of the raptors fled. Most of the humans had already fled through the ground-level exits. The stink from smoke fires that had been used (ineffectively) against the raptors still clogged the hall. The sudden quiet in the massive space had an unpleasant weight. With the immediate threat past, the magnitude of what had just happened settled upon me: the Protector of Ni-Yota was dead. Arrogant as he was, Aragor had been a fighter, the leader of millions. Yet I didn't think his death the worst of it. Betal had claimed the wizard Drasu had also fallen. Just days ago, I would've rejoiced at the news of the death of my mother's murderer, but now my emotions were far more complicated. I had come to understand that Drasu's magic had been all that held the hollowing horde at bay. Without him, an invasion was imminent. Or maybe it had already begun. The thought chilled me. I had gazed across the waste of the land across the Tayo River, a domain that had once been known as Illium, seeing nothing but rust and a hostile army of humans and other creatures more numerous than anything I could have imagined back in Rolm. And for all the dread the sprawling horde conjured, something worse was behind it. Something that had driven my mother into exile, sending her on a quest that had lasted until the day of her death.

In the wake of Aragor's death and the betrayal of one of their fellow dragons, I expected the terrible threat in Illium to be the immediate focus of the remaining dragons of Ni-Yota—the so-called Sworn. I was wrong. It happens.

Gia came at me before Aragor's dead body had cooled. The massive black storm of a dragon never liked me. He had been my sister's guardian. Perhaps that made him overly suspicious of me since I'd come to Ni-Yota to take her away. There was also the nearly fatal melee in which I'd fought against him alongside his mortal enemy, Elasu. We would never be friends, but I had hoped for some respite from the animosity. I got none.

Gia took only a cursory sniff at Aragor's corpse before pushing his giant head so close to my nostrils, I could smell the flesh of the blood raptor on his teeth. "Light Stealer," he named me with a growl.

I hated the label. It implied I was a thief. As if light could be taken. As if I possessed anything of Aragor's. As if I'd been in the wrong to do what I had done.

I didn't care what Gia thought about me, but my sister, Kiata, arrived next. She glided to the floor beside Aragor. The look of horror in her eyes as she stared at the bloody form of her hero, the late Skyking, made me dread what came next. Sure enough, her expression turned to horrific accusation when she gazed at me. Her gaze sent a pair of spears through my hearts.

"It was the only way," was all I managed as Kiata's eyes tore through me.

She turned away rather than continue to look at me. I had come to Ni-Yota for her, I'd battled Elasu for her, I'd tolerated Aragor so I wouldn't lose her, but I'd ended up making it all worse. I needed Kiata to understand why I did what I did. I turned my head toward Rinxia, the beautiful silver dragon who'd fought beside me, desperate for her assistance. She had heard Aragor's final words. I needed her to explain what had happened to Kiata. But Rinxia was already in the air, soaring into the gap in the roof, into the sky in pursuit of the blood raptors. I again faced Kiata.

"Sister, it was what he wanted. He knew what..."

I didn't get to finish, because she flew away, out of the hall. I intended to go after her. Not just because I desperately wanted to explain myself, but also because I was fearful. There might still be blood raptors lingering in the vicinity. Kiata was young and vulnerable. I didn't want her out there alone.

A deep voice rumbled, a sound so low only the largest of dragons could've made it. "You've done enough harm, Light Stealer. Leave her be."

The night-scaled monstrosity loomed over me, a void of darkness interrupted only by the bloody wounds made by the raptors he'd fought. I would've ignored him and flown off in pursuit of my sister, but he'd pinned my leg to the ground with his own massive claw. If I launched skyward, Gia would rip off my scales—if he wasn't bluffing. But staring at the giant mass of scales gave me the feeling that Gia wasn't the type to make idle threats. I would have to deal with him.

"Leave her," Gia intoned. "You bring only darkness with you, much as Elasu once did. The human taint is within you—your mind is unstable. Human avarice and emotion run through you. Kiata must be shown the Way of Dragons. You cannot help her with that. You should leave this place before you end up like the Pretender."

The human taint? Was that true? "Do not seek to blame me for the deeds of the traitor Betal. That dragon was one of your world, not mine. I'm not the cause of your ills." I showed my teeth.

"You may not mean to be an agent of the dark," Gia allowed. "Some cannot help it. Or perhaps your hearts are black inside from the human taint. The result is the same. An ill wind flies with you."

I snorted with contempt. "What ill wind?"

"Both the Pretender and Aragor are dead by your act, and both within the same moon. I call that an ill wind."

He had a point. "I'm not your enemy, but do not make it otherwise." I steeled my eyes, hoping to look convincing. Harlan would've called it a lame bluff, because the truth was, I had no desire to tangle with the massive dragon beside me, particularly in this place, with Aragor's corpse beside us.

"You killed the lord to whom I was sworn, yet you claim to not be my enemy?" He roared out an approximation of a human scoff.

My blood sizzled. I didn't want to explain myself to Gia, nor did I wish to fight. The battle had been quick and chaotic. Gia might not know all that had happened. "The poison in Betal had spread to

Aragor. He would've become a hollowing and he knew it. I did him a mercy."

I hoped that would end it. It didn't.

"Play no games with me, Light Stealer. I've no patience for spun tales. I do not deal in lies as did Elasu, nor do I have the vanity of Betal. I have dragon eyes, and with them I see clearly."

I had no idea what he was talking about. "Congratulations?"

Gia snarled, showing me his teeth. Blood raptor flesh. There were raptor bones in the cracks. "You mock, you kill, you lie. Now, it is time you fight."

The giant dragon pressed down even harder on my trapped claws, but that wasn't how Gia intended to hurt me. He merely didn't want me going anywhere as he brought his huge tail around. Thicker than two pairs of mated tree trunks, his tail came at me faster than anything that size had a right to move. I could've tried to rip my claws free, but I didn't think I'd have the time, even if I was willing to take the additional pain. I could've tried to duck under the blow, but that would've required me to lie almost flat on the ground at precisely the right moment, a position that would leave me terribly vulnerable to another attack. I wasn't sure if Gia intended to kill me or teach me some kind of lesson, but I wasn't willing to take the risk of leaving myself at his dubious mercy. I whipped my own tail to meet the onslaught, gritting my teeth in anticipation of the collision. I had no illusions about my strength being equal to that of Gia's.

Our ends collided with raw barbarity. Strength met strength. My bones trembled from the impact. I wasn't Gia's match in brute force, nor did I surrender from the contest. I parried his blow and kept my balance. My tail gave ground, but the danger of his attack had been blunted. Even as he pushed himself closer toward me, I waited for the next assault. Would he dare unleash his fire upon me? With Aragor gone, he had nothing to fear from any other dragon. There was no Protector of Ni-Yota now. If there had been a law against dragon killing dragon, there were none to enforce it.

Gia glared at me with contempt, but (I thought) not hate. I realized he was still contemplating how far he'd take this. Despite his claim to be a simple dragon who believed only his eyes, there was plenty of calculation in his amber stare. Thinking hard thoughts was probably new for Gia. I watched him carefully. Unfortunately, it seemed that Gia's final decision was to try to roast me. His jaw opened. I twisted my neck, intending to go for his throat and sink my teeth into his scales, even though I didn't want to do that. Enough dragons had died already on this ugly day.

Rinxia thought the same. My engagement with Gia had distracted me and I hadn't heard her return. "Hold your flame, Gia."

The black dragon was startled by her presence. He flared his nostrils, his eyes flicking away from me to track Rinxia's flight as she shot past him. She circled back, dancing through the air in a staggered approach toward her larger companion. Gia shut his mouth, tucking his teeth and flame away for another day. Relief pulsed through me. Rinxia set herself down beside me.

With the immediate crisis averted, I belatedly noticed another presence lingering behind a crashed chunk of stone: a human. He had skin far darker than any Mizu, despite its golden hue, and he carried a crossbow that wasn't his: the Farlighter smuggler, Harlan Dor. I also suspected his purpose here. His weapon would've been near useless against Gia's armor, but I couldn't help but be tickled by the gesture of preparing to defend me. For Harlan's sake, I was relieved he hadn't fired his weapon.

Gia removed his claw from me, backing up warily to a more comfortable distance. He looked at Rinxia, puzzled.

"You care nothing about the Protector's death, Rinxia?"

"Stop acting the fool, Gia," Rinxia snapped, sounding like an annoyed mother. "You know me better than that. There has been enough pain on this day to last a lifetime; do not add stupidity to the sad tally. We are the chosen of Haven. We carry a burden and must be better than other creatures."

If I had said that, Gia probably would've bathed me in fire. To Rinxia, he merely blew some snot from his huge nostrils. "You believe the outlander's fibs about Aragor being tainted?"

Something in Rinxia shifted. Her neck slumped with sadness. "I saw it, Gia." The silver dragon growled with displeasure. "Somehow, Betal succumbed to darkness. He brought it into our midst. It spread to Aragor from a bite. Just as we were warned…it spreads. Somehow, an infected dragon is even worse than the blood raptors."

Gia's eyes turned distant and dark. He waited several long moments before speaking again. "There was always a darkness to Betal's ambition. Such desire was not of the Way. Finally, it consumed him."

Rinxia's tail swept the ground. "Worse even than that. If the blood raptors are here, it means the barrier at the River Tayo no longer holds. It means that Drasu is truly dead, or gravely wounded. We must prepare to meet the hollowing horde when they come. That is what is most important."

Gia eyed me warily before offering a reluctant grunt. "The empty ones will come, but I do not fear them. They walk on legs; they carry blades or spears. They shall be stopped. They shall be killed, like all enemies of Ni-Yota." Gia once again fixed his distrusting eyes upon me. The anger in him flashed like the sun at its apex. "And you…I know you scheme for some purpose of your own, even if I do not know yet what it is. You claim you are not responsible for the deaths of both Elasu and Aragor, yet you killed both of them, Light Stealer. That is no coincidence."

Gia unleashed his words with as much force as he did his fire. I recognized his angry determination just as I recognized his stupidity. I also knew my words wouldn't sway him, but I tried anyway. "I scheme nothing. Drasu stole my sister. I came to get her. I trust you would have done the same."

Gia didn't hear me. He'd already made up his mind. "Know this: you shall never take Aragor's place."

My eyes bulged. I didn't understand, at first. I should've rebuked him immediately, but I was too shocked for coherent words. Perhaps I had misheard. Gia's Avian was different than what was spoken in Rolm. But the black dragon spoke again when I remained silent, this time even more plainly.

"You shall never be Skyking of Ni-Yota."

TWO

The Skyking of Ni-Yota.

Gia was worried I wanted to rule Ni-Yota. I hadn't seen that coming. I had no response ready. My mind reeled at the insanity of the accusation. Gia may have misinterpreted my silence as a challenge. Or perhaps his mind had come to a place where nothing I said would make any difference. I didn't get a chance to discuss the matter with him.

Gia turned from me, toward his fallen Skyking. He lowered his neck, examining the dead dragon, sniffing. Did he suspect that Aragor still lived? I would've assured him that wasn't the case. When I kill someone, I'm thorough. Just ask Brindisi. I had dumped the remains of my former ryder out through my bowels over the sea with all the dignity that the slaver deserved. Aragor was just as dead as Brindisi, although I presumed his body would be treated with more dignity (on the other hand, few humans in Rolm have become dragon crap, so such exclusivity could be seen as an honor).

In the midst of all this, Harlan edged ever closer to the collection of dragons gathered around Aragor. I was still shocked by Gia's accusations, so I didn't immediately comprehend what the crazy human had in mind. Gia kept sniffing, studying Aragor's body, while Harlan drew nearer. It was only a matter of time before Gia noticed. In his current mood, the giant dragon might decide to end Harlan with a flick of his tail if Gia thought the human intended disrespect. I didn't really want Harlan to end up as a bloody stain on the ground.

I opened my mouth to ask the smuggler what he was doing but held my words at the last moment as the answer belatedly came to me: the necklace. The so-called Torlich of Haven that Aragor wore. I realized that Gia wasn't looking for signs of life in the fallen king. He wanted the Torlich. Aragor had mentioned that he had decided to wear it as a symbol. Perhaps Gia thought that made the Torlich the equivalent of King Mendakas' crown, but for Protectors. Maybe it had other uses as well—it was apparently made from aurathorn flowers. My mother had used those to blunt the slave magic of the Sculptors of Rolm, so it was clearly powerful. Harlan wanted it as well. He'd told me he'd traveled the world in search of the strange vine. It was his quest, the way back to his wife, and I suspected much more. Indeed, the more I thought about it, the more certain I became that the Torlich was more than just a symbol. Harlan wasn't the type for a fool's errand. Despite his obvious disadvantages in confronting Gia, I didn't expect that Harlan would easily be denied, either. I quickly became concerned the smuggler would do something foolish. He was no match for Gia.

The giant dragon found what he was looking for before Harlan arrived. Gia lifted the Torlich with a single digit of his foreleg, his head tilting as he examined it. It looked like a large, wilted vine to me. Gia lifted the artifact still higher, at an angle that would allow him to slide it onto his neck, to wear it as the last Skyking had. Harlan's fingers twitched on the crossbow at his side. Surely he wouldn't be so foolish as to match himself against Gia with only a toothpick shooter as a weapon. I'd be forced to whisk my foolish companion to safety if he provoked a fight. I readied myself to fly, but Rinxia was even faster than me, and she had sharper eyes.

The silver dragon jumped toward Gia like a pouncing cat. But she didn't move to save Harlan as I thought. Instead, a tight stream of fire shot from her mouth. The sudden violence of her attack took me completely by surprise, as it did Gia and Harlan. Rinxia aimed true. Gia released a terrible roar of anguished rage as the Torlich disappeared, turning to ash before his eyes as Rinxia's fire consumed it. I was shocked. Why had she destroyed the Torlich?

The silver dragon had aimed well, but even her precise line of flame inevitably caught part of Gia's claws, since she'd incinerated the necklace he held. The massive dragon came about, facing me, his eyes pulsing furiously. Never had I been so certain that another dragon intended to kill me. He obviously assumed I had done the deed as part of my nefarious plot to be Protector of Ni-Yota. I was really having a crappy day.

Gia noticed Rinxia's presence belatedly, even though she was closer, her mouth open. Somewhere in his thick skull, Gia must've remembered I wasn't a fire breather. Confusion mixed with anger in Gia's gaze. I understood how he felt. He didn't expect a dragon he'd known for all his life to betray him suddenly and without apparent reason. Still, apparently Gia wasn't one for pondering mysteries. He loosed a wave of fire at Rinxia. She saw it and leapt to her left. Gia's angry breath caught the end of her tail as she took flight, but nothing else.

"Rinxia!" He called out her name as a curse, the roar shaking the walls of the massive chamber.

She twisted in the air, bringing herself to a near stop, beating her wings to keep herself in place so that she might face him. She was no fool; Rinxia kept a healthy distance in case she needed to escape again. "Let go of your anger, brother." Her voice was composed. "The taint was on the flowers, spread by Aragor's and Betal's blood. I could smell it. To hold the Torlich was to embrace the fate even worse than death—that which Aragor feared far more than even the void."

Gia unleashed a storm of roared rage anyway. If the din was a measure of a dragon's greatness, I'd have been licking Gia's claws after that roar. It was the cry of lost dreams, of betrayal, of having a roasted pig snatched from your mouth. Even worse than that. But he held his fire in check. Gia thrashed his head about in frustrated impotence. He looked ridiculous.

Eventually, he regained control of his faculties. His eyes finally settled on the flaking ash that had once been the Torlich. Only a few twisted hulks of silvery metal remained—Rinxia's fire burned hot. Harlan was at the pyre, on his knees before the ruin that had been his quest for untold years. He wore a look of anguish that was unfamiliar on his face. But Gia was my more immediate problem.

The angry dragon's gaze swung to me, then back to Rinxia. "Are you with him—the Light Stealer—in this? Do you plot with him?" The dragon's eyes glinted with accusation. "What has he promised you?"

Rinxia kept her voice steady, hard. "Your words are rot on the wind to me, my brother. Remember me and remember yourself. Aragor lies dead. His blood has not yet cooled, and already the madness to take his place consumes you. A true Protector thinks first of the people. An ancient trinket of vine and metal means nothing."

Gia yanked back his neck like a scolded hatchling. Heavy breaths escaped his nostrils. A moment of uneasy calm stretched ever longer. Finally, Gia unfurled his wings, his hot eyes finding mine. "Remember your place isn't here, Light Stealer. You are no Protector. You never will be."

Gia flew off after making his declaration, the power of his wings lifting broken shards of glass into the air. He hadn't lingered long enough for me to tell him we finally agreed on something: I didn't want to be Protector or Skyking or whatever else that involved my being responsible for this land that wasn't my own. I'd come here for my sister. I intended to leave with her. The rest had just...happened. I wanted nothing else to do with Ni-Yota if I could help it. This encounter merely reinforced my certainty on that.

Gia left Rinxia, Harlan, and I in the ruined wreck of the hall.

Blood decorated the seats where the raptors had harried the human occupants of Aragor's court. Two dead dragons lay among the devastation. A morbid sight. Harlan still knelt before Aragor's corpse, his face hidden from me. Rinxia landed softly beside me, a question in her eyes as I continued to stare at the back of my friend. I didn't know what to say to him—he'd traversed the world for that strange vine. I, too, needed it. I didn't know precisely what he'd sacrificed, only that it had been substantial. But, as a former slave, I did understand about being in the darkness. When I finally found some words, they came out in a voice that wasn't quite my own.

"Sometimes you are so lost you do not even remember there was a destination. If you endure, you may still find the way."

Harlan slowly turned to look at me, as if wary that someone spoke to him. Rinxia too twisted her neck to examine me. I found their surprise at my advice mildly insulting.

Harlan's eyes still hinted at the pain he felt, but already he was hiding most of it. He summoned his crooked smirk, although it wasn't quite the same. "For a child of the sea, the voyage never ends."

"Was that truly the last of the aurathorn?" I asked Rinxia.

"As far as I know, the Torlich was forged from the last that remained, but even that was just rumor, a story told by Aragor. The Skyking was…at times, he succumbed to his darker instincts. Insecurity was one, fear that he lost the favor of Haven. At such times, he would produce items of supposed significance, such as the Torlich. It seemed to calm him, so we were happy enough not to question the tales."

"So, it might not even have been aurathorn at all that burned up?" Harlan asked.

Rinxia seemed annoyed at the question—or perhaps at being questioned by Harlan. "The line of the Keepers of the Radiance—Bayloo's mother's blood—would've known better than I."

My mother. She had gone to Rolm to find the aurathorn, to find a way to use it. Bethy Rann had told me there was no more on Maricopa, but it had to be somewhere on the other side of the Wall of Fire. I was proof of that.

"Why do you both care so much?" Rinxia asked.

Harlan kept his mouth firmly shut for once, but I had no such reticence. "My mother used it to break the runes of control that held me as a slave for so many years."

"The vine?" Rinxia asked with surprise dancing in her eyes. "The histories say it could be dangerous to us...a weapon. But I've never heard of it being used to break a rune of control. Those bonds are supposedly unbreakable, our enslaved kin lost forever, or so the magi claim. Although, I am not a creature of magic, of course." Almost as an afterthought, she asked, "Where did your mother obtain it?"

I wanted to tell her, but I could feel Harlan's stare on me. It wasn't time to share speculations and false hopes. I merely said, truthfully, "I do not know. I hope to find out."

"The world is large, your wings are strong," Rinxia assured me, her eyes glowing with approval. "If we can free our brothers and sisters, I will help you find what you seek."

For some reason, I felt the urge to twirl and sing, although I knew it wasn't the time. Aragor's corpse was starting to stink.

Harlan's expression lightened. "Well, you dragons are certainly exciting company." He pulled himself to his feet. "Rinxia, I'm surprised to hear that Bayloo is a contender for the captain spot, given he's a newcomer to these parts."

"In Ni-Yota, such a thing isn't so outlandish: the Protector is dead. Aragor had no offspring, and his closest relation in blood was Betal the traitor. Despite the exile of his mother, Bayloo's own bloodline is ancient—he is of the ember dragons and therefore a descendant of Shihan of the Sky. He would have a legitimate claim."

I could do little more than gape. I'd heard the words, but didn't really believe them. *A slave dragon as ruler of Ni-Yota?* After a few moments, I realized that Rinxia and Harlan were both staring at me expectantly.

"Gia is crazed, but more importantly, he doesn't know me at all. I don't want to be Skyking or any other king."

Rinxia studied me before dipping her head ever so slightly. "Someone must be Protector. Without a dragon chosen with the favor of Haven, Ni-Yota will be adrift while the threats to our people are greater than ever before."

"I am supposed to care for the humans of this place?" It came out worse than I intended. This was Rinxia's home.

The silver dragon didn't take obvious offense at my words. "You speak gruff, but your hearts are softer. This human...an Islander, you seem to like him. You allow him to ride you." She inclined her head toward Harlan. "You fought bravely today, Harlan Dor, risking your own life to help the Skyking. Bayloo, you did even more, risking yourself for us. Your actions betray you. I think you have within you the essence of a Protector. This may be your Way."

I snorted my displeasure at this notion. "You should take up this so-called honor of service, this burden to Haven, Rinxia. You are from here, you clearly care for this land. If a dragon must rule this place, then it should be you."

"That is not my Way." She sounded rather sanguine about it. "I am not a leader. I lack the vision."

Harlan asked the question I had in my own mind. "I've known many a sailor who, a few cups into their drink, screamed with certainty that they knew they were fated for riches, when the only true certainty was a splitting headache come the next morning. Perhaps dragons are different. You speak of the Way, as if it is your destiny, your fate. How is it that you know that being Protector is not your Way, mighty Rinxia?"

Rinxia raised her chin. "The Light of Haven has shown it to me."

I'd really liked Rinxia before that moment. I tried to keep my skepticism from my voice. "What did they show you?"

"I've seen the coming of a new Cataclysm. If it is to be turned aside, we all must play our roles. My role is not as ruler of Ni-Yota. More than this, I will not say, so end your questions." A bit more gently, she added, "Besides, although I could fly circles around Gia, I cannot best him in battle. He is too strong, and my fire would not be enough against his armor."

I was confused. "Why do you need to fight Gia?"

"I would've thought that obvious." Rinxia stared at me. "He intends to be Protector. If any dragon wishes to challenge that, there must be a Judgment—a battle to the death."

I choked as if I had a chicken foot stuck in my throat. "Oh, definitely don't want to be Protector."

"Do you fear him?" She sounded surprised. My chest might've puffed a bit.

"It isn't a question of fear. I can handle Gia. But it seems a bit foolish to risk my life in battle for something I don't want."

Rinxia's eyes darkened. "I respect Gia. His hearts beat with the spirit of Light. But he will make a poor Protector. Even worse than Aragor. For while his intentions are truer than the late Skyking, he sees only that which is in front of him. A Protector must be more, see more." I pretended not to notice her invitation.

Harlan cleared his throat. "The Protector must always be a dragon, then?"

Rinxia's eyes glowed with amusement, though she kept her voice serious. "There is no law against it, but no human has ever made a claim. And they would fare poorly in the Judgment against the likes of Gia, I think."

Harlan tapped the tips of his fingers together. "I've been to many lands. Ni-Yota will not be the first to be graced with an imperfect ruler."

Rinxia tilted her head as she regarded Harlan. I was impressed at the courtesy she showed him. Gia never would've done that. He judged everyone based on physical strength. "You speak true, Harlan Dor. Despite the favor of Haven, it seems that dragons are no more perfect than humans. But at no other time since the Cataclysm has the land faced a threat such as we now have here. At such times, leadership is needed."

Rinxia seemed about to speak to me once again, but a high-pitched whistling interrupted. It was an unfamiliar sound—something reminiscent of the music of a hummingbird's wings, but far sharper and less pleasant. The noise was followed by another and another. I counted at least a dozen.

Rinxia was in the air a moment before me. We flew together. Once again, I readied myself for battle.

THREE

The strange noise wasn't a threat.

It was just some birds—not blood raptors. I could barely see them at first. I used the unusual sounds they made—a subtle whine of air channeled through their stiff wings—to hunt the incoming fliers. I adjusted my course toward the noise, but even with the birds' rattling to guide me, they weren't easy to spot. I almost smashed into one of the mysterious flying objects because I could practically see right through them.

When I finally got a clear look at one of the incoming birds, I found them bizarre, even by the standards of birds. They flew like no other creature I'd ever encountered. The so-called birds were slightly bigger than a sparrow, but with the wingspan of a hawk. Their wings flapped with unnatural stiffness, more like the ingenious crafting of a magnificent blacksmith than fleshy beings infused with true life. Yet the strange birds did indeed fly, their wings locked into place as they glided toward the palace. These had to be the infamous glasswings—the magically-created messenger birds of Ni-Yota. I counted four in all. They arrived from the west, where the hollowings massed. That so many birds had been sent could only mean they carried ill tidings.

Rinxia followed the glasswing flock as they approached the palace, slowing her pace to match theirs. I did the same. We were giants hovering above flies. The strange birds made a circuit around the tallest of the spires that rose from the great lake—the massive tower with a seemingly ever-burning flame at its top—before streaming into a smaller tower wholly engulfed by the larger structure's shadow. A walking bridge connected the two constructions. I judged the smaller tower to be the least grand of the various spires of the Protector's water-and-tower-centric palace, but its windows were the largest.

Rinxia and I followed the glasswings into a large circular chamber that occupied the top portion of the tower. Like the rest of the palace's structures, the room we entered had been appropriately sized for dragons, although the tables and chairs inside were clearly for human use (or a brief game of stomp-the-wood for dragons).

The tower's interior walls were lined with doorless compartments, each with a single perch. Several dozen of these tiny cubicles held more of the glass-like birds. The creatures held still even as Rinxia and I entered, as if they were glass statues.

At the chamber's center was a tree carved from pink granite, its two dozen or so limbs devoid of leaves or life, except for the newly arrived glasswings that had landed atop them. Like the other strange birds inside the tower, the new arrivals made no sound or movement except for a soft whistle, which they chirped out at a regular interval of once per ten beats of my hearts. The synchronized noise quickly got annoying. There were also two humans shuffling around in azure robes, one with a gray beard and another boyish figure with a face so plump and pale I suspected he might have spent the entirety of his short life within this tower, doing nothing but eating and tending glass birds.

The younger human jumped when Rinxia and I appeared suddenly in his workspace, his eyes wide. The elder barely looked up. He was focused on the stone tree and its newly-arrived occupants.

Annoyed at being ignored by the older human, I gave a meaningful snort. The man looked up enough to raise a bushy eyebrow at me. "Biggest glasswing I ever saw," he mumbled to himself.

I supposed he meant me. I further supposed his words passed for humor among humans.

After the old human had fussed with a couple of the glass birds, he fixed an eye on the dragon beside me. "Nice to see you, Rinxia. It has been a while. Not sure I know your companion."

"You may call me Bayloo," I answered for her.

"Interesting name. Interesting accent."

Rinxia gazed at the newly-arrived glasswing flock. "Master Haxi, we have come to hear the tidings of the messengers."

The human, Haxi, positioned himself behind one of the translucent birds. "It seems someone in the west has something important to say." With a fleet swipe of his hand, the old man snatched the glasswing. Bird in hand, he carried it over to a burning brazier a few steps away. The younger human hurried over to add a few stones to the flame, which turned a shade of blue, then handed Master Haxi a pair of metal tongs which the older man used to hold the glasswing over the fire.

"You need to torture it to get it to speak?" I wondered.

Haxi didn't look at me. He was too busy roasting the glass bird. "They don't feel pain, but they need to know when it's time to release their message and complete their purpose. Now, be quiet or you'll miss it."

My eyes darkened. I preferred the slobbering deference of Elasu's human servants to the scolding pretensions of the ones in Trishan.

When the glasswing's body darkened to a smoky gray, Haxi pulled it from the fire, holding the glowing tongs and its captive before us. Remarkably, the bird spoke, its voice unmistakably human.

"*Great Protector, I must report that mighty Drasu is dead. The hollowing horde now seeks to cross the river. All reserves have been committed but we cannot hold the bank for much longer. Come* *quickly or all is lost. Reported on the 18th Day in Cycle of the Monkey by Avix, Lord-Knight of the Edge Legion."*

The speaker's words were controlled and authoritative, but even in the mimicked sound repeated by the glasswing, I thought I heard suppressed panic. At the message's conclusion, the captive glasswing emitted a brief cry, a last gasp of its phantom breath, then shattered into a hundred pieces, its remains falling onto the floor like a shattered window. The old master barely noticed the mess. "Do see to that, Kix." He shuffled over to snatch another bird. Were these things alive or not?

Rinxia looked at me, her eyes flooded with concern. "They will all carry the same tidings. The hollowings come. Lord Avix is perhaps the most experienced human commander in all of Ni-Yota, the victor of dozens of battles against the horde. If he says the river cannot be held, we had best heed his warnings and expect an invasion."

I noticed that Rinxia said "we." She assumed I would be part of this war. If it had been anyone but Rinxia speaking to me, I would've dissuaded her of the notion immediately. Did I really want to fight the countless hollowings, their beasts, and their blood raptors? Or would I rather find a naïve, juicy pig to eat? It shouldn't have been a difficult choice. Yet, within me was turmoil. I already knew Kiata would want me to stay, to help. That seemed to be what my mother had intended as well. But what did I want?

Rinxia sensed my hesitation, if not my thoughts. "Bayloo, there is little time for us to act."

"Based on that message, I suppose that is correct," I said carefully. "Does this mean you intend to fly off to the west to start burning these hollowings?"

"Without Aragor, there is no one to command." Rinxia's tail twitched about as she thought. "We must speak with Gia as well."

"He doesn't seem like he wants to chat with me."

Rinxia considered this before craning her neck so her eyes were level with the old human. "Master Haxi, you must carry this message to Gia without delay. Tell him...tell him a council meeting shall convene in the Highflame tower without delay. Gather the rest of the late Protector's council as well. They are all to attend."

Master Haxi grunted, more interested in the glasswings than Rinxia. "You heard her, Kix. Get moving." With a flick of his head, he sent his assistant scurrying off.

I watched the pale human waddle out. He reminded me of a featherless duck. I had my doubts about how quickly Rinxia's message would arrive. "How long will it take this council to gather, assuming the little man does his duty?"

"It will take the humans time to find Gia and the others." She craned her neck so she could see the sky. "When the sun is at its apex, we will meet in the Highflame tower. I'm sure you've noticed the fire. It's the highest of the palace towers, the dwelling of the Protector." She brought her head closer to mine. "You will attend as well, won't you?"

Oh. Putting me on the spot. I didn't really want to see Gia again, but Rinxia's gaze was such that I knew I was going to end up at the meeting one way or another. Best to be noble about it.

"Of course. It's just …" I hesitated.

"You worry about Gia? He will have calmed himself by the time we meet. He knows Lord Avix well, and will understand the importance of the message's warning." She sounded confident.

"I'm not worried about Gia. It's just that I haven't eaten …"

Rinxia's gaze darkened.

"If there is to be fighting, you understand, I must have my strength."

Rinxia flew out of the tower without another word. I found Master Haxi staring at me after she'd departed.

"What?" I asked.

The old human shrugged and grabbed another glasswing. Looking at the bird, he mumbled something that sounded like, "Not the brightest of your kind, are you?"

I decided he was speaking to the glasswing. Probably.

I left Haxi in his tower with his glass birds. I flew back to the hall to seek out Harlan. I hoped the human would have some ideas about how to get us out of here, enticing my sister to come with us.

As I hoped, he still lingered in the Hall of Glass. A few other humans had returned. The Mizu attended to the corpses of Betal and Aragor as Harlan watched silently from a distance. I told him of the message that came from the west, of the hollowing horde and the confirmed death of Drasu.

"Those creatures, the hollowings, as they call them...and the taint...there is lore remembered by my people, as well. You should hear Rinxia's words and Gia's as well, before you make a decision. You should go to their council."

I growled with annoyance. "Aragor is dead. Perhaps now Kiata can be persuaded to leave this place. You seem rather skilled at the art of talking."

Harlan paid me no mind. "You underestimate your sister. She's like a young landling aching for her first voyage. I've felt the passion of her conviction in the few times I've met her."

"She is so young," I protested. "If she were human, she'd be a helpless babe."

"Aye, but she's a dragon, last I saw. And, dragon or human, in the young is the certainty that comes with ignorance. This is her home. Everything she has been told all her life has been about protecting it. The roots of her beliefs are already deep. I think you will find it hard to persuade Kiata to abandon this place, even with Aragor dead. Nor will she want to abandon Gia, who followed her around like a huge shadow throughout her short life. You had best face that, or you'll lose her."

I considered Harlan's unhappy theory with a snarl. The Sculptors of Rolm always stole hatchlings young—and that probably had a lot to do with the development of the mind as well as the hardening of scales. I wondered if it was something even more than that—something unique to dragons, something related to the so-called Way. Kiata already seemed set on a path, as were all the other dragons of

Ni-Yota. Only I was different; only I seemed confused about my mission in this life. My mother had said the Way wasn't for me. I had been a slave. That could be the explanation for my otherness. But it also meant I wouldn't be able to take Kiata away from the danger she faced here.

I gave a petulant growl. "I will go to their council." Harlan nodded happily. His pleasure at persuading me irked. "Don't be so satisfied. I'm not going to save them from the hollowing horde. I may not know my true Way as some of the other dragons here, but I've seen enough battles to know I don't want to fight that army."

Harlan smirked. "Let me tell you a story about a little girl who thought she would get what she wanted when she grew up. She was a princess, you see ..."

I unfurled my wings, flying to the sanctuary of the sky.

FOUR

At least there was lunch.

It wasn't pig. I wondered if Rinxia had arranged for my favorite animal to be excluded to spite me. That seemed petty. I'd gone out of my way to be kind to Rinxia, but I hadn't gone along with what she apparently wanted—for me to put myself forward to be Protector of Ni-Yota. I was still shocked she would consider it. I barely knew this land, and she barely knew me. The dark voice in my head reminded me that perhaps Rinxia simply didn't have anyone else to support for the position. If Rinxia actually thought there was some divine reason she shouldn't be Protector, that left Gia and me as potential candidates. Urging me to take the role didn't seem like such a tough choice when I looked at it that way. Still, no matter how much I liked Rinxia, I wasn't going to step into the mess that had gotten Aragor killed.

When the servant laid out massive trays piled high with chicken feet, any doubts were dispelled—this had to be Rinxia's work. Feet, feet, and more feet. What had the cooks done with the rest of the birds after they removed these small appendages? I glared at Rinxia as she devoured dozens of chicken ends, slurping and nearly purring with delight. In addition to Rinxia, Gia, and Kiata, there were four other humans joining in the so-called council feast, as well as Harlan. They actually seemed to be enjoying themselves as my stomach rumbled. Even Gia ate. The giant dragon hadn't spoken to me, but he hadn't attacked me either, so that was something.

"You really should try these, Bayloo," Rinxia said between bites. "They are a delicacy. The flesh helps smooth our scales and adds shine."

"I'd rather chew upon the stone of this tower."

Rinxia laughed with her eyes. Even mighty Gia seemed amused, which soured my mood further. Rinxia signaled with a foreclaw and another wave of dishes appeared. Finally, she showed me some mercy. Fresh lake fish arrived on long ceramic platters, the fillets prepared in a tangy sauce of citrus. Not bad at all.

The other attendees found morbid discussions of Ni-Yota politics more interesting than the food, but that arrangement suited me. I got extra fish while they jabbered. Only Harlan was uncharacteristically quiet. He didn't eat either. He just watched.

The late Skyking's council chamber occupied the lower levels of his impossible high tower. The room's dimensions were equal to the entirety of the tower, forming a great circular chamber filled with cushioned areas for dragons and uncomfortable-looking high-backed chairs for humans. A rather ingenious multi-level table dominated the center of the room, allowing both dragons and humans to sit around a common surface. The raised dais of the Protector remained empty, although Gia had claimed the spot nearest on the right. Rinxia had left the space to the left empty, but I'd chosen the far side of the chamber to enjoy my meal rather than fall into her trap. Gia seemed pleased with the seating, if not the company. There was plenty of extra space in the chamber. Too many dead dragons; too many dead humans too, it seemed.

Kiata sat beside Gia, which annoyed me. The opposite portion of the room held a total of five humans, four of whom I didn't know. Harlan was the fifth. Rinxia introduced each of the bipeds to me, but I was so annoyed by the chicken feet I didn't pay very close attention to their names (none of them were named pork or pig, I was sure of that). When it came time to focus on non-food matters, I decided to call the male humans Shorty, Doughy, and Angry. Doughy and Angry had thick necklaces with fist-sized medallions that signified their titles of knight-lords, much like the man Avix who'd sent the glasswing messages, but Doughy and Angry were apparently responsible for different Mizu armies. The other human male—Shorty—had a name (which I'd also forgotten), but no additional title. He wore a simple tunic of gray, and had let his flaxen hair grow long, like a female, but had a stubble-covered chin and a wide face unlike any of the others I'd seen in Ni-Yota—I guessed he was not Mizu, but from one of their conquered territories. The lone human woman made the strongest impression, though. She possessed an air of power that drew my attention away from the lake fish that was on the table. She was burly, with a hairless head, and wore a robe in the style of the wizards like Drasu. Rinxia named her Legao. She was of the Conclave of Magi.

Harlan kept a wary eye on the woman as well. She hadn't spoken yet—like Harlan, she seemed inclined to listen for the moment. But this Legao had presence in the way an inferno mountain had presence even when sitting quietly. I got the impression she was dangerous.

Harlan sat closest to me of the humans, in a chair he'd dragged over from the other side of the room. He hadn't been invited to the council, of course, but I'd brought him anyway. Since he arrived on my back, there wasn't much of an opportunity for objection. Of the gathered humans and dragons, only Angry had made a bit of a fuss, but everyone ignored him. Even Gia didn't seem to care, although I caught him exchanging glances with Rinxia.

Angry did the most talking at first. After complaining about Harlan—a foreigner and an Islander—being present at this august council, Angry glided smoothly into his next grievance. Something to do with supply wagons. The others ignored that complaint as well. Finally, the discussion turned more serious.

"We must march now if a substantial army is to arrive in time to make a difference at the river." It was Doughy talking. His chin swayed a bit off center when he spoke. I found myself staring at him. He had a piece of fish stuck in the corner of his mouth, but I quickly decided it was too little to bother with.

Angry's red face became hotter. "We shouldn't even contemplate withdrawing our forces from Hundra Pass. Elasu's death is fresh and the east is far from pacified."

Doughy scoffed at that. "The eastern lords will walk to Trishan on their knees without Elasu to stiffen their backs."

The human I named Shorty raised one end of his left brow at Doughy's pronouncement, but somehow that mere motion silenced the other humans, drawing their attention to him. He didn't speak, though. Not until Angry prompted him: "You have something to add, Master Jinu?"

Shorty—Jinu was his proper name, apparently—turned his head, a motion that revealed the longest ears I'd ever seen on a human. He looked like an alarmed rabbit. Fascinated, I extended my neck closer to examine the strange things. I expected to find a lot of hair growing on them, given Jinu's prominence as a member of the council, but the great ears were bare. He glared at me.

"I am not from Ni-Yota," Jinu told me, answering a question I had not asked. "My people were the Kahali of Illium, but the Protectors of Ni-Yota were good enough to take us in. It was a custom of our people to attach weights to the bottom of the earlobes of certain children to stretch them, as large ears were thought to denote wisdom."

"Humans can enlarge their ears?" I asked. "Why do you all not do that? You would hear so much better."

Jinu cleared his throat and turned his attention back to the other humans without answering. "I had word this morning from Lord Viza that he lost an entire mounted company as they made their way toward Sothxia. He suspects the tigris are responsible." Jinu glanced toward the empty dais before stopping himself. He spoke toward Gia instead. "We must not underestimate the danger to the east."

Angry seized on this, also addressing Gia. "Let us heed the words of Jinu's spies. In any case, it is folly to weaken ourselves by trying to march men for weeks to join a battle that will be over before they even begin their journey."

"Jinu's spies always seem to say whatever he wants them to say," Doughy countered. "Aragor liked to hear what he wanted to hear. But now ..."

The tip of Jinu's tongue licked his top lip, a gesture that reminded me of a serpent. "If you have an accusation to make, Lord Hera, then do make it. Yes, do."

Lord Hera's mouth opened, even as his eyes danced around the room. No one met his gaze. His lips trembled, then he shut his mouth.

"Yes, I see," Jinu said with satisfaction. "As I was saying, the tigris remain a significant threat. Elasu may be dead, but so is Aragor. The eastern lords bide their time to await the new Protector." I kept my eyes on the fish bones and not Rinxia.

"You are not a soldier, Jinu," Lord Hera declared, finding his voice again. "You are not even Mizu. Perhaps you do not care about the loss of Gaminer, or even Trishan. But I do. We need more troops at the Tayo River to hold back hollowings."

Angry replied to this. "Even cavalry will take too long." Doughy looked hopefully at Gia. "Unless the soldiers can be moved by air."

Gia shifted his giant bulk, brushing the table enough to move it. "Even if every dragon here loaded themselves to capacity and flew till they dropped from the sky, we could not carry enough soldiers to the Tayo River to make a difference."

Angry nodded and his face lightened. "Well spoken, mighty Gia. Even a thousand men won't be enough if the hollowings bring those damn blood raptors. Swords are little use against behemoths. I was at the river the last time we tried to go on the offensive two years ago, fighting alongside my men. We lost a thousand soldiers and a hundred horses just to keep two of the huge...things at bay until Aragor and you arrived."

Gia grunted. "I have not forgotten the battle. The beasts' hides resist fire. Worthy adversaries, I must admit."

"Then we dragons must go and rout this horde, drive them away from the river." It was Kiata who spoke, her voice sounding ridiculously innocent and tiny, at least to me.

Gia looked at her, his eyes pleased but amused. Like a doting parent. Something unpleasant turned in my stomach, and it wasn't the fish (probably). "Yes, brave Kiata, it must be dragons who will take this burden. You need not worry yourself, though. I shall go with Rinxia. We cannot risk losing you." Slowly, reluctantly, Gia turned his head toward me. "We would accept Bayloo's help as well, if he has the courage."

I had two fish in my mouth; Kiata answered before I could. "My brother will stand with you."

I swallowed without chewing. Seriously, Kiata?

This was ridiculous. I didn't want to fight the hollowings. But I also didn't want to come off sounding like a cowardly fool in front of Rinxia and Kiata. A tricky balance.

Rinxia spoke up. "The last time I flew along the Tayo, the hollowing numbers seemed near limitless. There are too many even for us, Gia. We are only three, even with Bayloo, and he is not a fire breather."

Oh. That. Again. Suddenly, I wasn't hungry anymore.

Gia answered, his eyes and voice mocking. "You doubt the power of the mighty ember dragon, returned to us with suspicious good fortune?"

"Fire alone wins no battles," I told him.

Rinxia spoke as Gia snarled. "My point is, three adult dragons are not enough to defeat the hollowing horde."

Gia's eyes blackened. "Shall we surrender then, Rinxia? Run to the other side of the Pillar Mountains, leaving millions to fall to the rust and join the hollowing horde?"

"I did not suggest that."

"We need only to hold the Narrows," Gia insisted. "Without a physical bridge from one side to the other, the rust cannot cross the river. It does not fly, it does not travel in boats or move along with its hollowing servants. It can only spread where the great blight mass can touch adjacent land. We must hold the river to hold back the rust. And we will."

"We need a better plan than flying blindly in the west, intending to burn our enemies." Rinxia's gaze swept the room but landed on me. "For years, Drasu held the horde, helping us turn them back each time they tried to cross the river. He is gone, but we still need magic to win this fight."

Magic.

My chest tightened. I began to understand more of Rinxia's cunning. Is that why she wanted me to be Protector? I didn't even really know for certain I had any magic; I didn't want to even discuss trying to use magic in battle against those hollowings. I could never form a shield as Drasu had, or summon that terrible lightning as he could. Rinxia needed to understand that. I was about to tell her, when the silent woman on the other side of the room spoke for the first time.

"None are equal to the task, mighty Rinxia," Legao told her. "There was only one Drasu. A wizard such as he comes along once in a hundred years, if we are lucky. Our Conclave can muster four windmasters if we recall them all from our waveships. There are two master binders at Kolum, but I doubt a fully grown adult behemoth could be tamed even if we could capture one alive. I expect hollowing behemoths may well be unbindable, in any case."

Legao said *tamed* rather easily, but I had no doubt what a so-called binder really was. Binding was just a cute way to describe enslaving another creature. My jaw hardened.

"And what about you, Master Legao?" Rinxia asked pointedly. "Were you not the most senior of Drasu's magi before you ascended to lead the Conclave?"

Legao's face became stone. "Never have I claimed to be Drasu's equal. No human wizard has ever rivaled his power."

"Why is that?" asked someone beside me. All eyes turned to Harlan as he slouched in his rigid wooden chair, looking like a dark, spineless lizard.

Harlan's question did nothing to brighten the wizard's face. Legao's tone turned from dry to hot. "Who are you to ask that, Farlighter?"

The hostility seemed to come from nowhere. Even Gia didn't have such open hate for Harlan. "I am called Harlan Dor, Master of Sea, and of late, Master of the Sky as well." He flashed the infamous smirk without moving a single other muscle in his body. "I'm at your service."

Gia stirred his massive bulk, expressing his displeasure with Harlan's self-proclaimed title with a single, massive snort. I found myself rather amused by it all. Harlan's newly-bestowed honorific was actually true. He'd ridden on my back and sailed the seas, perhaps farther than any other person alive. I liked his boldness, particularly since Gia did not. Kiata stared at Harlan, fascinated.

Legao's gaze was as sharp as a dragon's claws. "If only I could grant myself power as easily as you grant yourself titles. But magic is a far more demanding master than ego, Harlan Dor. Manners are just one reason your people are not welcome here."

Harlan straightened himself into a more presentable posture, dipping his head respectfully. "I meant no offense. My intent was only to highlight that I'd traveled more than most and hope to be of some assistance. Of mighty Drasu, I have heard the legends, of course. Yet the other magi of Ni-Yota are no less famous. Your windmasters are feared throughout the world's seas. My understanding is that the silver trim on your robe marks you a master of your craft—a master wizard, even as Drasu was, able to command the elements of the sky."

Legao looked at her own garb with something akin to embarrassment. "No human has ever rivaled the power possessed by Drasu. None have even come close. While others might learn the arts of wind taming or binding, he alone ascended to status of Weaver, able to command all the physical forces of the world by his own cunning and will, something previously only thought achievable by ember dragons. He was a magi in the true sense—a master of all the known magic paths. Those available to humans, that is." She gave a polite nod in Kiata's direction but not mine. "To your question, Harlan, I do not know why Drasu was so gifted, or why he lived so long, or why he never succumbed to the pain of the mind, as so many other wizards do. There are some who believe his mother mixed the blood of a dragon with the milk she gave him when he was an infant." Legao shrugged. "It is as good an explanation as any other I've heard."

Harlan's smirk widened. "Still, you wear the garb of a master. You now lead the Conclave of Magi. I presume that means we should not contend with each other in dice at the very least. So, what can you do?"

Legao flushed. Her hand rose, a finger pointed at Harlan, who didn't flinch. "I can rid the world of your mocking disrespect."

Gia's voice echoed throughout the chamber. "Bayloo's pet is out of line, but the question is a valid one. You hold the office of First Servant of the Conclave and wear the robe of a master of your craft. What can you do to aid us in our time of need, Legao? Even a partial shield, say, to hold back the blood raptors, would be invaluable in a moment such as this."

The wizard shook her head with regret. "Such a casting...You must understand, most magic is the manipulation of a single force. A windmaster might coax the breeze to change direction for a time. A wizard might direct lightning on a stormy day. A binder can tame a single beast, but only in its infancy, when the mind is malleable. But to weave a spell such as the Great Barrier, as Drasu did...it is both power and artistry combined." There was no mistaking the awe in Legao's voice as she spoke of Drasu's work. Or the envy. "Wind and water were bound with the sky. To disturb the barrier brought down the wrath of lightning. Even from afar, Drasu's power sustained the barrier without need to constantly re-weave the spell." Legao shook her head in astonishment, as if she were a child shown fire for the first time. "A near permanent weave of the forces of the world. Even among the ember dragons of lore, only a precious few could manage such a thing."

Gia didn't share Legao's awe. "Can you aid us in battle or is your power confined to useless stories, Legao?"

The wizard raised her chin. "I am a wizard. I can summon the power of the skies regardless of weather."

"Enough to penetrate the hide of a behemoth?"

"I don't ..." She stopped and met Gia's gaze. "Yes."

"Then you come with us. I will carry you on my back to the river." The huge dragon got to his feet. "The time for talking ends. We waste our breath here. Is there any here who challenges my right to lead in battle?"

Rinxia looked at him sharply. I understood—it was a step toward claiming the status he coveted. I kept my jaw firmly shut, so Rinxia spoke. "I've still heard no plan, Gia. Flying west to burn isn't a battle strategy. Bringing a wizard isn't a solution. Aragor would never have been so reckless."

Gia roared at her. The dishes on the table shook (luckily all the ones near me were empty). "You would have us talk until the hollowings reach Trishan, Rinxia. My fire and Legao's magic will handle the behemoths. You and the soldiers must turn the tide against the human empties—those hollowings. Maybe you can persuade Bayloo to help you with that sweet tongue of yours."

Rinxia held her ground in the face of the larger dragon's fury. "I'll not see our warriors slaughtered, their lives wasted, because of a lack of thought, a lack of leadership."

Gia smashed his tail into the wall behind him, shaking the room. His eyes burned. The two dragons locked gazes, neither giving ground. Gia's tail twitched. His jaw tightened. Terror swept through the humans, except for Legao. And Harlan.

"Excuse me, but might I ask a simple question?" Harlan spoke in an offhand voice, yet it managed to cut through the tension as thoroughly as Gia's roar. The black dragon turned sharply, ready to bite Harlan's head off. Then Kiata spoke up.

"Ask your question, clever human, friend of my brother."

Harlan winked at my sister. Her eyes glowed back. I was jealous. "Can the hollowings swim?"

Gia laughed in contempt, when comprehension came to Rinxia immediately. "They are shells of the men they once were. Whatever the shell could do, the hollowings can do. But they have never tried to swim the river."

"In my experience, most people can't swim. I doubt the people of Illium were any different. Even a remarkable number of sailors never learn. In the north, men are terrified of the cold water. Anyway, swimming a river as wide and swift as the Tayo would be difficult."

Rinxia nodded in the human manner. "Go on, Harlan."

He leaned forward in his seat, but still didn't sit straight like the other humans. "If the bulk of their forces cannot swim across the river, then they must either use a bridge or be carried. Since this river has been your defense for years, am I correct that there are no bridges?"

"You are correct," Rinxia confirmed.

"And the Tayo is crossable only in a few places—with the rest protected by steep cliffs, terrible currents, or other natural defenses?"

"Correct again. Other than the Narrows, the river is nearly uncrossable by land dwellers."

"That means that the hollowings will have to build bridges and move them to the river. Such bridges would be flimsy things, likely made of wood. Wood burns. You seem quite good at starting fires." His gaze slid toward Gia.

"That is your plan, human?" Gia dripped contempt. I didn't think it was such a bad idea.

Harlan smirked. "There's more." He glanced up at the ceiling. I didn't get his purpose, but he sounded confident. Of course, Harlan was also a smuggler and a liar when necessary. "I think you'll like the plan."

FIVE

I prepared for battle on the shore of the palace's great lake.

The water was calm, the smooth surface barely rippling in a gentle breeze that couldn't last. The afternoon was wearing on. Humans dressed in colorful tunics of red, orange, and green fiddled with my claws, fitting me with those deadly metal spikes that I had only been a victim of until now. I learned that the Mizu called them *sai*. The coverings felt strange on my claws, their weight disturbing my precise balance. And they were cold —they felt like dipping my legs in the water of a freezing lake.

"Master Bayloo, may we beg you to keep still?" It was one of the human tenders. Kashar was his name, and he seemed to be in charge. The man spoke to me with respect, his words soft and thoughtfully selected. Kashar handled the *sai* with reverence. His expression told me that he was delighted to have another dragon to fix these devices upon. "We are almost complete with the foreclaws."

"Why do these devices feel as if they have recently been pulled out from the Ice Sea, Kashar?"

"It is a result of the process by which they were created." He offered me a smile as wide as his face, obviously pleased to educate me about these weapons while his assistants continued the fitting. "These great *sai* were made in the ancient Forge of Uta, deep beneath Trishan, forged from a special metal like none other in Ni-Yota."

I could tell he wanted me to ask more about his weapons, and I was happy to oblige. "And how was this mysterious metal found, Kashar?"

"Ah, well, I must admit, it was indeed I who finally devised a way to utilize it. Pardon my saying so." I wondered if a human smile could grow so wide it became painful.

"Please tell me how this happened."

I wasn't just passing the time; I was actually somewhat interested in Kashar's story. I knew it wouldn't be as interesting as the story of the delicious black pigs that lived only in Changsha, but not every story can be about delicious-tasting animals, unfortunately. Still, it would take a while for my back claws to be fitted with *sai,* so I listened.

Kashar placed his hands together. "The metal was first found long ago in the tower of the Keeper of the Radiance during the last years of the reign of Alatel. I know you are perhaps not so familiar with all of our history, so I will add that this event occurred after the last of the line of Keepers was exiled from Ni-Yota."

My hearts thumped. My mother had been the last Keeper and had once dwelled in that tower. "There are many stories of how the ore came to be in the tower. Some say it was brought to Ni-Yota by the Jiax-Lo, the first Keeper of the Radiance in the time of Shihan of the Sky. Others claimed it came from Illium, from the mysterious Artificers of that place, or said it was an object from the Doomed World, before the Cataclysm. There are other tales as well. The records of the Keepers still have not been fully deciphered to this day."

Time to flatter some ego. Humans loved this even more than they enjoyed having their hair groomed. "But you are the one who finally made use of the mysterious ore—you are the one who forged it, are you not? What do *you* believe to be the truth, noble Kashar?"

I could tell by the gleam in Kashar's eyes I'd asked just the question he wanted to answer. "There is a story in the archives of an expedition sent by Nihan Who Follows, son of Shihan, to the Forest of Fallen Night. Nihan was obsessed with prolonging his own life, and sent many expeditions to that haunted forest in a vain search for the oasis that is rumored to lie deep within its heart."

I remember the dark, forbidding place—that Forest of Fallen Night. It was a thicket of impenetrable black where Elasu had somehow been at ease, but no one else. "I know the forest, but I've heard that no one ever returned from there. Not until the coming of the tigris at the time of the Schism."

Kashar's head bobbed. "True. True enough. However, men have only the history of their own lives. Only their stories live beyond them, and those change over time. Only the written word is immutable."

"You're saying someone did return from there?"

"There is an account in the Protector's archives. It recounts the testimony of a merchant from Changsha who had been sentenced to death for attempting to dishonestly replace a ruby entrusted to his care by the lord of the city of Piro with a stained glass replica. In an ultimately unsuccessful attempt to win clemency, he offered the Justicar of Changsha a chest of wood carved with a dozen stages of the moon as it waxed and waned. Inside this box were ingots of a reddish metal that shone unlike any other the justicar had seen. The condemned merchant claimed he found the box in the possession of a dead man—a soldier dressed in the yellow-crested armor of Protector Delima—near the far southern border of Ni-Yota, not terribly distant from the Forest of Fallen Night. This I believe to be the true story, and that the fallen soldier was the last of the doomed expedition in the forest."

"Why do you believe this tale above the others?"

"Because the metal I used to forge the *sai* was indeed found in a wooden box. The carvings had faded over the years, but I believe I could make out a crescent moon on the back. I mixed it with iron and other metals, but the edges...the sharp edges of the *sai* are pure."

I tapped my *sai*-tipped claws lightly against the ground as I considered. "And no one could work with the metal until now?"

Kashar shrugged, trying to seem humble, although his sloppy grin betrayed his pride. "Metal being as rare and expensive as it is, few pursue the study of its forging. In any case, the chest was in the possession of the Keepers of the Radiance for hundreds of years. Also, the Protectors who ruled Ni-Yota before the coming of Aragor the Skyking wouldn't countenance experimentation of such an ancient artifact. It was only with the rise of Aragor and the Schism that the need of the nation was greatest. But even after Aragor began his relentless search for weapons he might use against his enemies, no one could manipulate the metal. Not until I figured out the secret."

I studied Kashar. He wore a robe somewhat similar to Legao the wizard, although its hue was emerald with white trim. "You are a user of magic? That is how you were able to make these *sai*?"

Kashar's grin grew wider. It was almost wrapping around his head. "You flatter me. I have studied the Art of the Forge. I have learned the Way of the Flame. But there are others who have done that." He stepped closer. "I will tell you alone my secret, Master Bayloo. It was the fire that was the key. Others tried their arts on the metal itself, but that is impossible. It is something special. Greater and stronger than steel or anything else we here know today. I suspect it is from the time before the Cataclysm. To work this metal, it is the fire upon which magic must be worked. Only with a magical forge can the *sai* be created. With the blessing of Aragor, I obtained special materials from the Conclave of Magi, which made the flame of the forge hotter than any other."

I nodded in the human fashion, moving my claws about, newly appreciative of the weapon that had been bestowed upon me. "I will put them to good use, Master Kashar. That I will promise you."

The tenders finished their work. Daylight was precious, and I was anxious to begin this journey. Gia had already left with Legao to prepare for the attack. They would coordinate the human cavalry. Rinxia and I, along with Harlan, had a stop to make before we joined the others.

Rinxia sat next to me, her claws also now fitted with *sai*. Her face was annoyingly serene as a saddle was strapped onto her back. In addition to Harlan, we would carry cargo and human engineers with us. It was all part of Harlan's mad scheme. I don't like complicated plans, particularly those that required me to rely on anyone other than myself to succeed. Gia, Rinxia, and even Kiata felt otherwise. I had to remind myself that I had no interest in being Protector of Ni-Yota.

Harlan approached us, a heavy crossbow across his back. I knew he'd have at least two daggers on him as well. I was often contemptuous of human contributions to my battles, but with Harlan I had to concede the lethal effectiveness of his aim. Betal would've killed my sister but for Harlan's bravery and throwing skills. He had an excited spring in his step as he climbed easily onto my back, as if he'd ridden dragons all his life. His overly pleasant demeanor irked me. One should not be cheerful on the eve of battle.

"Why are you so intent on helping these people?" I asked him. "They hate you. The members of the council could scarcely conceal their contempt."

Harlan only needed to consider for a moment. "Do you believe in a higher purpose, Bayloo? A reason to live beyond just eating and getting through the day?"

I hated when this human answered my question with another question. At least I had an answer to this one. "The dragons of this place speak of the Way—their path in life. I'm unsure if I follow a necessary path, but for now, I am certain that I wish to free my sister from this place. I wish all my brethren free of their magical slavery."

Harlan huffed in delight, as if he'd proven a point. "I, too, have a higher purpose. But quests for these lofty goals are like sailing a ship around the world. The course isn't a straight line. But if your heart is true, it will lead you through the roughest seas to the place you were meant to find."

I grunted. "Sometimes when a ryder flies upon a dragon too high in the clouds, and does so too often, his brain becomes permanently damaged. It could happen quickly to someone who wasn't accustomed to the thin air. A sailor, for example."

Harlan laughed as if I were joking.

The human engineers arrived and climbed onto Rinxia's and my backs with some difficulty. I carried a total of three passengers, as well as two large barrels of cargo in my hind claws, while Rinxia carried two more humans and still more supplies. Fully loaded, we took to the sky.

Harlan had gone from terrified at flight to regretting he'd not been born with wings. He cackled with a mad joy as we soared into the sky. I understood his love of flight, but not his delight to head into battle against the enemies of Ni-Yota.

Rinxia flew beside us. "Thank you for standing with us, Bayloo. You are truly becoming one of us."

I stopped my instinctive snort before it escaped my nostrils. I was here. I'd made my choice. I had to make the best of it.

"It is my honor." I sounded awkward.

Rinxia's eyes glowed with approval. "We must fly northwest, to the place where the waters coming down from the mountains meet, their flows combining to form the mighty Tayo River. It is well inland, away from the Narrows, where the armies clash. Follow me and listen to the engineers. They've actually done this before —sort of."

Listening to humans. Not my strong area. "I'm sure Harlan will have plenty of advice for me."

"Bayloo, this can work. We need it to work."

Rinxia's words reminded me of the battle I'd fought beside Elasu. She had counted on me. I'd given her my promise, then I had let her down. Following orders just wasn't my strong area. Maybe I'd followed too many while I was a slave. I didn't say that, though. Rinxia sped northwest and I followed.

She led us to a hidden valley of trees within the massive peaks of the mountains that loomed behind us in the distance. The source waters of the Tayo came down from the peaks as snowmelt, flowing through the valleys and foothills. The river was even stronger here than at the Illium border, its waters a steady rush of power. Tall trees grew in the valley near the river, their trunks thick, but not too thick. The site was well chosen.

"The materials here will serve our purposes," Rinxia declared.

Harlan dismounted and nodded in satisfaction as well. "The river current is strong, quick. This will do, indeed."

The human engineers climbed off my back, as did Harlan. He spoke excitedly, waving his arms as he spoke with the Mizu. Their facial expressions told me I wasn't the only one who thought Harlan was slightly mad. Harlan returned and put Rinxia and me to work ripping trees from the surrounding wood and placing them on the ground in neat rows for engineers. The last of the day's light was expended as we worked.

After dark fell, I sought out Rinxia. The day's toil had offered few chances to speak, but I had grown increasingly impatient. "Let us be gone from this place. Gia and Legao will be ready for battle at first light. We must be there to join them."

"We are not far by way of wing," Rinxia assured me. I envied her calm. "Rest first, Bayloo. We have time to meet them at first light. The engineers here will work through the night by torchlight as best they are able. It is dangerous to do what they do in the darkness—they are only human. We should be ready to assist."

I wasn't patient. "While we delay, the hollowings fight to cross this same river further downstream. They may already be across in sufficient numbers, and all this will be for nothing."

Rinxia's eyes glowed bright against the night. "You sound concerned, Bayloo. Are you in such a hurry to join the fight?"

I let go of a long breath. "If I must fight, then I wish to win. Even when I fought as a slave, that was part of me."

"You must curb your impatience," she chided. "Haste can be our undoing. Precise timing means more than speed now. We must strike with Gia and Legao and the human-led cavalry forces. Only together do we have a hope of succeeding in this."

She was right, but that didn't make waiting any easier. I had always been anxious before battle, and those fights hadn't been of my choosing. Also, in Rolm, I'd known my enemy. I'd been fighting creatures I understood. Even the griffins, war wolves, and furies of Oster were just lethal soldiers of King Galt. These hollowings were something else. I'd never faced behemoths or blood raptors or whatever other unnatural allies they had waiting. This wasn't a war for territory or power. Even Aragor seemingly had no idea what the hollowings wanted. That made them dangerous.

I shuffled about as the human engineers swarmed over the trees that Rinxia and I had collected for them. I checked my wings and my *sai* until deep in the night, my thoughts relentless.

Sometime after everyone else slept, Rinxia approached. She moved so quietly I barely heard her. Only her scent alerted me to her presence. We had no trouble seeing each other even in the dark.

"You are nervous." She said it kindly, as if surprised.

I wasn't going to admit that. "I itch for battle. Even if my body wishes to rest, my mind does not cooperate."

"Perhaps I can help with that."

The sleek, beautiful silver dragon slid beside me, her scales rubbing against mine. I could feel the heat of her body. Her scent filled my nostrils and my head. A wave of dizziness struck me. Rinxia curled her neck against mine. Every part of me tingled with warmth. Every part. She wrapped her tail around mine.

I stopped feeling anxious. I forgot all about the battle to come. We spent the rest of the night in that pose and others, then spent more time curled together. I cursed the sun when dawn finally arrived.

SIX

I followed Rinxia into the sky.

In that moment, I didn't care where she was leading me. I'd have followed her into a bath of chicken piss. What a dragon!

She had said nothing to me in the morning. Just before the first light of the new sun reached us, she disentangled herself from me. I wanted to chase her, to grab her, to beg her to come back to me. I was a bit pathetic, but I held myself in check. She knew what she was doing and I didn't. I copied her silence.

On this new morning, we both flew without saddles or human passengers, for which I was grateful. Harlan was capable, but he was extremely human. I was relieved not to worry about taking care of him while in the air. He would face his own dangers, but I could do nothing about those for the moment.

Rinxia pulled further ahead of me, her lean body and powerful wings cutting through the wind. I admired her grace in the air. I vowed that nothing would happen to her in the forthcoming battle. I would protect her, even if she didn't need it. My blood surged, singing in my head. I almost felt sorry for the hollowings. We were going to smash them.

As the sun cleared the Pillar Mountains far to the east, I saw Gia. He awaited us at the appointed location like a great pimple of black on the face of the horizon. On his back, he carried the wizard, Legao, who looked as out of place in the air as I did in the sea. Gia made his foul mood evident without delay.

"The battle rages while you waste your time on human schemes."

Rinxia danced around the larger dragon. "The outcome of the battle will decide if the time was wasted. I see that the horse riders advance as they should."

I followed her gaze to the ground. Below was a massive formation of human cavalry. They flowed toward the gap in the mountains where the Tayo River narrowed. They moved like ants in neat rows, their mounts kicking up dirt and dust as they galloped to battle. The huge mountains to the north and south were silent sentinels to the carnage that would follow.

"They ride, but we must lead," Gia growled, beating his wings. "To battle!" he roared, already pushing for speed.

Rinxia and I beat our wings. The cause of Gia's impatient consternation appeared immediately. I saw the River Tayo and our enemy. My hearts sank. We were too late.

The hollowings had already crossed. Their army had formed a dangerous salient on the Ni-Yota side of the river in two places, the leading edge of the formations slowly growing, reaching toward each other like lusty lovers. Between the attacking spearheads were desperate Mizu foot soldiers locked in combat, their lines uneven and erratic. The hollowings looked like human soldiers to me, except for their movements.

The hollowings were many, but it was the terrible behemoths that formed their vanguard. The beasts towered over every other living ground creature, each of their four legs as long as a horse and as thick as three men, their heavy, forked tails packed with nasty-looking spikes as long as a human leg. Their heads were crafted of three armored plates joined together, creating a triangle, with tiny eyes located above a pair of curved tusks that jutted outward and upward.

If I'd been a human, I'd have run from such a beast. The Mizu were braver than I. Or stupider.

The Mizu mostly held their ground despite the onslaught. Many on the front wielded long halberds, while others slashed their blades. Archers held fast behind the crumbling lines. But for all the courage of the defenders, they appeared doomed. The peril of impending encirclement was obvious from the air. In the chaos of battle, the Mizu troops might not have realized what was happening. Or they were indeed stupidly brave.

I have seen many battles, and I knew this battle would not be won on the ground. I looked to the river. There were two bridges spanning the length of quickened waters. The passages resembled huge wooden barges strung together to span the width of the river, their ends held in place by the strength of four massive behemoths to which great cables of a metal-like rope were attached. Hollowings streamed across the tenuous floating corridors in a continuous line. The living shells looked almost like a regular army, except for their strange, synchronous movements. It was as if the hollowings were connected to each other like string puppets, each soldier's legs moving in lock step with the others. They moved with neither obvious urgency nor reluctance. If they had commanders among them, it was not apparent to me.

The non-human hollowings were even more unnatural. Wolves intermingled with the human hollowing troops, the lupines also marching along with the same steady motion as the humans. The sight fascinated and repulsed me. It was a terrible alliance. The war wolves of Oster were trained animals. They obeyed, but they were not slaves. These creatures were something far more disturbing.

I drew closer to Rinxia. I caught her scent, which sent tingles through me. I had to force myself to remember the battle. I didn't know how much fighting Rinxia had been involved in, but her demeanor made me confident that this was not her first battle. "There are easily a thousand Mizu soldiers caught between the advancing hollowing salients. Those men will be trapped and slaughtered."

"I see it," she assured me. "We'll save them."

I supposed her words were meant to reassure me. They didn't. They meant she intended to engage those armored monstrosities and the horde accompanying them. She intended to risk her life for those humans.

Gia roared to us from across the sky. "Bayloo and I will each take one of the salients. Rinxia, you burn the bridges on the river and any other creature that tries to cross." I felt Gia's gaze across the sky that separated us. I met the challenge in his eyes. "I expect I'll have killed my first behemoth of the day long before you have, Bayloo," he sneered. "Prove me wrong."

The giant black dragon plunged into the fray, his great wings casting a shadow over the field of battle. After a reluctant moment, I did the same.

"Be careful!" Rinxia called to me as I dove. Those simple words meant far more to me than they should've, but they wouldn't make me more careful. Quite the opposite. I intended to win this battle for Rinxia. I wanted another night like the one I'd just experienced. I wanted to find out what came next. That meant I needed to beat the hollowing horde.

Gia plunged toward the upstream salient, flying on a direct line toward the behemoth at the forefront of the attack. I was more cautious, first circling over the downstream formation as I observed the hollowings' maneuvers. I wasn't familiar with this enemy, nor this type of battle.

The horde fought with the same unnatural synchronization they displayed when they marched. Human, wolf, and behemoth each pressed forward on the line of attack without fear or apparent regard for their own life. When a soldier fell, another took his place. The wolves attacked in formation, charging forth in a bold manner completely unnatural for their kind. In the wars I'd witnessed, formations maneuvered erratically, lines buckled, commanders improvised, and soldiers panicked or overreached. The field was a swirling mass of barely organized chaos. There was none of that among the hollowings. The hollowing soldiers barely made any noise. However the strange army coordinated their actions, it wasn't by voice command.

I heard a roar in the distance. With one eye I saw Gia unleash his fire at the behemoth within his salient. The blaze washed over the creature like water over rock, with about as much effect. The armored beast didn't even look up. Flames were not the answer to defeating this foe. That was fine with me.

The salient of hollowings beneath me had two behemoths among them. I saw no obvious vulnerability to the creatures. I made a final circle around the hollowing force before swooping down to attack, keeping away from the massive creatures on the front line. I was noticed by the enemy, but there was no panic among them. A dozen fighters turned about in unison, as if on parade, raised crossbows, and fired. I banked enough that most of the fusillade missed, except for a pair of bolts that deflected off the scales of my underbelly. There was nothing special about their weapons. I'd survived their initial attack.

My turn. I grabbed two hollowings in my foreclaws on my initial dive, then knocked about half a dozen more to the ground with my tail as I swept across the formation. As I flew, I squeezed my claws together, crushing the creatures in my grasp. They gasped, but didn't cry out as a normal human would. I dropped the mangled bodies into the river.

The two behemoths continued to plow forward without regard to my antics, their thrust supported by a hundred hollowings. Buoyed by the new presence of powerful allies in the sky, the Mizu soldiers struggled valiantly to hold their ground. Their halberds shattered against the behemoths' thick armor and their blade edges drew no blood, yet they didn't flee. I was impressed with the discipline under such conditions. King Mendakas' soldiers would've broken long ago. Humans were such strange creatures, capable of such bravery and such treachery. I would try to make the efforts of these soldiers worthwhile.

Executing a sharp turn, I beat my wings, coming at a behemoth from the rear. It didn't turn its head, seemingly focused on the Mizu soldiers in front of it. I had a perfect chance to engage it, maybe rip through its armored hide with my *sai*-tipped claws. That was the problem: it was too easy. My life wasn't meant to be easy. I never believed easy when it was offered, not anymore.

Indulging my cynical suspicions, I turned away from the tempting target just before my claws got close enough to reach the behemoth. Sure enough, its massive spiked tail snapped with preternatural speed into the space I would've occupied had I kept on my original course. The beast finally turned its head to watch me after its whiff. I was already soaring into the sky, newly wary of my formidable adversary. The behemoth's anticipation of my tactics made me realize that it had other ways of tracking my movements beside its own eyes. I suspected it had something to do with the strange movements and behavior of the hollowing horde. They shared observations like any other army, but faster and quicker.

Perched high above the fray, I had the opportunity to survey the rest of the battle. My eyes searched for Rinxia first. I found her quickly, her silver form nearly a blur as she ripped through a cloud of acrid smoke rising from one of the hollowing bridges. A few flames burned along the passage, but not enough to doom it. The hollowings hacked away at the edges of the bridge that had caught fire, severing the damaged portions to prevent the flames from spreading. More hollowings continued to cross, including another behemoth, its massive weight sending parts of the wooden bridge underwater as it took each step. But even the behemoth's weight didn't collapse the construction. The hollowings had engineers among them as well. This was no mindless horde. It was merely a different kind of army.

I soon understood why Rinxia hadn't done more damage: blood ravens. Two distinct flocks consisting of hundreds of the vicious birds pursued her through the sky. She was fast enough to evade them, but by dividing themselves, they made it difficult for her to make clean dives or concentrate her fire for very long. The hollowings had also wheeled massive ballistae to the river's edge. Dropping to an altitude low enough to hit the bridges put Rinxia within easy range of their projectiles. In my mind, I urged her to stay near the clouds, to stay safe. I couldn't bear to lose her. I also knew she would do no such thing. Rinxia had too much courage for that. More courage than me.

As for Gia, he'd been true to his nature, boldly engaging a behemoth with mutually devastating results. The giant tusked creature was missing part of a rear leg, while Gia had streams of blood leaking from his belly from where the behemoth's tail spike had apparently penetrated. But Gia showed no sign of quitting or caution. If he would rule as he fought, Rinxia was undoubtedly correct that Gia would make a poor Protector. He was reckless, even with his own life.

From the east came the thunder of hooves. The Mizu cavalry we'd passed on our way to the river advanced at a gallop, surging in two groups toward each of the hollowing salients. They punished the ground as they came. I noticed the wind shift as they neared the hollowing lines. A steady easterly breeze suddenly intensified, swirling into tornado funnels that led the advancing horses. The twisters concealed the size and direction of the cavalry attack behind a wall of dust and sand. That had to be Legao's work. I watched with satisfaction as the tornados hit the hollowing lines a moment before the cavalry charge. The battle was truly joined. I took my opportunity.

I came straight down into the fray. Legao's magically-summoned storm made it impossible for even my eyes to see the ground clearly, but I remembered where to find the behemoth. With the entire hollowing army blind, I gambled that I could take the beast by surprise this time. It would probably be my only opportunity, and I intended to make the most of it. I beat my wings, increasing my speed. The wind ripped past me; flying dust clattered against my scales. I was committed. I doubted I could've pulled up completely even if I had wanted. I flexed my claws, enjoying the feeling of the cold *sai* on their tips. I hoped the metal of their tips had indeed come from the Forest of Fallen Night. It was fitting that something from the tigris' home would lead me to victory.

Swirling dust cascaded over me. I guided myself with memory

and sound and instinct. I found my target. My enhanced foreclaws dug into a rough hide as thick as dragon scale. The behemoth's hide tore. I felt blood flow, even if I couldn't see it. The beast reared upward. It even made some kind of hideous noise, like a choking roar. I shoved myself back into the sky, using the behemoth's torso for leverage. I lifted to safety just before its invisible tail swept through my airspace. I came down again, this time with all four claws descending onto the behemoth. I dug deeper and deeper until I felt bone. The creature's tail came for me. I beat my wings, keeping a firm hold on the behemoth's vertebra. It didn't snap—the bone might as well have been metal—but something cracked. It sounded like the biggest walnut shell in the world being broken. Hollowing or not, that couldn't have been pleasant. The behemoth jerked violently, its legs collapsing. Still holding its spine, the dying beast's terrible weight yanked me toward the ground as it toppled. I held tight, beating my wings as I struggled to maintain my altitude. The beast weighed as much as a small mountain. I couldn't lift it, but it didn't matter. Its spine finally snapped into two pieces. I clutched the upper portion of the bone in my foreclaws while the rest of the behemoth's spine remained inside its shattered body, ending what remained of the beast's empty life. The behemoth twitched violently on its side. I plunged down to finish my work, slashing the dying beast's throat with a claw. Legao's dust tornado subsided, the last sand and debris falling onto the corpse of my foe. But I wasn't done.

From every side the hollowings advanced, men and wolves alike, all newly appreciative of the danger I presented to them. Arrows came from the sky, launched by unseen archers. The ground shook to my left. There, the attackers parted in perfect unison, forming a corridor for the second behemoth. It hurled itself forward with surprising speed, considering its bulk. I estimated I had barely enough time to hurl myself upward out of the reach of its tail spikes. That was also what it probably expected me to do. Instead, I leapt directly at the charging behemoth. It didn't slow. Given its size and speed, I doubt it could've stopped even if it had realized what I intended.

The trio of armored plates protecting its head opened, revealing a face that was mostly a three-sided mouth lined with knife-like teeth, along with a single, hideous suctioned tentacle. I came directly at that long, deadly jaw with its whip-like appendage, beating my wings for speed but hovering barely above the ground. I pulled up only at the very last moment, shoving the first behemoth's shattered spine into its brother's jaw. Instinctively, the beast snapped, pulled back its tentacle, and shut its armored plates. Or at least it attempted to shut them. The ends of the bone wedged between two of the plates, leaving a gap in the behemoth's armor. It flung its head about wildly to dislodge the obstruction, its tentacle wrapped around the bone, trying to remove it.

I didn't give it a chance. I fell from the air onto the behemoth's head, reaching inside its mouth to the soft flesh. I shoved my *sai* through the soft palate of its mouth. Blood gushed from the wound. I severed the wet, fleshy tentacle as easily as I could pierce a chicken's neck. I would've been proud of myself, except for the beast's tail. It took me in the flank. The air rushed out of me. But the blow didn't penetrate my scales. The behemoth was hurt. Its strength already was failing it. I pulled my foreclaw from its mouth, along with a satisfying hunk of flesh, even as my hind claws dug into the wounded creature's backside. With a mighty roar, I beat my wings, tearing off still more of the behemoth's hide and flesh. The beast still flailed about as I rose back into the air, hollowing arrows sliding off my belly scales. I flew a tight circle, accelerating as I came in for a final pass. I tucked in my foreclaws and racked the behemoth's bloodstained skull with my hind *sai*. That was the end of it.

I roared in triumph as I once again soared high above the field.

The Mizu warriors hadn't missed my victory. Their cavalry-led charge had hit the line as I'd grappled with the behemoths, with deadly effect. The mounted warriors had cut a swath of destruction, killing hundreds as they rode through the hollowing lines. Of course, the hollowings didn't flee. Even as the Mizu riders cut them down with blades and spears, the unnatural enemy reformed their lines, trying to hold the salients. Mizu horsemen galloped along the hastily formed front, some standing in their saddles, firing arrows from curved short bows at the flanks of the salient. Hollowings fell by the dozens. The horde might be fearless, but the Mizu were superior warriors in every other way. The emotionless husks that had once been men fought with instinct, but not intensity. That element—the human element—was the difference in the ground battle. With the behemoths dead, the Mizu warriors slaughtered the outnumbered hollowings. That would've been the end of the salient, except for those cursed wolves.

The fleet-footed predators formed themselves into wedge-shaped packs and charged at the Mizu horsemen, their eyes the color of rotten oranges. The wolves ran low enough to the ground to make it difficult for the Mizu riders to defend themselves adequately with swords. I heard their commander shouting orders for men to dismount, to save the horses and engage on foot.

I dove back into the fray, attacking the hollowing lines from behind. I extended my legs, dipping my *sai* down so low that their tips nearly touched the ground. Then I flew over the enemy at speed, chasing down the wolf packs from behind, slicing open a dozen skulls on a single pass. I came about a second time. Crossbow bolts greeted me, but couldn't stop me. More of the unnatural wolves fell. The Mizu saw the waste I was making of their enemy and pressed their attack. I swung back once again. I was their doom.. The hollowings figured that out quickly—I came out of my turn into a black cloud of blood raptors. They didn't really attack; the birds simply threw themselves at me. Beaks and claws smashed into my face, my body, my wings. I couldn't see, there were so many. I pulled up, hard. The air whistled angrily as a massive bolt fired from an unseen ballista shot past me. I flew still higher.

The blood raptors followed, harrying me. There were so many. Each time I flapped my wings, I struck more birds. They disrupted my flight path, although there must have been a heavy cost to the raptors. I must've maimed a hundred as I circled about.

How many are there?

Finally, I dove again, beating my wings for extra speed. That enabled me to put the suicidal birds in my wake. I saw the battlefield again. The blood raptors hadn't only come for me: they harried the Mizu cavalry as well, flying about like a huge locust swarm. The soldiers swung their blades, but it was like trying to cut through the sea—one bird fell and two more took its place. I heard more shouts. Fires were lit—more of the acrid smoke that had been used in the Hall of Glass to keep the birds at bay—but they wouldn't be effective out in the open. Worse, the behemoth I'd seen on the bridge earlier was almost across the river. Still another beast traversed the second bridge. Rinxia dove and swerved about as no less than three massive swarms of blood raptors pursued her. Gia belched fire as the birds flew overhead. I couldn't see the behemoth with which he had tangled. He must've triumphed as well. I wondered which of us had been quicker?

More hollowings crossed the river on the still-intact bridges. I roared in frustration as the battle continued to unfold. For all the success of our tactics, the hollowings were too many. They kept coming faster than we could kill them. I looked to the river at that moment and saw the first sign of salvation.

Harlan Dor had finally arrived.

SEVEN

Harlan sailed down the river atop a tree.

Actually, there were four boles, each tied together to form a crude barge. A second, identical craft trailed him. He sat at the rear of his makeshift vessel, maneuvering the rudder as the relentless flow of the River Tayo propelled the craft. Harlan smirked as if enjoying a leisurely afternoon pleasure cruise.

The hollowings must have seen him coming. There were easily ten thousand of them on the far bank of the river, waiting in deadly silence for the opportunity to cross to the other side. But they did not react to the strange new arrival. At least not initially.

Again, I wondered at the horde's decision-making process. Two river barges might not have seemed like an immediate threat because there were no soldiers aboard, no supplies, no ballistae or other weapons. Or perhaps it took a bit of time for the horde to adapt to an unexpected situation. While the hollowings ignored Harlan and the battle raged on my side of the river, the twin barges drew closer. I kept watching, my eye flicking from the barge to the hollowings standing on the far shore, then back again. Men and hollowings continued to be slaughtered on the near side of the Tayo. Still, the horde paid no mind to the barges, not even sending blood raptors to investigate the craft. I willed more speed to Harlan and his vessel, but to no avail. Even with the river's stiff current, his progress was agonizingly slow.

I dodged through a swarm of blood raptors that came at me from below, maneuvering behind them but keeping out of range of the arc-bolts being lofted at me from the hollowing war machines below. As I executed a sharp leftward bank, a chill swept through the air more suddenly than even the swiftest-moving winter squall. A tingle tickled my tail, then snout, the feeling of something familiar but distant. The wind seemed to stop. There was a sound from somewhere in the sky, the hiss of a giant exhaling. The breeze shifted. Magic was at work.

I searched for Legao. It took me only a moment to spot her. She sat on a horse adjacent to the salient where Gia fought, well behind the front line. A pair of Mizu soldiers in full armor flanked her on either side, looking as dangerous as tiny humans could manage.

I wasn't the only one who sensed the magic—or at least the sudden change in the wind. The flock of blood raptors pursuing me broke off. The dark cloud of killer feathered creatures turned immediately toward the barge. Another group separated themselves from the formation pursuing Rinxia, their new course putting them on a path to Legao.

I called out with a tight roar, loud enough for Harlan and Legao and everyone else on both sides of the river to hear. "Blood raptors incoming."

Harlan's grin didn't drop. He stood on his barge like a captain on his deck, his eyes fixed on the approaching raptors. The birds came quickly, forming themselves into an arc of feathered unpleasantness. The river's waters quickened, perhaps propelled by Legao's magic. Harlan nodded at the added speed—his barge would be at the first bridge in moments, although not before the blood raptors reached him. But Harlan didn't budge, didn't make any obvious effort to protect himself, as if such a thing were beneath a captain's dignity.

He put both hands on the rudder. The hastily constructed barge must have been unsteady in the quick waters of the Tayo—he didn't want it to go off course and collide with either bank. I realized that Harlan intended to pilot the barge all the way to its target. The fool.

I roared again, and he heard it. "Get off!"

Harlan didn't obey me—at least not at first. Instead, he waited, holding as still as a statue as the blood raptors came ever closer. The human had ice for blood. Only when the vanguard of blood raptors was close enough to crap on his head did Harlan react. With a talon about a pinky length from his nose, Harlan, in an unnecessary flourish, took a backward step off the edge of the barge, bowing smartly before plunging into the swift flow of the river. A hundred raptors swept across the barge in the next moment, flapping in a furious circle over the water as they searched for their missing prey. Harlan didn't surface. The stupid, bloodthirsty birds didn't notice the tiny flame he'd left behind on the barge. At least, they didn't notice it in time to get clear.

The barge ignited just as its bow struck the first of the hollowings' bridges. We'd packed the carved channels inside the trees used to construct the raft with the same fire oil that the palace staff used to keep the ever-burning fire atop the Protector's tower lit. No one had ever thought to use it in such quantities or for such a purpose, but Harlan had been confident it would work. He was right. The fire raced along the cut channels in the long, oil-soaked trees of the barge. Moments later, the wooden craft was a smoking inferno, the fire crackling over its surface. Even the newly-felled wood of the raft crisped in the intense heat created by the fire oil. Accelerated by Legao's magic, the rushing water of the river shoved the flaming barge into the first bridge with enough force that the vessel broke apart, sending each section sprawling along the width of the span. The oil-driven fire crossed hungrily onto the wooden bridge with satisfying speed. The hollowings reacted as best they could, but nothing could extinguish the flames of fire oil.

The behemoth that was already three-quarters of the way across the river quickened its pace. Rinxia was ready. With most of the blood raptors that had been harrying her diverted to Harlan's raft, she finally had a chance for a clean attack. Rinxia made the most of her opportunity, coming fast for the remaining bridge. She dove so quickly she was little more than a streaking silver light until the orange flame sprang from her mouth. She pulled out of her dive with no more than the length of a single human between her and the river. Rinxia streaked along the water's surface with the speed of purpose. I knew her target: the behemoth on the first bridge. Rinxia needed no fire now. The flames had already spread. Instead, she pulled up as she neared the hurrying beast, shoving the behemoth with her *sai*-tipped hind legs as she ascended for the sky. Her claws cut its hide as she passed—deep, ugly gashes. The massive creature was already off balance, struggling on the wobbly, flaming bridge. Rinxia's strike was enough to send it tumbling into the waters of the Tayo. But the falling behemoth was quick—even quicker than Rinxia. Its forked tail whipped at her even as the beast toppled into the surging water, a deadly spike on its edge catching Rinxia's hind leg. The blow shattered a scale. Even at a distance, I could hear her gasp in pain as she dipped a wing into the water. For a terrifying moment, I thought Rinxia would crash, but instead she righted herself by curling her tail. But the blow also distracted her for a precious moment. Rinxia didn't see the ballista bolt until it was too late.

    I cried out at the same time as Rinxia, both of us roaring in pain. The velocity of the hollowing projectile was enough to propel it through the scales protecting Rinxia's right side near her rib cage. The top third of the shaft slid into Rinxia. I dove for her, but she hit the water before I could get there. If she was like every other dragon I knew, Rinxia couldn't swim, particularly not with a wound like the one she'd just suffered. The Tayo's harsh current grabbed her, yanking Rinxia downstream with anxious fury, toward the bridge. Another behemoth wading across the far bridge saw her coming. He ignored the spreading flames around him, disregarding his own safety for the chance to finish off a dragon. No way I was going to let that happen.

I came for her, swiveling like a corkscrew as I descended, using my wings to change my speed and direction as the ballistae opened fire on me. A bolt sailed past my head. Another grazed my right wing. I heard shouting. It might have been Harlan's voice. Arrows rained down upon me. I didn't care. I was in a funnel of desperation, my eyes fixed only on Rinxia. Everything else was lost in the background.

Within three heartbeats I had her clutched in my hind legs—gently because I still wore the *sai*. Lifting another dragon, even an undersized one like Rinxia, was no easy task, and the covering of my claws made it even more difficult. I didn't quite get fully airborne. Instead, I dragged Rinxia through the water toward the Mizu-controlled shoreline, targeting the area between the shrinking remains of the hollowings' salient. I would've made it, except for the damned behemoth. I'd snatched Rinxia just before she'd fallen into the beast's clutches. It didn't occur to me that the thing would dare to leap into the Tayo after us.

As the behemoth crashed into the river, the three armored plates protecting its mouth retracted to allow a suction-clad tentacle to come forth like a living whip. The slimy thing caught Rinxia's right hind leg, curling itself into position. Then it yanked her—hard. The force almost pulled me out of the air as I dragged her along the water. Rinxia and I jerked violently backward, toward the behemoth's thrashing tusks and tail. Even as the rest of its body sank under the current of the river, the behemoth's deadly appendage hunted us. I beat my wings, but I could make no progress. Rinxia cried out again. The behemoth and I were yanking her in different directions, which couldn't be doing her punctured side any good at all.

I had to end the stalemate. My only option seemed to be to release Rinxia and kill that thing before it pulled her under and drowned her, or worse, turn her to a hollowing. I hated the idea of letting go, but I didn't seem to have a choice or any more time. I was about to release my grip when Harlan called out again.

"Hold on. We're going to light it!"

His words jarred my memory. I remembered Harlan's plan. I turned my head upriver. The other exploding barge had broken apart, just as it had been designed to do. It had been made of smaller, narrower trunks. The Tayo's magically accelerated current had sped the pieces into the gaps in the damaged upstream bridge, but also underneath its supports. More importantly, the fire oil contained inside the logs had leaked into the river. It was everywhere now, a thin film coating the surface of the river.

Flaming chicken piss.

Gia swooped down, spitting his fire onto the polluted water of the Tayo. The whole river along the battle line of the hollowing horde caught fire, including the water all around Rinxia and I. But dragon scales repel fire. Behemoth skin, while tough, wasn't quite as durable. Rinxia had also punctured several holes in its hide when she'd attacked it. The beast in the water caught fire. It writhed about as its tentacle crisped. I beat my wings again. The slimy whip holding Rinxia snapped. I dragged her along the flaming surface to the near bank, onto the shore.

I looked at Rinxia. She still drew breath, but with distress. Smoke from the burning river filled the air. My roar shook the ground.

"Healer, to me!"

EIGHT

Rinxia wouldn't die.

That is what I promised myself as I gazed at her bloody body, at the bolt rammed in her side. But I couldn't stop myself from shaking. I kept remembering my mother and the emptiness that had come to me following her death. I couldn't clear my mind. I couldn't focus. I had failed Rinxia when she needed me most. I needed to fix this.

My eyes were aching as I stared down at this beautiful dragon. I supposedly had power inside me. Something as great as Legao's power, or maybe even Drasu's, if I just found a way to use it. I had found a fleeting glimpse at that strange place—the Latticework—when I'd tried, and failed, to heal Aragor. I needed to do better for Rinxia.

I tried to remember my way back to the place I had been before, which wasn't a place at all. It was a state of high perception that allowed me to sense the underpinnings of the mundane world. I needed to concentrate; I needed to focus. But I couldn't do that. My hearts were too panicked. I hadn't cared about Aragor. This was altogether different—this was Rinxia. No one else was like her, no one else connected with me like her. I wanted to help her so badly my bones ached. I kept flailing my head about, trying to find the singular determination to sense what I knew was around me, to summon the power that was supposedly within me, but whatever I had once found now eluded me. I failed Rinxia yet again.

That was when the human healer arrived. Yali was her name, and she had a waterfall of twisting hair that was the color of Rinxia's scales. She took charge immediately, her confident voice and condescending tone a comfort to my wounded mind. Yali directed the quartet of robed minions who followed in her wake with precision that the knight-lords of the Mizu army could learn from. The robed humans applied their poultices at Yali's command, then fed potions into Rinxia's mouth, while I gaped at them from behind. Finally, Yali herself removed the bolt from Rinxia's side. I winced as the blood poured from the wound. Rinxia moaned with pain, still unconscious but obviously alive, for which I was grateful.

Yali and her assistants quickly applied a salve that stopped the bleeding. I held my breath while Rinxia's wound was bandaged. When Yali finally turned away from her patient, I was quick to share the worst of my fears with her.

"What if the hollowing weapon carries the taint of the rust upon it?"

Yali glanced back at her patient, her face serene, as if caring for a dragon with arc-bolt wounds was a common occurrence. "I've examined the tip of the bolt—fired ceramic. It appears no different from any other weapon we use in Ni-Yota." A weight lifted from my chest, but only until she added, "Of course, there is no way to be sure until she fully recovers."

"Is there nothing else you can do?" I asked, hating the desperation that crept into my voice.

This time Yali gazed west in answer. "No one knows how to stop the rust."

I told myself I would find a way to heal Rinxia if the hollowing disease had infected her. I had utterly failed with Aragor, but I wouldn't fail Rinxia. I just needed to calm myself. Up until that moment, I hadn't truly needed magic. I hadn't wanted it. I had grown quite able without fire or magic. Now, I had purpose. I just needed to stop shaking. I needed to find peace. Then, I would return to the Latticework, that place that was apparently part of the inherent power of my kind.

Yali and her fellow healers tended to Rinxia within a tenuous island of safety carved out by Mizu soldiers on the eastern bank of the Tayo River. At the same time, nearby, the last of the hollowings on the shore were being slaughtered, their corpses soaked in fire oil brought on supply wagons, then dumped into the river. The burning water sent plumes of smoke into the sky, obscuring the far bank. Mizu soldiers continued to feed the flames with additional barrels of oil, although the supply would be exhausted soon enough.

While the river burned, I stayed by Rinxia's side, nervously attempting to peer through the wall of smoke for signs of danger from the horde that remained on the far bank. We were still perilously close to danger, and still without Drasu's shield for protection. Despite the damage that had been done to the hollowing army, they still had battle engines with more than sufficient range to reach the ground upon which Rinxia lay. But for now, the enemy held its fire.

As time passed, I gradually grew more confident that Rinxia was out of immediate danger. Yali stayed by her side anyway, walking in slow circles, occasionally glancing at me with an amused smile. I watched the steady breathing of Rinxia's chest. It didn't falter. Gradually, my thoughts turned to the fate of the reckless human, Harlan Dor.

The fool had voluntarily leapt into the raging waters of the Tayo River. If he had been any other human, I'd have assumed him drowned, dead, and probably eaten by whatever creatures inhabited the waters of the river. But Harlan was a Farlighter, a man of the water. His people had an uncanny talent for all things connected to water, and I presumed that meant swimming as well. I comforted myself with the memory of Harlan's face as he'd jumped off his raft. He had entered the water with aplomb. I told myself he would be fine. It would not be a mere river that claimed the sailor.

Sure enough, sometime before dark, Harlan approached, emerging from the masses of Mizu soldiers. He had not a scratch on him, although he wore different clothes from when I'd last seen him—likely something borrowed from the supply master of the Mizu army. His lips were turned downward in an uncharacteristic frown when he saw Rinxia.

"How is she?"

"She will live," I promised him and myself.

The healer, Yali, approached warily, her features hard. "A Farlighter?"

"Is that all you see?" Harlan replied. "I can sing and dance as well."

Yali looked him up and down. "I heard a Farlighter rode a burning barge into the hollowing bridges, then jumped into the current of the Tayo River. I didn't believe it."

Harlan looked sheepish. "The barge wasn't on fire until after I jumped off."

"You look remarkably well for a man who swam in the Tayo," Yali noted. "Those waters are quick, powerful, and deadly."

"Every seahand I know had to swim a league in the Ice Sea before their thirteenth year. The Tayo is a calm bath compared to that."

Yali shook her head almost imperceptibly. "The Firelighter who swims rivers now comes to inquire about the health of dragons. Now I have lived a full life. I thought your kind hated dragons."

Harlan smirked. "The first dragon I met saved my life." He motioned toward Rinxia. "She seems a good sort as well. I'd take either of these dragons here as my first mate over any human I've had serve me on any ship. I hope you know healing better than you know me."

Yali answered with a cold stare. "What do you want?"

"How much longer till Rinxia can be moved?" he asked.

I didn't like the sound of that. "Why?"

"I've checked on the fire oil supplies," Harlan told me. "We can't keep the fire going much longer."

"So the hollowings will come again?" I would fight to protect Rinxia, but I had no illusions about the challenge ahead. The behemoths were formidable, the blood raptors seemingly innumerable, the horde's hunger insatiable.

Harlan rubbed his chin. "I've spoken with the Mizu commanders. We've hurt the horde badly this day. Five behemoths dead, along with hundreds of blood raptors and thousands of soldiers. They still outnumber us, but their forces are not unlimited. More importantly, it takes trees and time to build bridges. The Mizu knight-lord, Avis, thinks we'll have a reprieve of sorts."

"How long?"

"He doesn't know. Days, perhaps. Probably not a week."

"The blood raptors could still fly across the river." I looked at the Tayo with distrust, as if my words would summon an attack.

"Aye, but that would be tactically foolish. Alone, the birds can do no real damage. Their value is to provide cover for the soldiers, wolves, and behemoths. If the horde is intelligent, they would do better to hold back and attack in force."

I considered that. "The hollowings act with discipline. They communicate. They are strategic. But they will come if it offers them the chance to finish off a dragon."

"I've already sent for a dragon-cart," Yali assured me. "Rinxia is not the largest of you. We'll be able to move her to safety."

"How soon?" I pressed.

Yali rolled her eyes. "Soon enough. But I'll see to it."

She stomped off into the swirling chaos of the Mizu army.

"I like her," Harlan said to me. "But time grows short. We need to move ..."

Harlan trailed off as a great blot of darkness with wings came toward us: Gia. I saw immediately that he, too, had spent time with the healers after the battle. Salves and bandages covered portions of his neck and torso. He landed beside Rinxia without looking at me or Harlan. I studied his injuries as he studied Rinxia's wound. Gia had been mauled. I saw a tear on his right wing that had been stitched back together with some kind of animal gut, the stitching far less fine than the work that had been done to me back in Rolm. Entire scales were missing on his right side, and in several places his armor had holes, undoubtedly made by behemoth tusks and spikes.

His amber eyes ran all over Rinxia. He sniffed at the terrible wound in her side. "She fought bravely, as always." Gia said it with approval, but I doubted that Rinxia would've cared for his praise. She fought for duty and the purpose of her Way. Gia just wanted to fight for its own sake.

"What happens when the fire oil is done and the hollowings come again?" I asked. "How do we stop them next time?"

Gia twisted his thick neck, bringing his head back to look at me. He moved stiffly. "You fought...courageously, Bayloo." He sounded only mildly surprised. "We are stronger than the hollowings. Each time they attempt to cross the river, we shall hurt them more. Until finally, like a stubborn hound, they learn to stop coming."

"Courage and fire will not be enough next time. Harlan's trick with the fire barges will only work once. I saw thousands of Mizu die. They do not have the numbers to keep fighting the hollowings."

Harlan echoed my advice. "The horde cannot be cowed. This is no army seeking conquest. They come for another reason."

Gia flared his nostrils at him. "And what is that reason, human?"

"I don't know," Harlan admitted. "That is one of our greatest problems. It is difficult to defeat an enemy one does not understand."

Gia growled as his tail shifted behind him. "They seek to invade our land, kill us, consume us. We will fight them with all we have. We are stronger. This Light shines on us." He looked at me. "Rinxia will recover. Get your rest, for there will be another battle."

I stretched my neck high to survey the camp of the Mizu army. The signs of another fight to come were all around us; soldiers and horses dragged themselves across the battlefield. Healers attended to the human soldiers. The army, at least, seemed well organized. The humans here knew the grim tasks of war. Only a single group seemed out of place. To the north, I saw a procession of unarmed humans attired in robes of black surrounding a single covered wagon, its top draped in cloth that matched the color of its attendants.

I indicated the wagon with a nod of my head. "What happens there?"

Gia stared at the distant wagon. He didn't turn back toward me for several long moments. "They bring he who you came to kill back to Trishan, to be put to final rest beneath the Light."

My blood surged. "Drasu? That wagon carries Drasu's body?"

"The shell that held his spirit is there. We shall burn what remains of his flesh in the fire, releasing him back into the Light to find his place in Haven."

"You intend to honor him?"

"For decades he served. Without his magic, the hollowings would've overrun the Tayo years ago to march on Trishan. We would've been caught between Elasu's minions in the east and the horde in the west, to be ground to dust in its center. He served the Protectors for decades, not just Aragor."

"He was a hatchling stealer." Bile filled my mouth. "He was a murderer of dragons. My mother's killer."

Gia's eyes became wary. "Kiata is our deliverance. Aragor foretold it was the will of Haven that she be brought here." He paused, perhaps considering my charges against the wizard. Gia had no love for humans. "He acted on the orders of the Skyking. They are not orders I would have given, had I been Protector. But there can be no vengeance against the dead."

I blew contempt from my nostrils (and a bit of snot as well). "I wonder if that is so." As I said the words, I remembered my conversation with the ghastray back on the island of Alahu. The predators of the sea wanted Drasu. I had promised to deliver him. Gia seemed intent on burning his body in some ceremony for the masses back in Trishan. He'd try to stop me if I took Drasu now. Did I care?

I took another look at Gia's wounds. They were many, and deep, but he would heal quickly, as our kind always did. The damage to his wing didn't look as extensive as what I had recovered from, and he was still flying. But there wouldn't be a better time to fight him than now, if I inevitably had to do so.

Harlan interrupted me, I suspected with deliberate intent. "Do not forget what awaits across the river, beyond the fire."

We all turned to the Tayo. The flames fed by Trishan's fire oil had begun to fade, although the smoke still rose.

Gia showed his teeth as he imagined his enemy on the far bank. "I must ensure the humans are prepared. You should make yourselves ready to fight again."

With those fine words, the huge black dragon flew off toward the larger army encampment to the north. I watched Drasu's funeral procession begin its long journey to Trishan before turning my attention back to Rinxia. Her breathing remained steady, but I still counted each of her breaths, willing the next to be stronger. As I counted, the remaining day faded, as did the flames that shielded us from the horde on the opposite side of the Tayo River. The smoke was still too thick for human eyes, but I was able to peer through the thinning plumes, and what I saw brought no comfort. Tens of thousands of hollowings massed at the western bank of the Tayo, silently watching, poised to march across once again. Only the swift current and deep waters of the Tayo prevented that. The hollowings did not look defeated. They looked formidable. Worse, their numbers seemed undiminished—indeed there might have been even more of them.

Harlan confirmed my unhappy suspicion. "I counted eight large ballistae during the battle. Now there are twelve."

"I will take to the sky to have a closer look."

Harlan let go a reluctant sigh. "I would accompany you."

"I mean no offense, but it is an unnecessary risk for you. I can see better and fly swifter without a human on my back."

"Your dragon eyes do see further, my friend. But that is not the same as seeing better." Harlan tapped his forehead. I had no idea why. "I've seen plenty of this world. Some things were almost as strange as the hollowings. And while my dear departed mum would be thankful for your concern about my safety, I think there is little risk so long as you don't attempt to cross the Tayo."

Harlan's assumption that I didn't intend to cross the Tayo was interesting. I hadn't said that. Indeed, I'd been contemplating the opposite. He seemed to have guessed my thoughts. Harlan's eyes narrowed.

"Don't do anything that might provoke another battle we aren't ready for, Bayloo."

I tried to make an innocent face. That's hard for a dragon.

"There is no saddle on me. In Rolm, ryders practice for years before attempting to mount a dragon without a saddle. Are you ready to cross the line between brave and foolish?"

Harlan waved away my concern. "I'm sure you'd never let anything happen to me. But as it is, Legao rode Gia here, so there must be a dragon saddle in the vicinity. I'll find it."

He set off before I could tell him I was in no mood to wait. However, shortly after Harlan disappeared into the mulling mass of horses and Mizu soldiers, an entire supply wagon packed with food pulled up next to me. The meat was mostly dried, but they had fruits, nuts, bread, and water, so I didn't complain. I wished Rinxia had been well enough to eat, for I knew it would help her heal.

Not long after I had replenished myself by consuming most of the contents of the Mizu wagon (but not the driver, who was scrawny anyway), a giant transport similar to the one that had lugged me to Changsha arrived. This one was accompanied by Yali and a score of other human healers. Part of me was reluctant to let Rinxia out of my sight, but I knew that was foolish. She was safer away from here.

"Where will you take her?"

Yali seemed surprised by the question. Or maybe she wasn't accustomed to speaking with dragons. "To Jahatta." She pointed east. "High walls, fresh water. We have no time to dally."

I couldn't very well argue with that. The smoke thinned as we spoke. "Do as you must." I took a long look at Rinxia. She was no less beautiful for being unconscious and wounded. "Her safety is more important than your own life."

"We shall not fail she of the Sworn." Yali bowed. She sounded confident.

I let them take her away, anxious to finish my reconnaissance so that I could be with her. As if sensing my heightening impatience, Harlan chose that moment to return, coming at a full sprint, accompanied by two Mizu carrying a dragon saddle. The human was resourceful. In short order, I was ready to fly, Harlan secured to my back. I lifted us into the air with a great push of my wings.

For a dragon, it was better to be in the air than on the ground. That was just the way of things. Above, the air smelled better and the world became more obvious. In this case, my ascent made it obvious that the hollowing horde had indeed grown in size. Their ranks were ten deep in places. Worse, two great streams of men and machines flowed toward the Tayo from the vast emptiness of Illium. Several of the coming war engines resembled nothing I'd seen before. Behemoths pulled them, two per machine. I hovered, watching the approaching storm. Their progress was slow, but dreadfully steady.

Harlan put it succinctly. "More monsters, living and made."

"The large ones aren't ballistae. I see nothing that releases a projectile. They resemble siege towers, but far larger."

"They aren't ballistae, nor are they siege towers," Harlan confirmed. "Look at the mechanism on the front of each. It resembles the hoists we use aboard ships to raise and lower sails."

Sails? "So what are they?"

"They are rolling bridges. Huge ones."

NINE

Behemoths weren't fast, but they were fast enough.

The Mizu commanders thought the hollowings would have to build new bridges. They thought their enemy would have to find more trees in the wasteland they'd created, cut them, craft them, and do whatever else humans do with their little hands to engineer their clever creations. All of which should've taken time. The Mizu knight-lord thought his army could rest, plan, and prepare for the next assault. All that was, apparently, wrong.

I confined my flight path to the human-held bank of the river. There was no point in going any farther yet. Harlan started whispering some words while I continued to fly along the river's edge. It sounded like gibberish. Or at least it wasn't Avian that he spoke.

"What's that you're up to?"

Harlan made me wait for his answer. "Just a little sailor's trick for measuring time and distance. Assuming that those behemoths don't need to rest, I'd judge they'll reach the river by morning. I don't think the hollowings will wait any longer than that to attack again. They don't seem to need rest, and they are intelligent enough to deny it to us."

I gazed again at the giant towers. They were the largest war machines I'd ever seen. I wondered if even the engineers of Ni-Yota could've created such monstrosities. How long had they been in the works? Surely, it had taken more than an afternoon to assemble such machines. They must have been readied long ago, but were being deployed only now, when the original attack was defeated. What was their original purpose?

I didn't relish fighting an enemy such as this. The enchanters of Ulibon had been formidable, the griffins and furies of Oster even more so, but the hollowings were something else entirely. Their battle tactics spoke of their intelligence, but the great moving bridges coming across the Illium waste betrayed practical engineering expertise as well. Harlan was doubtlessly correct that the hollowings did not seek conquest in the manner of the kings of Rolm or Oster. Whatever the reasons for this battle against Ni-Yota, the enemies in the west were even more determined in their ambition than the most relentless human monarch.

Harlan spoke aloud the conclusion I was trying to avoid reaching. "To stop them, we'll have to burn those giant bridges. Best to do it long before they reach the river."

"They are expecting that," I said reluctantly. "They move ballistae with the towers. I do not see the blood raptors, but they must be close, waiting. The hollowings will protect those towers with everything they have."

We both watched the behemoths pull the looming machines closer for a time, the wind whistling an ominous song. Harlan finally spoke again. "You should speak to Gia."

I groaned even though I knew Harlan was correct. If the latest hollowing advance was to be turned back, we dragons needed to act together. A fire breather would be necessary for this. Rinxia's speed would've been invaluable as well, but she would be in no shape to fly in the time we had remaining. I worried about her, but I was also glad that she wouldn't be taking this risk. Let Gia do it. Let him act as the protector of this land.

I turned back toward the Mizu army. As I descended, searching for Gia, I caught sight of Drasu's caravan, a lonely wagon with its escorts drudging slowly east. It wasn't lost on me that fate had spared me from having to make the terrible decision of killing the wizard and creating the very situation that now faced Ni-Yota. That didn't make fate and I even. Throwing me a meatless bone didn't come close to compensating for my upbringing and years of slavery.

It wasn't hard to find the giant black dragon amidst the sea of humans and horses. Gia saw me as well, his great neck craning upward as I circled in the sky above. The humans with whom he had gathered began staring upward as well, alerted to my presence by Gia's attention. Several stood from their chairs.

"The humans below look nervous," Harlan remarked.

"Perhaps they fear I intend to open my bowels."

"Please don't."

"Do not fear. That dried meat from the Mizu supply wagon was too salty to be ready for evacuation so soon. The best I could do would be to spray them with a bit of pungent golden rain."

"Bayloo, that's too much information. Let's just go speak to Gia without provoking him first."

I landed among the gathered commanders of the Mizu army, deliberately placing myself directly opposite the other dragon. Of the four humans gathered around Gia, I recognized two: the wizard Legao and a tall, long-limbed man I'd seen leading the cavalry charge against my salient in the battle earlier. I didn't know his name, but I recognized his eyes.

Gia greeted me with his customary warmth—none. "This meeting is of no concern of yours, Bayloo. I will summon you when your assistance is needed."

Oh. That's how he wanted to play. If this was the reception he offered, I should've just crapped on him. Gia was living proof that dragons could act as stupid as humans.

I let a low roar rumble up my neck. "I take no commands from you, Gia. I accept no summons from anyone. I go where I will; I fight as I must."

Gia showed me his teeth.

Harlan scrambled off my back. "Enough...enough. We come not to bicker amongst ourselves, but with information that must be heard."

Gia kept the edge of his jaw curled in challenge. His eyes saw nothing but threats from me, because that was all he expected to receive. Some among the other humans were wiser, at least.

Legao paced to the center of the council. "We are in need of allies and information," she proclaimed. Gia whipped his head toward her, but he did nothing to stop the wizard's speaking. "We gather to speak of this battle and the next one that will inevitably come, Bayloo. You should know these others." She swept an arm along the gathered. "Here sits Avix, Knight-Lord of the West." Avix was large for a human, with a flat face and no chin. It wasn't lost on me that this knight-lord sat closest to Gia among the humans of this council. The rider I already recognized was next. Legao named him Tia, Master of the Horse. The last human was a smaller, squatter man, with arms almost as long and thick as his legs, and a face with enough divots that it looked like a bird had been pecking away at his flesh for most of the morning. "Dianti, Lord at Arms," he was named. Dianti squinted at me as he bowed his head politely.

Legao wasn't done with introductions. "This war council should all know the outlander who rides upon this dragon's back. He calls himself Harlan Dor. Let there be no doubt: he is a child of Farlight. But also know this: Aragor welcomed him to this land. Although his heritage is not one favored in Ni-Yota, let us not dismiss Aragor's decision. The idea to pack fire oil into the barges was his."

Tia gave Harlan a knowing nod. "It was brave to stay with the craft, battling the current until the end. I welcome your presence here, Harlan Dor."

Gia's eyes flashed with annoyance.

Legao made a final introduction. "And as you all undoubtedly know, this is Bayloo, from beyond the Edge."

Avix stood. "What have you come to tell us, Bayloo?"

I didn't like his tone much more than Gia's. I was deciding if I should answer when Harlan spoke over me.

"The hollowings prepare another attack. More bridges are being brought from the west."

Avix waved a hand. "This is expected from them. They are persistent. But even with the hollowings' ability to marshal their collective manpower, it will take considerable time to construct and transport the materials from their nearest forest they haven't already consumed, which is at least one hundred leagues—"

I had no patience for this. "They come now." I said it loud enough that there could be no doubt that Avix could hear me, even through his human ears.

That silly human held up a finger. "Not possible, given the distance and time."

Harlan answered more calmly than I would have. "They come even as we speak, with huge bridges that resemble siege towers, except far wider, seemingly designed to cross rivers. They are the size of wheeled fortresses, allowing for more of their forces to cross more quickly than they did on the bridges we burned today. And they bring at least four this time."

Avix's nose scrunched, as if he was trying to retract it into his head. "How could such things as you describe even move?"

I told him, but I was watching Gia's reaction. "Behemoths pull them far faster and for longer than could your horses. By tomorrow they will likely reach the river. Already, the hollowings mass for a second assault. As we speak, more ballistae line the river."

Grim silence descended upon the council. Finally, Gia forced his gaze to meet mine. "You have seen all of this?"

"Just now. It is as Harlan says. The hollowings come again."

Dianti opened his mouth. "My men aren't ready, Avix. Wounded still litter the camp. The able-bodied are exhausted. Reinforcements from the east will not arrive for another week. The foot soldiers will take even longer, and that's at a forced pace."

"We have the river." Tia's voice was measured, determined. A warrior's tone. I approved. "Even if they bring four bridges, that is still only four points they can cross. They outnumber us, but we can concentrate our forces, particularly the mounted horses."

Dianti let out the sigh of an exhausted man. "Their lines cannot be broken. Their soldiers have no fear. Even with mighty Gia tearing their behemoths to pieces."

Oh, it was mighty Gia who tore those beasts to pieces? All by himself. Remarkable indeed.

Dianti wasn't done. He was the most animated of the humans, and apparently the newest to join the battle. "Those wolves are even more lethal. I could scarcely believe it. The stories do not do them justice..."

"Do not lose hope, Dianti." Avix's lips spread into a thin line. "It is true, as you say, that the hollowings do not behave like a regular army, but they have weaknesses as well, which we can exploit. For example, the hollowing foot soldiers do not pull back when they should. And holding a full line is not always the wisest course of action. We can concentrate all of our remaining horses on a single bridge." He looked to Tia. "Most likely the hollowings will fight relentlessly, trying to hold their position even when vastly outnumbered. They die just like our men do. We might take and destroy each bridge, one at a time."

Tia bobbed his head with approval. "It is wise to use their stubbornness against them, but I fear we won't have time. They will come hard and fast, and we do not face just the human soldiers. It is the behemoths and the wolves that pose an even greater threat. To say nothing of those nightmare birds."

Finally, Gia spoke again. "Better they never reach the river at all." He looked at me, not hiding the distrust that smoldered in his eyes. "This all supposes that Bayloo and his human speak the truth." He spread his wings. "I will return shortly."

Gia beat his great wings. A torrent of air and dust swirled as the massive dragon lifted into the air, headed toward the river. I hoped he only went to confirm my information and not to do anything so foolish as to cross the river to attempt to attack now, on his own. That would be idiotic, but it was also Gia.

We all watched him fly, a black blot on the sky. Soon he would be nearly invisible to any except me. Or maybe Legao. Her face remained impassive, even as her eyes took in every detail around her. She seemed wary.

"You have some idea as to how to stop the hollowings?" I asked her. "Is there something else we must know?"

Legao took her time before answering as the others stared at her, none with warmth. "No."

Avix huffed. "The master magi indeed. Drasu was an irreplaceable loss." Deep lines crossed his forehead. The man was tired.

Legao fixed her eyes upon him without moving her head. "To stop the horde, they must be destroyed. That is the only way. Otherwise, they will come. Again and again, until we are dead or flee. Even Drasu could only delay them."

"We all know you are not Drasu." Dianti puffed his chest. "Aragor put too much faith in the old spellcaster. Using magic to keep them on the other side of the river was a mistake. It is like locking your door with a hungry wolf outside. The longer you wait, the hungrier and more desperate the wolf. Now, the situation is far worse."

Legao merely arched her brow, her face cold and dangerous. Dianti shut his mouth.

It was Avix who explained it. "You are new to the river, Dianti. I assure you that there was never a way to defeat that horde with swords. Whatever aid we can get, from whatever quarter, we must use." He looked at Legao, then me. "Dianti, I hope you live long enough to understand that."

The soldier paled.

Gia's return saved Dianti from embarrassing himself further. He set himself down close to me, far closer than I was comfortable with. The only creatures I wanted that close to me were Rinxia and the black pig I was about to eat. An even deeper distrust blazed in Gia's eyes.

The huge dragon flicked his heavy tail dangerously.

"I see the hollowings—a great horde still remaining across the river. I have flown back and forth along the Tayo, flying high so that I could survey the wasteland from afar. I looked deep into the land that was once Illium, Bayloo. I saw nothing like what you have claimed."

TEN

Gia named me a liar.

At least that was what I thought just happened. While I did sometimes lie, I wasn't lying this time. Why would I bother to lie about a forthcoming hollowing attack?

The air between Gia and I heated from the glare of our locked gazes. I don't know how long the standoff lasted. Long enough that one of the humans might have peed himself, based on the odor in the air. I got tired of wasting my time with this gigantic, overly proud oaf of a dragon.

"Four bridges and towers, Gia. They look like rolling palace spires being dragged by behemoths. Even you can't miss them."

"I did not see them. Do you say I lie?" He slung his tail ominously. Despite his wounds, he sounded anxious for a fight. What had he seen up there?

He was turning this around on me. My hearts beat with outrage. I unfurled my wings in challenge. Gia didn't flinch, but I definitely sniffed a bit of human urine. Not a lot, but enough.

"I saw the hollowing bridges," Harlan assured everyone, as if the word of an outlander would carry any weight with the self-important personages of Ni-Yota or with Gia. "My eyes are not those of a dragon, but these constructions are so massive they cannot be mistaken."

I sensed the confusion and fear of Gia's council. They would follow his lead—he was in charge. Not even Legao would challenge him directly. The wizard kept her silence, although I doubted it was from fear.

My thoughts flashed to Rinxia. She wanted me to be Protector of Ni-Yota—or at least she didn't want Gia to have the title. She was right. Gia's head was filled with rot. It would be easy to provoke him into battle. I was pretty sure I could win a confrontation. But what was the point? I had nothing to gain. Even Rinxia would not want Gia and I fighting now, not with the hollowings about to strike again. I sucked a whirlwind of air into my lungs, then released it slowly.

"What did you see out there, Gia?" I fought to keep my tone level.

"There is blackness to the west. Nothing else can be seen."

Blackness? The sky had darkened considerably since Harlan and I had done our reconnoiter, but for Gia's dragon eyes that shouldn't have been a true impediment. Not with something so large and obvious as those rolling bridges.

"Come with me again, to the sky," I urged him.

"I do not need you to tell me that my eyes are wrong. There is blackness. It is...unnatural. Not the blackness of night, but something else. I cannot see beyond it."

I looked over at Harlan. I found his face lined with concern, a rare enough situation. I decided to be the grown-up dragon at the council. I just hoped Rinxia appreciated this. "Together, let us make what we can of this, Gia."

Gia sniffed suspiciously but still didn't answer.

Legao spoke into the gap. "I would ask to come as well, if one of you would consent to carry me. I suspect other forces may be at work here. I may be able to be of some use."

I liked how she spoke as if my idea would go forward. Cunning. I broke away from Gia's gaze to take the measure of the other humans of the war council.

Avix kept his expression blank, waiting for Gia to guide him. Dianti looked scared, as if someone was about to suggest he ride up into the air as well. The stocky human's eyes shifted uneasily between Gia's huge form and the darkening sky.

"We must know what we face," Tia urged. "Bringing the magi is prudent."

Finally, Avix nodded as well. Whatever his loyalty to Gia, the eastern bank of the river was his to defend.

With everyone except Dianti having spoken in favor of my proposal, Gia relented. "I will return to the sky." He looked at Legao. "I've no saddle, nor is there time to fit one before the last of the light fades, making your human eyes completely useless. Bayloo must carry you."

There probably was a dragon saddle nearby. Gia deliberately put me in this situation rather than send for one. He wanted me to carry the wizard while he was seen as unburdened.

Carrying Legao didn't thrill me. I wasn't sure how horses felt about their riders, but allowing someone into that position on our backs made dragons particularly vulnerable, since it was out of reach of both our tails and our claws. With most humans, I was confident I could deal with any situation, but Legao was a wizard. I hadn't had good experiences with human magic. I barely knew this wizard, and I certainly didn't trust her. Legao stared at me expectantly, her look a mixture of challenge and expectation. She had fought well against the hollowings.

"Get on and let's go."

Legao climbed onto my back without hesitation or misstep. "Don't cross the river," Harlan reminded me unnecessarily just before I took off. Having Harlan nagging me was almost like having a mother at times. I took to the air, Gia close behind.

It didn't take us long to reach the river's edge. The sun was passing under the horizon in the west, spreading a malevolent crimson glow across the wasteland that lay beyond the horde. Our altitude was sufficient to see far past the hollowing horde at the far bank. The bridge-towers should've stuck out like wolves in a chicken coop, but they didn't. Instead, I saw endless waste, ripped and torn over the years by the hollowings. But that wasn't the end of it. Something wasn't right about the sight. I continued to stare. Part of the distant wasteland was darker than the rest, as if covered by a veil of shadow.

Gia either didn't see the abnormality or chose to ignore it to prove his point. "There are no rolling bridges, Bayloo."

"Look at the horizon, Gia. What is that darkness?"

Gia stared outward, his massive wings catching the air, keeping him almost steady beside me. "There is something strange," he conceded reluctantly. "I saw something similar earlier. As I said, it is not natural." Gia beat his wings, flying higher. He then turned southward before returning a short time later. "I cannot see around it. Above it is more darkness. It is…strange. It is there, but not there. Like a wave in the sea, not quite solid but real."

For once, he wasn't wrong. I couldn't easily explain what I saw and what I didn't see. The tower-bridges had indeed vanished. "The hollowings must have noticed my earlier reconnaissance. As always, they adapted. The rolling machines I spoke of must be hidden behind that wall of dark."

It was the logical explanation. Surely, Gia must realize that. Except he didn't trust me, and he didn't want to acknowledge I had been telling the truth all along. "We have never seen this from them before. They never bothered to disguise their movements. They had overwhelming forces and didn't care that we knew."

"Before, there was Drasu and his barrier of magic," Legao pointed out. "Perhaps there was no need for such measures before now. The number of their forces didn't matter because few managed to cross."

"Is that magic out there?" I asked Legao. "Some kind of spell?"

I couldn't see Legao shake her head, but I was pretty sure she did so. "The hollowings have never used magic in all the years we have faced them. Drasu would've mentioned it. This is something else."

"Can you do better than that?" I was annoyed. "This ride isn't for fun."

She snapped back at me. "What would you have me do, Bayloo?"

"When humans are curious about something, don't they usually just poke it or something?"

Legao sighed loud enough for me to hear it. "They are still quite distant. However, I still might manage a little...poke, as you say."

Legao began to whisper. It sounded like the first few notes of a song, a dreamy melody barely remembered. She swayed in her saddle as the words grew louder. Something within me stirred as well. My blood surged, the pumping of my hearts ringing in my ears as I listened to the wizard on my back speak to the wind. She kept adjusting the song until she found a harmony with the air at that moment. Legao sang her request to the wind; the gusts answered. The air barely stirred nearby, but as a dragon, I understood enough about wind currents to know that was how such things worked. A change in wind direction and speed in one place would push the air around it in that same direction. In this case, Legao had started a small storm. Not high in the clouds, but closer to the ground. The wind she unleashed began to pick up speed as it sped from the riverbank, moving across the waste that had once been Illium. It picked up dust as it went, swirling like a frantic dancer, headed toward the curtain of black. Faster and faster it moved, sucking dust and sand from the ground into its funnel. The debris turned the ever-quickening storm the same battered rust color as the ground of the wasteland. The magic tempest continued its journey, until finally the conjured wind smashed into the wall of shadow.

The curtain buckled, its surface breaking apart and then quickly reforming as it swallowed Legao's summoned storm. It was all over in a few moments. The curtain of night seemed solid once again. But it wasn't. It had never been solid, nor was it a wall in the traditional sense.

"It moves. It breaks, but it came back again. It's like a sea of night," Gia observed.

He was wrong. It wasn't a sea. I knew what we were looking at. I'd seen something similar the day Aragor had died. "It's a wall all right—a wall of blood raptors. The storm startled them enough to break formation, but only for a moment. Just like the hollowing troops. They come at us in rank, in this case packed so closely together they shield the great tower-bridges from view."

Gia stared. "There could be anything behind that wall. Or nothing at all."

He was being stupid. Again. He couldn't help himself. It took all my self-restraint not to tell Gia of his own foolishness. "You may not like me, but do not doubt the truth of my words. The obvious is directly in front of you."

Gia snorted, annoyed and ever distrustful. After taking a last look at the horde, the black dragon dropped from the sky without another word to me. I watched him land amidst his council of humans and Harlan. I followed in no particular rush. I wasn't a puppy to be led about.

When I finally rejoined the council, the humans were silent, staring at Gia, awaiting his decision.

Gia's first words were to Avix inquiring as to the total number of wounded. The knight-lord seemed surprised at the question.

"I still don't have an accurate count. Hopefully I will have it by morning. I would guess at least a thousand dead or wounded, probably much more."

Gia pretended to care about the answer. "Send a glasswing to Trishan. The late Protector's funeral is to be delayed for several more days until I can return to raise the fire myself."

Avix hailed a servant to carry out Gia's wishes. I was impatient with these games. I was tempted to announce that I would destroy the bridges myself. Except alone, I would probably fail. No fire, and only a single dragon, would make the task impossible. I needed Gia if

I was going to do this. He knew it. Finally, the giant dragon got around to saying the obvious.

"An unexpected danger approaches from the west. A new threat, most likely. I've decided it is worth the risk to cross the river to destroy it before it gets here. Let us decide how that is to be done."

ELEVEN

We decided to use the darkness.

No one really knew if the hollowings slept at night. According to Avix, they did appear to lie down as regular humans would. It seemed their empty bodies had a need for rest, just like ordinary humans. But even if the horde wasn't actually sleeping, we still decided that night would give us some advantage, because dragons could see better at night than humans. Gia's dark scales would make him particularly difficult to spot. I consented to having my own scales coated in dark war-paint to further camouflage myself.

"This won't be useful," I said to Harlan as several Mizu rubbed the dark chalk over me with thick brushes.

"Then why are you letting them do it?"

"Because Gia mocked the idea. I didn't like his tone so I wasn't going to let him stop me."

"Excellent reason."

I thought so as well.

I had also refitted my *sai* onto my claws with the assistance of Harlan and two Mizu attendants. The cold metal weapons felt like cheating in a way, but they had more than proven their worth against the behemoths in the previous battle.

A mounted Mizu rider carrying a torch arrived to inform me that Gia was ready to fly. We had decided we would cross as far apart as practical with the hope that at least one of us would get across the river undetected in the darkness. His starting position was sufficiently distant that I couldn't see him from the ground.

"It would be better if I was with you," Harlan commented as we both watched the sky for the flaming arrow that would be the signal to take to the air.

"Having a passenger makes me less maneuverable. Also, you are far more exposed to attack by blood raptors than I am. Most importantly, you don't add anything to this mission." It was a bit harsh, but true.

Harlan showed no sign of taking offense. "I learn from what I see. That can be useful even if the use isn't immediately obvious."

Was the implication that I didn't learn?

A crimson streak rose into the sky before I had a chance to ask Harlan precisely what he meant. I unfurled my wings. I didn't want him with me, and that was that.

As I was about to take off, Harlan spoke quickly. "The hollowings expect the expected. To outwit them, you must do the unexpected."

I wasn't paying attention. "Got it."

I hurled myself into the sky, with only a brief pang of regret. Why was I doing this? For Rinxia and Kiata, I told myself. This place mattered to them, so it mattered to me. But it wasn't just that. My head was skeptical of any duty to Ni-Yota, but something else tugged at me: the rust was devastating. I might not follow a so-called Way like the rest of the dragons of Ni-Yota, but I knew a threat when I saw it.

I headed north at speed, flying above the clouds, well beyond where I thought I would be visible to human eyes. As I traveled beyond the Narrows, the hollowing army disappeared from the landscape. North of the Narrows, the Tayo widened and quickened, its banks becoming a nearly impassible collection of jagged cliffs and ominous peaks where not even the hollowings could easily travel. Mizu battle engines that resembled ballistae but shot plumes of smaller projectiles designed to target blood raptors had been lifted onto the mountains on the eastern side of the river, along with cages filled with specially trained war hawks. It was here I crossed the water into Illium.

A chill ran through me as I passed over the far bank of the Tayo. I presumed that was just some silly jitters. I was in the sky. Here in the air, my kind ruled. Blood raptors might harry dragons at these heights, but they could not defeat us.

Beneath me were jagged rocks and craggy mountains. After the peaks came more wasteland, a landscape covered almost entirely by the ugly presence of the rust, as if some impossible giant had poured it from buckets from the sky until every bit of land below was covered. Even far above, the sight made me uneasy. I flew quickly; no alarm was raised, no arc-bolts were launched. I turned, heading southwest, toward the wall of blood raptors that traveled through the waste.

I kept a sharp watch on the ground below. I caught glimpses of what I thought might be movement: a rustling of ground, a flash of black at the fringe of my vision. It was hard to tell from my altitude. Whatever I saw could've been the wind, or perhaps the hollowing wolves who fought alongside the humans. I was moving quickly. Whatever was down there, in the sea of blighted rust, I heard no loud noises and saw no marshalling forces.

Each beat of my wings brought me closer to the blackness, and the bridge-towers I was certain were beyond the camouflage shield. I scanned the sky to the south, trying to catch sight of Gia. I saw only more night. That was either a sign that his natural darkness was an effective cloak, or an indication that I was in deep trouble. I didn't trust Gia, although I didn't think him dishonorable. I didn't doubt he wanted to destroy the hollowings, at least. I kept flying, deeper in their domain.

I pushed myself faster, anxious to be done with this. My scales prickled. Had I really come so far unseen?

I caught a smell on the air, something foul. The odor of decay, but not death. Then, I heard the noise of a thousand dark whispers. It was the mingled sound of countless feathered wings. Along with the whispers came the groan of wooden wheels, the crushing of stones on the well-punished ground. I was close. The hollowings would know I was here soon if they didn't already.

I still couldn't see Gia. He could've been in the clouds, silent and unseen, or something could've delayed him. His fire would be critical to the plan succeeding. I wore the *sai*, but I needed to drive close to use those. Gia's fire was the better weapon for this mission. I had to give the fire breather his due. So, where was he?

I flew even faster toward the black. I had thought Gia a fool, but it occurred to me that perhaps I was the true fool for coming here, for relying upon a dragon who resented my existence.

The notion that Gia wasn't going to show up kept gnawing at me, like a little beaver in my mind, destroying the dam of calm that held my fears in check. My hearts beat like lead, but I had no time for remorse. The malicious little eyes of the blood raptors appeared. Was there triumph in those little creatures' gazes? Did they laugh at my lack of foresight?

Gia ached to be Protector. He thought I was in his way. How badly did he want that title? Enough to see me dead in the wasteland. If he never showed up, who would ever know? He could make up any story he wanted for Rinxia and Kiata. But if I was wrong, if I turned back, I would be abandoning Gia. His wing was injured. He might not make it without me.

It was too late for such cynical considerations. I wasn't going to turn back. Either Gia would be where he was supposed to be, or not. I put all my strength in a decisive beat of my wings, extending the *sai* on my foreclaws. The raptors and I collided violently. I sliced some feathers. I carved through the bird wall easily. I'd expected scrapes and pecks and fury, but I received none of that. I'd anticipated the raptors to scatter when I struck the heart of the flock, as ordinary birds would have. They didn't. Instead, the blood raptors let me in like an invited guest and closed the door behind me.

Inside the blood raptor cage there was utter blackness. Even the starlight was blocked by the feathered ceiling above. I wasn't sure if I'd ever been anywhere so dark. And it reminded me of something I and other dragons don't dwell upon: we can't actually see in the dark. Our eyes simply require far less light than humans, and the regular night has plenty of light for us. In the total absence of any source of light, I was blind. The hollowings had somehow created a near-perfect void inside that flying box. I could barely make out the outline of my own snout.

It was a trap.

They expect the expected.

Some fire would've been very useful at that moment, but of course I had none. I didn't need to see to know that it was just me in here. I wanted to panic, and I was fully entitled to do so, but I didn't. If I lost control now, everyone else won. Gia won, the hollowings won, the tigris won, countless uneaten pigs of Ni-Yota won. I wasn't dying in the dark or falling to the tainted rust crap that had gotten Aragor.

Why had the hollowings gone to such lengths to lure me into the dark? It must've taken countless blood raptors to accomplish this. The obvious answer was because they didn't want me to see some kind of threat inside their trap. They expected me to be surprised by the utter darkness, to hesitate. So I didn't. I turned as quickly as I could, then dove. I heard a ballista fire, the snap of its torque. One, three, five shots. The bolts whistled dangerously through the air. I couldn't see them, but I could hear. Only one projectile came close. They hadn't anticipated how quickly I would adapt. Also, the hollowings didn't understand dragon senses. No other creature was our equal. I couldn't see, but that wasn't necessary for a dragon to fly adeptly. Our navigational sense didn't require sight. I didn't know exactly what was on the ground, but it didn't really matter. I could locate the sounds of ballistae well enough to know their location. Even if I didn't get everything precisely correct, I intended to destroy a wide area.

I dove. My claws sank into the wood of a machine. I caught it and closed my claws, lifting the ballista into the air with another beat of my wings. I dropped it where I heard the scurrying of rapid footsteps, leading to a shattering crash and even more scurrying. The hollowings didn't shout or panic. I swerved again, turning onto my side, just in case these creatures could somehow see better than regular humans. I listened for the sounds of arc-bolts being reloaded, pouncing as soon as I did. The hollowings did their best, but I was as fast as only a desperate dragon could manage.

Where were the bridge-towers?

The hollowings had stopped moving the massive machines I had come here to destroy. I heard no sound of creaking wheels. That was clever, but not sufficient. Behemoths were massive animals, and even hollowings make noise. They were still flesh, they drew breath, and that made noise. I could hear those great beasts even in the strange silence of the void. I flew at a sound I guessed to be a behemoth, hoping that they couldn't see any better in the dark than a human. If I was wrong, those deadly tail spikes would give my enemy a potentially fatal advantage, but fortune fought with me at that moment. My *sai* plunged into tough hide followed by softer flesh. Something sticky and warm coated my claws. A rush of air swept past as a behemoth tail came at me, but I was already gone, streaking upwards.

Arc-bolts clicked into place. There was more movement on the ground. The blood raptors fluttered. Too many sounds at once. This wasn't a safe place. I needed to flee.

I hated leaving the bridge-towers intact, but fighting in the darkness in this place, blind and alone, was madness. I flew for the blood raptor wall on the opposite side from where I'd entered the hollow trap.

Blazing light burst through the feathery barrier before I reached it. It was as if the sun had risen within the hollowing cage, furious at being shut out for so long. The smell of burnt feathers reached my nostrils soon after, shattering the illusion of daybreak. The sun hadn't risen. Gia had come. That big lug of fire-coughing dragon had actually arrived. Finally.

The light of the black dragon's fire revealed the clever trap that had been laid for me in this place. The great rolling tower-bridges were real enough, but after the hollowings had raised their feathered shield to block all views, they'd brought in a dozen ballistae I hadn't seen. These machines rolled on wheels and weren't as large as their cousins near the river, but their projectiles were no less deadly. Two of the machines had already reloaded. I gave a roar of warning as they loosed their bolts at Gia. He didn't have time to maneuver out of the way, but he was able to redirect his fiery burst of breath toward the incoming danger. The heat of Gia's fire melted the tips so the weapons were as lethal as pebbles when they finally struck his armor. That was a handy trick.

Reinvigorated by Gia's belated arrival, I broke off my retreat, executed something close to a flip in the air, and proceeded to visit havoc upon every ballista I could reach. They were easy targets, unarmored. A single hit from my tail or claws was sufficient to destroy them.

Gia cared only for the big targets. He flew immediately for the tower-bridges. Keeping well out of range of the behemoths on the ground below, Gia bathed the first of the massive constructions in fire. The flames embraced their victim, swirling and crackling with delight as they spread. I wacked another ballista, intent on giving Gia all the time he needed to set every tower ablaze. But it wasn't going to be so easy. When Gia's flames dissipated, instead of a smoldering skeleton of ash, the tower structure remained intact. His belch of fire hadn't ignited the wood of the tower-bridge as I'd expected. At most, he'd singed the exterior. Gia roared in frustration, circling back and dousing the tower yet again, this time with brilliant fire fueled with his unrivaled anger. The tower groaned, wobbled, but that wasn't enough. Once again, the flames faded, leaving the structure standing defiantly. It would take more than fire to destroy these new constructions, and the hollowings had no intention of giving us the chance to do more damage.

The walls and ceiling of the bird-box Gia and I put ourselves in collapsed. Thousands of blood raptors descended upon us from five directions. Being closer to the top, Gia got the worst of it, with the birds enveloping him in a blanket of vicious avian feathers, claws, and beaks. There were so many that the huge dragon disappeared from my sight, with only a feather-encased blob remaining. The birds grabbed at his wings by the hundreds. Gia began to fall from the sky, the birds weighing upon him. His wings moved, but the motion was balky—it was like trying to fly through water. He unleashed his fire, even daring to douse himself in flames, but that wasn't enough. There were too many raptors, and they were willing to roast to bring him down. The behemoths abandoned their position near the bridge-towers, each one galloping toward the area where it seemed as if Gia would fall. All this without audible shouts or other obvious communication.

A hundred or more raptors swarmed about me as well, all of them pecking and scratching. Dozens tried to latch onto my wings. I shook and twisted as I flew in circles, trying to keep the number that managed to get a hold on me manageable. I could still fly and maneuver. I could also see—and what I saw was four mean-looking behemoths waiting to kill Gia the moment he struck the ground. I didn't see any way for him to survive what awaited.

Chicken piss.

I flew at my fellow dragon, diving and twisting as I came to him. I wouldn't be able to lift him—two of me wouldn't be able to do that—but I needed to get the blood raptors off his wings. I didn't have the fire to do that, but I did have some other advantages: I had a really loud roar, I flew fast, and I was desperate.

The roar part was easy. I unleashed it, deafening in volume, enough to shake the air. That didn't stop the blood raptors, of course. To do that, I had to fly directly onto Gia. I swept over the giant dragon, scraping my belly against his back, my wings against his. It was the closest I'd ever been to another dragon I wasn't trying to kill— except Rinxia. I squashed a dozen raptors between us, and swept dozens more off his back and wings with my tail. Bird bones crashed, wings snapped. It still wasn't going to be enough to restore his ability to fly—there were too many on his wings. I latched onto the huge dragon, pulling him toward me as if I were inclined to mate with the brute. I beat my wings as hard as I was able. That slowed us, but not enough. Desperately, I wriggled and twisted. Gia did the same, unleashing his breath at the same time. He scorched me as well as himself. I couldn't take much more, but neither could the raptors. Our entire armored bodies heated, our scales becoming like flying ovens even as I continued to smash the birds. Feathers smoked and burned. We couldn't completely free ourselves from the latching raptors, but it was just enough.

Gia roared, and I knew what he meant. We shoved off of each other just before we struck the behemoths' killing area on the ground. Gia came so low he might have taken a tail to his hind leg, but it wasn't enough to stop him. I could sense his angry determination through the dark. His eyes burned nearly as bright as the fire he kept unleashing.

"We will finish those towers!" Gia called to me as he beat his wings, once again gaining altitude.

There were four towers. I had no idea how to destroy them, except to land on them and rip them apart. I also knew that the blood raptors would rally and attack again. Already, they were reorienting themselves, forming up into huge clouds of black to envelop us once again. This time they'd come in equal numbers at both of us.

"Gia, we have to leave. The raptors come again."

He didn't listen. Instead, he fell upon another of the bridge-towers, tearing at the wood of its upper layers. Gia's strength was tremendous. He smashed and shattered the upper portion of the tower with several brutal hits of his tail. So what? It wasn't destroyed. Whatever damage he'd done would be fixed. As he pummeled the tower, the blood raptors came again. He saw them and tried to escape at the last moment, using a spreading shield of fire to get himself the time he needed to evade the massive, flapping cloud that came to envelop him. It almost worked.

Gia managed to keep ahead of the blood raptors. He was faster, particularly in a dive. Unfortunately, I hadn't destroyed all the ballistae. The hollowings had already aimed an arc-bolt at the tower Gia had been assaulting. They quickly adjusted as he jumped off. I saw it. I flew fast. The bolt launched, springing at Gia even as he essentially dove toward it. It was too late for Gia to maneuver out of the way. I swept between them, my body passing through the narrow space that separated weapon and victim without a moment to spare. My tail whacked the projectile off course about a finger's length from Gia's snout. I roared in satisfaction. Gia pulled up just before the ground, barely above the outstretched swords of the hollowings below. The blood raptors followed like hungry chicks chasing their mother. I came at Gia as well, faster than the birds. I flew alongside him.

"This was a trap. We need to get out, now."

Gia growled defiance.

"Rinxia cannot defend Ni-Yota by herself. I'm leaving."

My wings ended any chance for debate with the larger dragon. I headed east, gaining altitude as I moved. I pushed myself hard. Again, Harlan's warning that hollowings expect the expected rang in my mind. The reminder came just in time. I swerved off my initial course, then did it again. A deadly pack of six arc-bolts, fired from ballistae hidden in pits dug into the ground, made me grateful for my friend's warning. I looked back to see Gia had wisely followed me eastward. The blood raptors remained in pursuit, but they couldn't match a dragon's speed. When I was confident that I was well out of the range of any human-built projectile hurler, I slowed to allow Gia to catch me.

I had one burning question for him that couldn't wait until we were safely back on the other side of the river. "What took you so long to get here?"

He didn't answer.

TWELVE

Blood raptors pursued us.

Gia and I were swifter. We put ever greater distance between us and the birds as we flew toward the Tayo. It had been a trap, and I felt fortunate to have escaped with my life. I wanted to return to Ni-Yota to fight another day and see Rinxia again. I sensed no such urgency in the giant brute who flew alongside me. Gia seemed to hesitate ever so slightly each time he beat his wings, as if reluctant to make the effort. It could've been that he didn't like retreating. Or that might have nothing to do with his hesitation.

Gia twisted his neck to survey our pursuit. The birds had fallen well behind us. Below there was only the rust, a lethal sea of waste, but it couldn't touch us in the sky. Gia snarled, a sour, cranky sound, as he turned his head back toward Ni-Yota.

The big dragon annoyed me like a chicken feather up my nose. He also might've deliberately tried to get me killed, although I wasn't sure. I certainly had no patience for him. "What's gnawing your snout?"

Gia growled. "We flee. Flee like little mice from a snake. We are dragons."

"The term is regrouping, Gia. We were outnumbered."

"The hollowings will always have greater numbers. What shall we do if they cross the Tayo with their bridges and greater numbers? Will we fly all the way to Trishan? Or perhaps you'll go 'regroup' across the mountains back in Elasu's old den at Changsha." I could taste his bitterness on the wind.

There was no answer I could give that would satisfy him. I should've just kept my mouth shut. "I prefer to fight battles I can win. Sometimes that means retreat. What is honor worth to the dead?"

"What is the point in living without being true to the Way?"

I could've made a list. Black pigs and shaojiu were near the top. And seeing Rinxia again. Food and drink didn't care if you were honorable or not. Rinxia was more complicated. I didn't bother to tell Gia about these things. He wouldn't understand. I just laughed with my eyes. Gia snarled all the way back to the river, but still he came along.

The blood raptors trailed us all the way, more relentless than a dog begging for dinner scraps. Would they follow us across? The Mizu had their war engines and many cages of hawks, but it wouldn't be enough to stop the blood raptors if this many chose to cross over.

As we neared the river, the wind changed. Indeed, it disappeared almost completely. The air pressure dropped. Dark clouds appeared where they shouldn't have. I knew magic was at work. I hoped it was Legao and not some more sinister force.

"Let us not dally," I said to Gia. In truth, I doubted Gia had much more speed than he'd given. I pushed myself harder, curious if the larger dragon would find the strength to keep pace. He did, so I beat my wings for still more speed, reminding Gia that I was swifter than he. I wanted to get across the river. I didn't know how much control Legao had over the forces she summoned or what she intended.

The cloud gave no warning of the fury it was prepared to release. One moment the skies were dark; the next, brilliant flashes of light tore apart the curtain of night. The blazes came in quick succession, as if flying archers lurked in the clouds, launching the lightning arrows in unison. The deadly light ripped into the clustered flock of blood raptors, their close formation enabling the lightning to inflict far more damage than against a conventional flight of birds. The raptors adapted quickly, splitting into several less-dense clouds. The flashes continued to come, but their pace slackened noticeably. I suspected we were witnessing the limits of Legao's power. By the time I crossed the Tayo, the lightning had ceased, but the birds still flew toward us.

I scanned the ground, looking for the wizard. She stood on a small hill beside Harlan, dubiously protected by a dozen wary Mizu soldiers with crossbows in their hands and huge shields on their backs. I landed nearby, leaving Gia to his own ends. He didn't follow.

Harlan came to meet me. "It seems you've angered them."

"It was a trap, as I think you suspected. The bridge-towers were there, but fire-proofed in some way. We failed."

Harlan looked into the dark night, its void now broken only by the light of a few stars. "I'd say you've grabbed a tigris by the tail." He chuckled. I didn't.

"Burning the bridges isn't the answer. It never was. You were right when you said the hollowings expect the expected. We must do the unexpected."

Harlan smirked. "You have a plan, then."

"Maybe I do. It will take time. A day or more, at least." I studied the great horde encamped on the river's far bank. "It is something I must do. Gia will have to hold them again. That will be a bloody affair."

"If a bit of time is all you need, there may be a better way to get some of that."

Harlan walked toward Legao, who had fallen to one knee on the ground. Her breathing was heavy, and dark shadows extended beneath her eyes. The magic had cost her.

"Great Legao, I know you have given your best to your efforts." Harlan cooed like a bard. "Have you enough left for one more task that may be the key to saving us all?"

The wizard pulled her head up from its slouch. She gave Harlan a piercing stare. "You have a way with words, Harlan Dor. You wield guilt like my mother."

"I merely speak the plain truth. This does sometimes tug upon the conscience of those who happen to have such a thing. If my words affect you, it is really a testament to yourself."

Legao blinked several times, then shook her head. "I don't understand what you just said. Name the task you ask, and please quiet yourself after that."

Harlan waved an arm expansively toward the river and the horde beyond. "Rain, my dear wizard. We need rain, a lot of it."

"Are the hollowings afraid of getting wet?"

"Hardly, but the ground across the river is nothing but dry sand and dirt coated with that horrid rust. It's been trampled countless times through the years. It should soak easily and become muddy."

Realization dawned upon me. "Wheels are wheels. Even if behemoths are pulling, they need traction to move those huge machines across distances."

Legao still didn't rise to her feet. "The horde grows close, I suppose. You'll need a lot of rain in very little time."

Harlan grew more serious, never a good sign. "We'll take whatever we can get."

Legao pulled herself upright. She swayed, steadying herself only at the last minute. She spread her arms wide and her irises flashed ever so briefly. She mouthed some words, little more than a whisper, but I did my best to discern them. A low hum followed the shifting tones, the connection of one sound leading to the next. The words themselves (if they were words) meant nothing to me, but somehow, I still had a sense of the power—these were sounds of command. I wondered what these chants meant to Legao, and how it was connected to the magic she wielded. As she worked, I tried, once again, to find the Latticework, that place of magic around us. I reached out with my senses, anxious to understand the power that Legao drew upon. My efforts yielded nothing more than a vague feeling of sizzling energy around me, as if a grand revelation was just out of my grasp. I looked at the sky instead.

Nothing happened immediately. The clouds and wind seemed unmoved by whatever it was Legao attempted. I realized she was weakened. Legao's previous casting had sapped her strength, and she was relying as much on willpower as stamina for this work of magic. Still, I knew by now that Legao had skill. She might have lived her life in the long shadow of the master Drasu, but she had plenty of talent in her own right. Her voice strengthened—and in that instant, I felt it too. The fabric of the sky answered a command, shifting in a manner not intended a moment before that. Clouds gathered as Legao ordered, drawing moisture from the surrounding air. I could sense the dazzling array of connections between the wind, the sky, Legao, and everything else—a magnificent puzzle that was both simple and incomprehensible. Not long after, it began to rain across the river. The drops came slowly, like reluctant tears. Legao swayed again. Her face grew pale. Harlan watched her carefully, poised to catch her if she stumbled. The rain eased to a faint drizzle.

Legao lacked the strength to complete the task. She dropped onto one knee. I had plenty of strength, but I had no idea how to use it. Even though I could neither see nor feel Legao's magic directly, I understood its effect on the Latticework. What she had done was akin to a new apprentice trying to alter a finely woven tapestry. Compared to the intricate elegance of the Latticework, which seemed to form the very structure of existence, her efforts were brutal and clumsy, but that still made her a master compared to me. However, even in my ignorance, I instinctively knew which of the dazzling cords of creation she had attempted to command. Somehow, I understood these weavings just as I understood the winds, just as I always knew my destination and could never get lost in the sky. All of this was part of me as a dragon.

I focused on Legao's work so far. Having used all the moisture in the vicinity, she was trying to pull in still more for her conjured rain storm. She just didn't have the strength. I willed the chords to move, to shift in a manner that would accomplish Legao's purpose, but could not. I could not touch them. I could not command them as Legao had. Something held me back. Heat surged through me, a bubbling power that demanded release, but I didn't know what to do with it. I tried again, attempting to reach out to the great Latticework around me, tracing the cords of light that connected me to the sky. Again, nothing happened. It was just out of reach. I roared in frustration, my anger at my impotence getting the better of me. In that instant, the Latticework was gone.

I thrashed my head around, but only for a few moments. I knew I needed to get my control back. I steadied myself, then tried to find the Latticework again, but could not. Whatever mistake I had made, it had cost me a precious opportunity. Fortunately, Legao remained determined. She pushed herself back upright, her jaw hard. Once again, her mouth moved. Reluctantly, the sky answered. The rains fell again, first a steady trickle, then a deluge.

I felt Harlan's eyes upon us both. Wind and rain ripped past us, cold and welcome. The drops pounded the ragged, thirsty dirt beyond the Tayo. Then, Legao crumpled.

Harlan caught her before she hit the ground. An instant later, three of her Mizu guardians were around her as well. They carried her off, but I didn't move. I gazed at the sky. The rain lessened, but it did not cease. Even without Legao, the clouds had been called, the weather's pattern altered. Eventually, what Legao had done would be set right again, and the Latticework would return the sky to its normal state, but for now, the effect of Legao's magic lingered to our benefit.

Across the river, the ground upon which the hollowings would have to pull their towers quickly became mud, a shifting, slurpy deluge that even a behemoth would have difficulty traversing. Runoff water flowed into the Tayo, raising its water level. There would be no easy crossing. As the water fell from the sky, I kept searching for the elusive Latticework, lurking everywhere and nowhere. I was desperate to understand its pattern and its power. To sense its presence was to enter a near trance. I forgot about the wet sliding off my scales and about the chill of the wind. I merely studied the magnificence of the workings of existence. A wizard had caused this rain. One day, I vowed, I would be able to do so as well. That and more. I knew now the power was inside me.

Only when the sun rose behind me did the rain finally quit.

Harlan was beside me, although I hadn't noticed him before. "Well done. I always knew the strength of the spirit within you. The magic that goes along with it is even more impressive."

I was surprised at his praise. "I did nothing."

Harlan's eyes widened. "Oh?" His tone told me he disagreed. "Legao looked ready to tumble before you roared, before you did whatever else you did. Then, during the night, the rain slackened, then came again as you sat here watching. Somehow, I think you helped with this."

"I don't think so. I am a babe bumbling in the forest." Harlan kept staring, so I added, "For now."

He nodded, seemingly satisfied.

"In any case, this rain won't stop them," I warned.

"No, it won't," Harlan agreed. "But it will delay them. Once Legao recovers, she may be able to continue the work, getting us even more time. Well done so far. What is the rest of your plan?"

My plan?

I'd forgotten all about it. I had been utterly focused on the magic being wrought. My balky mind only reluctantly returned to something like normal. I groaned as I remembered my original intentions.

My body ached. My eyes threatened to close themselves, regardless of what the rest of me wanted. I longed for rest. Delicious rest. But there wasn't time for that. I had to fly. There was much to do and time worked against me.

Still...whatever I had done through the night had not been sleep. My body was drained and I was horribly wet. My efforts deserved some sort of reward.

"Harlan, see if you can find me a pig or two, and we'll talk about what must be done over breakfast."

THIRTEEN

Harlan failed at breakfast.

I'd told him I needed food and rest. I went off to nap beneath a great tent that had been erected in the camp, and Harlan said he would take care of breakfast. But when I awoke, the human had procured only pig feet rather than the whole animal. Pig feet aren't a pig. Chicken feet aren't a chicken. I would've thought even a human with dubious taste in food would've realized that.

Justifiably grouchy, I turned my attention to what had to be done before the hollowings arrived. "We need to speak to Legao."

"You attract too much attention," Harlan said. "I'll go."

I didn't argue with him. He was correct, and my bones still ached from being out in the rain all last night. While I didn't quite trust the wizard, I needed her. I was pretty sure she wasn't one of Gia's lackeys, at least. I waited impatiently, staring at the overcast sky. Only a light drizzle still fell, but it didn't matter. We'd succeeded in slowing the hollowings.

Harlan wasn't gone long. "She wasn't glad to see me. She looked a bit like you this morning."

"Hopefully her breakfast was better. What did she say about the plan?"

Harlan smirked. "'At least we'll die fighting,' were her words."

I snorted. She wasn't wrong.

"I took it as a sign of agreement," Harlan said. "She is no friend of Gia's, and she understands the threat we face, I think."

I was actually glad for Legao's approval. I wanted to speak to her about the hollowings, but also about magic, but there was no time now. If we survived the battle to come, perhaps.

I took to the sky. I moved swiftly with the wind, my fatigue banished in flight. The morning was not yet old when I located the first part of my plan. A caravan of robed humans hauling the body of Drasu the wizard. They had left yesterday, but dragons were much faster than horses, particularly when the horses were hauling wagons.

Harlan called out to me from my back as I circled over the caravan. "Are you going to ask permission or just take him?"

It was a fair question, to which I hadn't given any thought. I had planned to snatch the body. That was how dragons did things—we swooped and took. It was simple and efficient. But I'd brought Harlan along for his more subtle perspective. "What do you suggest?"

"They'll never give him to you. Just swoop down and take the corpse."

Very helpful.

I landed in front of the caravan. Its escorts were justifiably shocked by the dragon that appeared before them.

I drew myself up, posing in my full glory with wings pulled toward the sky. "The wizard Drasu has been called upon to render one last service to Ni-Yota."

The robed men accompanying the corpse-wagon were surprised by my pronouncement, but not as surprised as they were when I ripped the canopy off to expose Drasu's body to the morning sunlight. They'd laid him down with a shroud, but I tore that off too, for good measure. I wanted to see the lifeless remains of my mother's murderer. In my memory, the wizard was a fearsome creation, with eyes that radiated power and a heart of stone. He had commanded the skies, besting even my mother in a contest of magic.

Dead, the once mighty Drasu looked pale and frail, an empty shell. Whatever power had lived within the body of that wizard had fled, perhaps to Haven, perhaps to someplace less pleasant. I had hunted this human across the world, my hate for him the fire that fueled the early days of my journey to Ni-Yota. Looking at this slowly decaying hunk of flesh, I found my inferno of hate had extinguished itself. The flesh of the dead wizard was just a hunk of rotten meat. But Drasu still owed me dearly for what he had done. He had nothing left to pay with except his remains, so I had no guilt about snatching the corpse and flying off to the north, leaving a group of gaping Mizu in my wake.

"Nice touch, telling them that Drasu had one last service to perform," Harlan commented as I beat my wings for more speed. I wanted this over with as soon as possible.

"It's true enough. I intend to make good use of his corpse."

"You really think the days-old body of some old man is going to be a sufficient exchange for what you ask?"

"That's why I brought you along, slick tongue. You need to convince them."

Harlan went silent, perhaps insulted or perhaps strategizing.

We passed a dozen villages and three smallish fortresses on the route north. I wondered if one of these was the Jahatta, where the healer had told me Rinxia had been brought. I saw no sign of any of those places hosting a dragon, and I wasn't inclined to stop in any inhabited settlement with Drasu's dead body in my clutches. We did our resting in open fields. By the late afternoon, the rugged northern coast of Ni-Yota came into view.

"Where do we drop him off?"

"Vengeance said that whatever one ghastray tastes, they all can taste. We just need to find a ghastray-infested shoal to make the delivery."

"The northern coast has plenty of treacherous shallows to rip apart the hull of a ship. Usually I try to avoid them, but it will be easy enough to find one."

"Pick someplace where I can land safely. Even with our stops, this has been a long flight. If there was game to hunt, that would be even better."

"I'll see if I can't find a deserted island with a fine inn located on it. Ghastray-infested waters are quite popular with travelers."

It took me longer than it should've to realize Harlan was jesting with me. I was weary, and even at my best, I didn't understand human humor. Food and rest weren't joking matters. Despite Harlan's poor attitude, I had no doubt about his knowledge of the sea. The man seemed to be able to sniff rocks beneath the harshest waves, pointing out shifting currents where I saw only water. He noticed miniscule specks of land that even my dragon eyes would've missed. In the end, he located as suitable a spot as I could've reasonably asked.

Harlan directed me toward a cluster of cresting waves just south of a patch of worn, broken rock barely large enough for me to lay upon.

"Cozy," I commented.

Harlan groaned a rebuke. "The tides shift due to the changes in the current. This is the island at its smallest. It will grow to many times this size by the evening, leaving a muddy beach where we might find crabs and clams. Besides, even now, there is enough room for you to land and rest, as you requested."

"Barely."

"Perhaps you have grown too accustomed to luxurious spires in the sky to accept such humble accommodations. I'm afraid no roasted pigs live on this speck of land, either."

I didn't think his rebuke was particularly fair, but it stung with enough truth that I shut up. I came in low over the shoals and dropped the remains of Drasu into the sea.

"Farewell, wizard."

The seas took Drasu without hesitation. A wave crested over the corpse. The dead eyes flipped open in the current. It was an unsatisfying end to Drasu. A moment later, a stinger flashed. When I looked again, the body was gone forever, taken into the depths. I couldn't see the ghastrays, but Harlan apparently could.

"The shallowings come for their meal." He sounded certain.

I made several more circles in the air above the shoals, vainly hoping that Vengeance would poke his hideous head from the water to strike up a conversation with me, but when that didn't happen, I settled down upon Harlan's puny hunk of an island to wait. My wings were grateful for the relief even if my stomach was less pleased.

"Does this place have a name?" I asked.

"Not that I know of."

"Then I proclaim it Harlan's Rest." It was the first time I'd named a place. Humans did it all the time. I got why they liked it—it bestowed a feeling of power, as if I was superior to the land itself. Maybe I shouldn't have so hastily named it after Harlan?

My companion looked shocked, then pleased. "It's as good a name as any."

Vengeance arrived sometime during the night. I awoke to his disturbing call—a high-pitched shriek that shook bones and chilled the air. Upon hearing the claxon, my blood surged as if anticipating battle. Harlan was on his feet a moment later.

We didn't have to move far on the miniscule island to find Vengeance. The ghastray's frightening eyes protruded from the waters of the shallow beach directly in front of us. His translucent body shimmered just beneath the waves, reflecting in the starlight. I looked up to find that Rima had appeared in the sky, its broken form adding to my unease as I came before the ghastray.

There were no introductions, no pleasantries.

"A corpse is not a kill." Vengeance's voice reminded me of the Abyss, of cold death.

"The wizard Drasu is dead, as we both wanted. He will cast no more spells, weave no more magic, nor will he help to enslave any more of your kind."

The eyes shut then reopened in quick succession. "We tasted the marrow of his bones. This was as it should be. But slavers still live. The legacy of Drasu continues in those they call the binders."

The ghastrays wanted no more slaves. I couldn't blame them, but my war was now even bigger than that. I needed the Mizu and the ghastrays on my side. "Ni-Yota has suffered. Even their so-called Skyking is dead."

A wave hit, but the ghastray remained perfectly still. "There is always another."

"Perhaps not this time. All of Ni-Yota stands on the edge of annihilation."

Two of the ghastray's eyes closed while the rest remained open. "This bothers you, dragon? I thought them your enemy."

It was a fair point. Why did their fate bother me? It just did. There was something about the rust, something that filled my insides with an awful peril. "A grave threat arises, a darkness that poses peril for the last of my kind." I struggled to reconcile my feelings with my words. "When compared to this fate, old grievances fall away."

Vengeance opened all of his eyes again. "For your kind...perhaps. It was correct for you to bring us the wizard; even if the *chi* within him had fled, he was luscious to consume. There is nothing more here, dragon."

I realized he intended to leave. "Wait, we have need of your help."

I could feel Harlan wince beside me. Perhaps this was not the best way to begin a negotiation. But if the human didn't like it, he should've spoken earlier.

The ghastray's eyes shut and opened in sequence. "The strange dragon still does not understand."

Vengeance's head began to sink into the sea. I didn't know what else to say, but Harlan apparently did. He spoke to the ghastray.

"This threat is not merely a war between humans, nor is it a battle among land-dwellers for territory or food. It is not even a clash of magic. It is something more. It is connected to the *Iraliss*."

The ghastray stopped his leaving. Every eye opened, seemingly wider than ever before. A stinger-laden tail appeared from the depths. Slowly, its deadly edge approached Harlan, the threat obvious. The human stood his ground, although I heard his heart pumping ever faster.

"The...human...speaks so much." The stinger moved even closer, its edge less than an arm's length from Harlan's throat. "It uses stolen words it does not understand. Words from the distant past. Words it should not know, much less offer to us."

I had no idea what they were talking about. Harlan's mouth was like a leviathan's belly; you never knew what would come out when it was opened.

Instead of cowering as most might have, Harlan tilted his head upward, as if in pride. "I am of the Farlighters, the denizens of the sea, wanderers of the world. We of the Drowned Isle know the old lore."

Vengeance glided further up the beach. "A child of the Drowned Isle, yes." The stinger quivered with excitement. "Indeed, you among all humans should know this. Among all humans, your kind has killed more of us than any other. Among all humans, your kind are the worst. The curse upon your people is well deserved." Harlan's face hardened like an edged rock. "Why should I not avenge my brothers and sisters now?"

"Because Bayloo speaks the truth." Harlan struggled to keep his voice even. "A grave threat comes to all of Inkra. It is the concern of all living creatures, your kind as much as mine. Whatever our pasts, we can agree on this."

"Your kind are liars. All humans are liars. Humans brought the great death, and you Farlighters are their closest kin." The ghastray's stinger actually brushed Harlan's neck.

I figured it was time to leave. We'd have to find another plan. But Harlan didn't give up. "Look up, master of the sea. In the sky is my truth. The broken moon, Rima, comes portending the news we bring. Even your kind are a part of this. It is time for you to fulfill your duty."

Vengeance released a noise that could've been called a hiss, if a viper had been dragon-size and extremely pissed off. Perhaps Harlan wasn't quite the negotiator I'd hoped for when I'd decided to bring him along.

He wasn't intimidated. "Among my people there are teachings so ancient that they were first spoken in the time of the Cataclysm. Much of that is only fragments, bits of memory handed down. But among those tales, one of the oldest includes mention of something called the *Iraliss*—the emptiness."

Vengeance moved as if stung by a bee on the arse (if ghastrays had such a thing). His tail whipped back. The creature's shimmering body nearly rose out of the water. His eyes fixed upward, gazing at Rima's uneasy glow before settling again on Harlan.

"Speak of your need, human. If a lie leaves your ugly lips, I will stop the beat of the annoying thumping in your chest."

I heard Harlan's heart move still faster. "On the western side of the River Tayo, at that place called the Narrows, where crossing is possible through the mountain wall, a horde awaits, an army like none other. Tens of thousands of humans, accompanied by wolves who should be their predators, massive beasts unknown to this land called behemoths, and countless blood raptors. All of them acting in concert, as if all were obeying a single voice that commanded them."

Vengeance didn't sound impressed. "This may be unusual for creatures of the land. It may be the imagination of your useless eyes. It is not the *Iraliss*; it has nothing to do with the Purpose."

I really hated it when they used words I didn't know. It reminded me of my youth trying to learn Avian from the humans. I don't like being left out, either.

Harlan continued. "These creatures that look like humans and others do not eat, they almost never speak, they do not behave as they should. When captured, they quickly die rather than divulge secrets.

They consume the ground around them, even rocks, to sustain themselves. The Mizu have battled them for years. They have come to refer to them as the hollowings—because they are shells of the creatures they once were. Yet they act with intelligence, even guile, setting traps, building items that they need to continue their advance across the river."

The ghastray shuddered. "The river—these invaders seek to cross the water?"

"Yes, as I said." Harlan sounded excited. "The Mizu hold them at the Tayo, where there is but one place that bridges could be built and an army could cross. For years, the magic of the dead wizard enabled the Mizu to hold the line, but no more. As we speak, the hollowings come with bridges and other machines of war. Even the dragons cannot stop them."

I disagreed. "Well, that's not quite true. We—"

"This is not the *Iraliss*." The ghastray sounded angry and adamant, but also relieved.

"Without the aid of your kind, the hollowings will cross the river. Eventually, all of Ni-Yota will become as they are—shells without substance, the land covered by the rust. All creatures will be slaves to some dark, unknown purpose. The taint of the hollowings keeps spreading; by touch of blood, it seems to spread. Aragor himself died as the taint set upon him."

"The great dragon died of this...rust?" The eyes all blinked. "Why would it kill him?"

"Bayloo killed Aragor so that he wouldn't become a hollowing."

The ghastray shimmered in the waves. Without warning its eyes plunged back below the surface. Harlan and I exchanged a puzzled glance. When we looked again, the creature had re-emerged, its eyes bulging.

"The dragon king is owed to us. Bring Aragor here."

Something uneasy rumbled in my belly. I shouldn't have eaten those pig feet. You never knew where a pig might've walked.

"You want Aragor's corpse?" I asked.

"We shall feast on dragon. And we shall learn if this dark human who smells like the sea and claims to know of the *Iraliss* is a liar like the rest of his kind."

The night darkened further. Rima had disappeared mysteriously, its light gone.

"Bring the dead Skyking to us or die as he did. It matters not to us."

FOURTEEN

For some reason, Harlan was pleased.

"That went better than I expected." He spoke cheerfully as he again climbed onto my back. Night reigned in the endless sky, its blackness interrupted by only a few pinpricks of stars. There was no sign of Rima, that strange apparition in the sky that came and went without apparent pattern or purpose.

I couldn't tell if Harlan jested with me. "The ghastray called you a liar. Then it sent us to fetch the body of the former ruler of Ni-Yota. At no time did it agree to help us."

Harlan chuckled softly. "It wouldn't have asked us to bring Aragor to him if it thought I was just telling stories. I think we've got Vengeance hooked. Or at least smelling the bait."

"It is a ghastray. It may just want to eat a dragon corpse without having to go through the trouble of making one of us dead. The world is running short on dragons. He may just want to taste one before we are all gone."

Even without seeing him, I felt Harlan shrug. "That's not impossible, but I think not."

"Also, you are suggesting that I fly to Trishan and fetch the dead body of the former ruler of this land to deliver to the ghastray."

"It worked well enough with Drasu. It's that or fly back to the Tayo River to fight alongside Gia until you are dead. Or you could run away."

My answer was to launch us into the sky. I headed south toward Ni-Yota, but beyond that I remained undecided on my destination.

"Even if I wanted to deliver Aragor's corpse, the Mizu aren't just going to hand that over. And dragons are heavy, Harlan. Even dead, empty of water and blood, it would be difficult to fly him to the sea."

"We can find someplace closer. The ghastrays seem adept at finding us after you feed them."

I didn't like anything about this. Feeding corpses to ghastrays seemed like an odd way to win a war. Yet I had no other idea how to muster allies against the hollowings. I flapped my wings for more speed.

We soared through the rest of the night and into the next day, much of the time lost in our own thoughts. Harlan's conversation with Vengeance had been an odd one. Of course, I had long ago discovered that Harlan's guise of a simple smuggler hid a far more complicated man, but even so, I had underestimated the depth of the human.

Eventually, I tired too much to continue flying. We landed at a Mizu waystation. It resembled all the others, with low-rise buildings surrounding a central courtyard, although it was a bit smaller, its structure worn by sun and sand. The occupants were uncertain how to deal with us at first, but they quickly (and wisely) concluded that feeding the hungry dragon was smarter than fighting with me. They didn't have pig, but after a long night and day of flight, the juicy calf legs (without the hooves) they procured tasted almost as fine. As my hunger cleared, my mind regained its focus. Harlan, because he took the time to chew around bones rather than through them, ate slower than me. I didn't have the patience for him to finish. His mouth was still full of meat when I began with my questions.

"What is this *Iraliss* you spoke of with Vengeance?"

Harlan swallowed the bite he'd been working on. He still held a meaty rib between his hands. He looked up at me as fat dripped out of his mouth. "A bit of gossip I overheard one night, listening to a conversation I shouldn't have heard. I do that a lot."

I didn't like Harlan's dismissive casualness. Not this time. I replied with a displeased rumble in my throat. "Do not play simple with me, for we both know you are anything but that."

Harlan pushed a hunk of partially chewed meat down his throat. "You give me too much credit." He wiped his mouth with his sleeve. "I am born of a people who hold desperately to the belief that an island swallowed by the sea hundreds of years ago can somehow be saved, and that this is a cause worth devoting our lives to accomplish. For generations we've kept this belief, parents passing it down to children, telling stories of a non-existent patch of land laden with endless wonders, tragically sunk somewhere out on the endless horizon. Many actually believe it, although fewer with each generation. Among such a people, it shouldn't surprise you that many hold to various legends to support their beliefs. Indeed, when the task that is set before you seems futile, it's important to comfort yourself with fables far more fantastic and impossible than the reality you face. At least, that is the way it is among many of my people. And I'll add that my wife would throw me overboard with weights on my legs for speaking in such a manner." Harlan turned glum for a moment. "I have been away too long."

I released a sharp snort. "For once, I need you to keep talking. You knew to share these words with the ghastray. He recognized this *Iraliss* of which you spoke. That is more than a legend, if even the ghastrays know of what you speak. You have more to tell."

Harlan shook his head, reluctant. "I know less than you believe. I just know how to play my cards." He ripped some more meat from the bone in his hand, but I suspected he was stalling for time. When he'd chewed a bit more, Harlan spoke again, his mouth still half full. "I've spoken to you before of those among us who are best at manipulating things—the closest we have to magi—the people we call Meddlers."

"I remember."

"Among those, some are known as Tellers. They keep the lore of our people, as well. Some of it is in books, written. But, as you might imagine, boats are poor places for books. Water, storms, salt, drunks... with such a life, books are not the best places to keep precious knowledge. So much of our knowledge is kept in stories, tales passed on in families, held in the collective memories of our people."

"This is common in Rolm as well. There, families all speak of many of the same stories to their children, just as it was told to them. Even I've heard some of these tales, although many make little sense. In one story the humans speak of ancient ancestors who climbed up a hill merely to fetch a pail of water, but with tragic results."

Harlan grinned, revealing several meat scraps stuck in his teeth. "I'd be willing to wager my best sail that our Tellers are better at their stories than the people in Rolm. Their memories are near perfect, so much so that they could remember the position of the stars on a given day of the year, tell you of the wind's direction on that same morning, and recite nearly every word spoken to them since they turned five. It is within these people that our knowledge truly resides."

"Then tell me the history of the *Iraliss*."

Harlan sighed. "It is difficult to explain. You must understand that what we have left—seahands, like me—is not history, not a chronicle of events. What we have instead are a hundred loosely related stories of the horrors of the ancient times. The Collection of Chaos, those tales are called—they track the accounts of individuals who lived during and after the Cataclysm. One is the story of a town consumed by fire, every resident burned to ash except for the little girl who is saved by a talking mountain. Another is the account of a holy man and his efforts to persuade Haven to calm the wrath to which humans have been subjected, but instead, the man is transformed into an eagle so he may better witness the folly his fellow humans wrought around the world. As for myself, I prefer the tales of the ancient inferno staffs that could spray fire, the stories of heroes of the sea who used the ancient weapons to defend their ships in the darkest days of the exodus from Farlight, rather than these strange, darker ramblings."

I was at the limit of my patience. "Tell me of the knowledge you shared with the ghastray."

Harlan looked at his feet, then at me. "The particular tale involving the *Iraliss*—which is a term of the ancient language of our people that only the Tellers bother to learn—is one of the oldest of my people. It is a story of caution, of the old magic of our ancestor run amok. This is one of the most haunting stories, which is why I remember it and its strange words. I heard the tale from the Teller on our ship when I was but a child of seven. It terrified me, but it also became a matter of fascination. I had my mother retell the tale to me many times after, even though I often couldn't sleep afterwards."

"I will have no trouble sleeping," I assured him.

Harlan smirked. "The story is told as entries to the log of a ship's first mate. In it he describes a fabulous ship, a vessel far larger than anything we could conceive of today. It was so large a man could get lost aboard, or spend the entire voyage without going above the deck. It had light even at night, and could sail against the will of the wind. This great ship was sent from one of the ancient kingdoms to aid a people who inhabited a distant land and were suffering from famine. What made it strange was that the starving land had some of the most fertile soil in the lost world, yet the people there were desperate for food. When the crew arrived, they found the great port town deserted—no people, no bodies. Indeed, the entire place was overgrown with weeds that burrowed through the streets and stones of buildings, as if the island had been abandoned for hundreds of years. The first mate describes how they found a lone survivor, an old woman who begs them to burn their ship and kill themselves. They think her mad at first, but then the crew starts to become ill. In his later entries, the first mate tells of crew members he'd known for years acting erratically, barely speaking. One tries to kill him. The crew begins to call their sickened fellows 'the empties who walk.' In the ancient tongue, this translates to the *Iraliss*. Somehow, the strange weed that infested the city spreads to the ship, perhaps brought by one of these *Iraliss*. The remaining crew who tries to stop it are killed by the *Iraliss*. The first mate's last entry is of this plague ship leaving port on the island, headed toward his homeland."

"So this ship spreads the plague. At least according to the legends of your people?"

"According to the stories, Bayloo. But those are not history. They are not even memories. Indeed, there is still another story that many believe is related to this tale of the ship. That one is called 'The Sacrifice' by my people. It is an account told well after the actual events, but it speaks of a group of people who have powers like wizards—practitioners of an unknown magic. They call themselves the Genies. In an effort to prevent the spread of something that story refers to as the Taint, they transform themselves into predators of the sea—creatures able to swim at speeds greater than any ship and able to communicate with each other almost instantly over vast distances. They do this in an effort to save the land from ships that carry the Taint from land to land, spreading its horrors. But such power comes at a heavy cost, as such things always do. The change they effect upon themselves is irreversible. It is a story of how a group of humans trade their humanity for the chance to save their fellow humans."

"Rather noble, for humans. Particularly human wizards."

Harlan dipped his head toward me. "Perhaps we were made from better stuff in those days. On the other hand, that's when the Cataclysm occurred, so perhaps not."

"Were these humans the first ghastrays? Is that the point of the story?"

"Do stories need a point? Not even our Tellers claim that all of their tales always have a basis in fact. They merely swear they are repeating the words that were told to them. Some indeed may be only stories. Others, perhaps, are more."

"Vengeance mentioned a 'Purpose.' Is there a legend among your kind for that?"

"Not that I know of, but I'm not a Teller. Indeed, my friend, I think you may know more about their kind than any other creature, except the ghastrays themselves."

"I know almost nothing."

"You know they hunger for the flesh of a dead dragon and that the Mizu aren't going to want to give that to them. I think you also know that Ni-Yota is doomed without the aid of the ghastrays. I think I agree with that."

Harlan lay back on the ground, weary, although I also got the sense he disliked the subject of his people's history. I too wanted to sleep, but I had at least one more question I needed answered.

"Why do they call your people cursed?" I asked. "It was not just the ghastray. Elasu said the same."

Harlan stared up at the stars twinkling in the sky. I realized that I had said something wrong. "It is not necessary to speak of it." I understood that not all thoughts need to be shared. Some pain was best kept inside.

Harlan didn't move, except for his lips. "Others will be happy to tell their rumors, but you might as well hear it from me." He gritted his teeth for a moment, then said it. "My people become ever fewer. Life on the sea is hard, and not appealing. Many leave the way. The number of ships dwindle."

"The same is true of dragons. We are but a handful. I had hoped to find more here, but we become ever fewer."

"Aye, our peoples are not without their similarities," Harlan said. "But with we Farlighters, those of us of the true blood, with this skin that glints in the light that marks us as true descendants of the original inhabitants of Farlight, our children are different. That is our curse."

My hearts became heavy. Even without knowing the answer, I wished I had not asked the question to Harlan in the first place. "I don't understand. Your children?"

"Always, Farlighter births are twins. Two children." He sucked in a great gulp of wind. "Within a year, one must die, or they both perish. The parents must choose within twelve moons, or both die. No one knows why. No healer has ever been able to prevent it. That is the curse."

I didn't know any words that should be said at that moment. I looked up at the sky as well. There were no answers there, either. Finally, I dared ask another question. "Is it...some magic?"

"No one knows for certain, and my people have no wizards. But the malady, as we call it—though curse is a better term—has been with us since the beginning. The people of Farlight were different, they tell us. Our skin resists burning in the sun. We need less water. Less food, even. We almost never get sick, which is necessary for a people to survive on the close confines of ships. Without these abilities, we would all die. But such traits are retained only by keeping the bloodline pure. My people never mate with outsiders, so we can keep these traits. But there is a cost. A great cost."

"Do you have a child?" I asked before realizing I should not have done so. Harlan had mentioned a wife, but no offspring.

"No. I have no children to worry about."

Some of the tension within me relaxed at his words. At least Harlan had not lost one of his offspring. I had only Kiata to worry over. With my own hatchlings...that would be difficult. The curse was heavy indeed.

"I have just begun to touch magic...this Latticework of existence. Yet it is powerful. It is everything I believe. If something exists, it can be changed. So know that if the magic of the ember dragons can help your people, I will offer it."

Harlan turned his head toward me; his eyes were glassy. "That is generous. For our people have not always been friends."

"Then let us save this world, and change that story," I told him.

I was very naive.

FIFTEEN

Clouds hovered over Trishan like a wary parent over a child.

I circled the city long enough to give the palace staff sufficient time to prepare for our arrival. Also, I wanted to inspect the wreckage of the Hall of Glass, to see if Aragor's remains might still be there. The glass roof still hadn't been repaired, but neither did I see any sign of the former protector of Ni-Yota. It seemed the people of Ni-Yota didn't leave their ruler lying dead on the floor for extended periods. Big surprise.

"You didn't expect this to be so easy, did you?" Harlan asked from my back.

I hadn't expected it to be easy, but that didn't mean I hadn't hoped that it would.

I landed beside the lake, just outside the multi-storied palace complex which also housed the hall in which Aragor had died. Despite giving the humans plenty of time to prepare to greet me, it was Kiata who arrived first, flying from her tower like an arrow. My hearts thumped with both pleasure and trepidation at seeing her again.

She landed with grace worthy of Rinxia. To my pleasant surprise, my sister greeted me by rubbing her neck against mine. "Brother, it is good to see you safe. The last glasswing from the west informed us that Gia had led us to victory, beating the hollowings back across the river."

My elation at Kiata's warm embrace faded quickly. My eyes darkened into the equivalent of a human frown. *Gia had led us?* "It is true that the hollowings have been driven from the eastern side of the river, at least for now. But at a great cost: Rinxia was injured in the fighting. It was Harlan's plan with the rafts that saved us in the end."

Kiata's eyes glowed with approval. "I knew it was right to have faith in the clever human. If the hollowings have been beaten, why then have you returned, brother, but not Gia?"

Harlan chose that moment to slide off my back onto the ground. He made a great show of dusting himself off. There was no dust on him. He spoke with flourish. "Because, noble Kiata, the hollowings do not accept defeat. We are merely in a gap between battles."

The joy in Kiata's eyes quickly evaporated. "Explain yourself."

Reluctantly, I told her about the huge tower-bridges being dragged to the river, as well as the failed raid where I'd almost gotten killed. I left out the part where her hero, Gia, arrived so late I'd been stuck alone in the hollowing trap with blood raptors and ballistae. Harlan's sharp eyes were upon me as I spoke; he was doubtless wondering why I'd passed on the opportunity to malign Gia. The answer was, I knew my sister better than he did, even if we had known her for almost the same length of time. Kiata would not change her mind about Gia because I or anyone else told her some story. I had spent considerable time in the mind of my human ryders, and not all of it had been wasted. Childhood heroes were not surrendered easily. She would have to learn Gia's true nature for herself. Until then, I wouldn't be able to fully sever the bond between them. It angered me, but that didn't make it any less of a fact.

"If the hollowings come again...why leave mighty Gia alone to fight against them? Especially if Rinxia is hurt, he will need you by his side."

Kiata sounded so anxious that I feared she'd at that moment fly to the river to help him.

"We have another plan," I said, my voice hesitant. I knew Kiata wasn't going to like what we had in mind. No one wanted to see someone they had looked up to chewed to pieces by a bunch of ghastrays. First I'd killed Aragor, now I wanted to feed him to the ghastrays. There was no easy way to explain that.

A human from the council—I forgot his real name, but he would always be Doughy to me—chose that moment to arrive with a small entourage. He'd changed his outfit into something much more elaborate and less martial since last we had spoken. He now wore a silk robe trimmed by inlaid gems. At his waist was a puny sword held in a dazzling red scabbard, more decoration than weapon.

Beside Doughy strode a bizarrely tall human, with legs making up most of the height. The man's chin hung from the rest of his thin, dour face, while each of his stick-like fingers was laden with a ring of metal. The tall man's body was draped in a gown of yellow, its length such that the end trailed behind him like a tail. Two other humans clad in silken robes trailed behind, their faces solemn and blank.

"Ah, welcome, welcome." Doughy put his hands together as if softly applauding my arrival. Then he noticed Harlan. "Ah, yes, you too. Welcome." Back to me he said, "I've ordered Otai to make the Wind Tower ready for your stay." He gestured to the tall human next to him. "Will great Gia be joining you soon?"

I was about to inform the chunky and tall humans that our stay would be short, but Harlan spoke more quickly. "Lord Heta, it is an honor to see you again. I wonder if everything is arranged for great Aragor's funeral ceremony? I know this was of great concern to Gia."

I noticed that Harlan actually remembered Doughy's name, but more importantly, I realized that he didn't answer Doughy's question, instead using the man for his own purposes.

Doughy—Lord Heta—turned his flabby jowls toward Otai. The tall human's voice was strangely quiet for such a large person. "All is ready, but we await Gia's return, for all know it shall be his fire that shall begin the cleansing journey."

Harlan glanced over at me. I got his meaning. I stretched my neck toward this Lord Heta. "I wish to see Aragor, now. Before Gia returns."

Doughy's face darkened, but it was Otai who answered me. "I assure you, all is as it should be. I've attended to the matter personally."

I pushed my head at Otai's stretched face. "I've no doubt that is the case to human eyes. Meaning no disrespect, but even for one such as you, there are matters among dragons you do not understand."

Otai shuffled on his feet.

Doughy coughed. "Otai will have everything ready, I assure you. Although recently appointed, he served the prior steward for many years. Great Aragor's *jing* will leave his body in the proper manner, returning to Haven."

I actually had no idea what he meant by *jing*, but it seemed important to the Mizu. I pushed in on Lord Heta, blowing air from my nostrils hard enough that it made the man's face fat move. "I trust no human with this. I wish to see Aragor. Now."

Doughy began to shake. His mouth didn't quite seem to be working.

"Why are you so concerned?" Kiata asked. She sounded suspicious. That was inconvenient, but at least my sister was no fool.

I pulled back from the trembling human. "Please, Kiata. I need to see him."

My words didn't allay her suspicions. That shouldn't have surprised me. I had killed Aragor, after all. It was something I had to do, but that didn't change what I had done. My sister had admired him, and she didn't trust me. My chest ached, but it didn't change what I needed to do. When Kiata spoke, she did so reluctantly.

"Come with me, Bayloo."

Harlan scrambled onto my back again as Doughy and Otai made strange gurgling noises of displeasure. I flashed a toothy, human-style grin at them before following my sister into the air. My wings were heavy as I followed Kiata. I didn't want the gulf between us to expand any further. I'd come here to Ni-Yota for her.

Kiata flew along the lake, heading north from the palace. The fading afternoon sun reflected off the dark waters, making the surface an eerie crimson. Kiata didn't fly far. Along the water's edge sat what looked like a giant stone bowl that was big enough to hold three dragons. Its interior was carved from a faintly translucent yellow stone. A single Mizu, his body almost completely wrapped in white cloth, stood rigidly at the base of the bowl, with only his dark eyes visible through a slit in his head covering.

Kiata landed just south of the bowl. The Mizu attendant stayed as still as a statue, but I knew he wasn't stone. I could hear him breathing.

Kiata indicated the giant bowl. "This is where the Protectors depart this world. When the shell that held their *jing* is burned, their true being is finally released to return to Haven, from whence they came."

Harlan jumped from my back to the edge of the stone basin. The Mizu guard unfroze, whipping his blade from its sheath as quick as I might snatch a pig from a platter.

"Hold!" I commanded. That was enough to keep the Mizu in place. "He means no harm."

In truth, I didn't know what Harlan meant to do—the bowl was empty.

After a cursory glance inside, Harlan jumped down from the edge of the strange structure. He winked at the Mizu guard after his feet touched the ground. Anger flashed in the warrior's dark eyes, but he didn't move.

"The Mizu believe that Aragor's *jing* is trapped within his corpse even now?" I asked as respectfully as I could despite my own personal skepticism. I'd seen plenty of dead creatures: dragons, humans, pigs, whatever. Good or evil, strong or weak, killed in battle or for dinner, I'd never seen any sign of anything within them after death. But Kiata had never been in battle. Her experience with death was limited to that which had been caused by others. I understood how she might believe otherwise.

My young sister contemplated my question. This was probably the first time someone had challenged her belief. She was so young, despite her increasing size. "This is what the Mizu priests said. This has been the way of the dragons of Ni-Yota for hundreds of years. Do they have a reason to not tell the truth?"

I looked at Harlan. Somehow, I thought the answer to that question would be better coming from him. Having killed Aragor, I was biased.

"Kiata, I have sailed the seas, traveling to the different lands of this world for longer than Bayloo has drawn breath. I've met countless men. I've spoken to other creatures as well. Recently, I had the fortune to meet dragons, but I know humans best. My kind and yours are obviously quite different, with customs and languages and beliefs as different as the mountains from the dirt. Yet what all humans—at least all the humans I've ever met—have in common, is fear."

My sister seemed surprised. "Even you, Harlan? You are among the bravest creatures I've known. Braver even than the knight-lords who claim to know no fear, only duty."

Harlan pinched his own arm. "I'm flesh and blood—an ordinary human. I fear all the time. I'm afraid of sounds in the night, afraid of failing those I love, and even more afraid of never seeing them again. When Bayloo snatched me from the seas within moments of my own death, I was even more afraid during that first flight than I was of dying alone in those bloody shallows." He laughed at the memory. "I nearly peed myself as he soared into the clouds."

"Nearly?" I asked. "Dragons have an excellent sense of smell."

"My point, Kiata, is that all humans fear. Death and what follows is among our greatest fears. It is universal to every human society, no matter how rich or poor. And all of them have stories to comfort themselves about what comes after. The priests of Ni-Yota are just men, like me. Perhaps dragons are not so different either. We all fear death. Believing in a *jing* that can travel to Haven to be reborn in another body helps to alleviate those fears. Saying that one's *jing* entitles a being to rule all others is even more appealing to a ruler. At least that is my guess."

Even in the fading light of the day, I noticed my sister's eyes darken. "You imply that Aragor was not the chosen of Haven."

Harlan shrugged in the face of her rising anger. I was glad he'd taken on the burden of explaining this to her. "It is a great comfort to believe that rulers are divinely chosen, that there is greater purpose to their actions, and we are guided by destiny. This is true of humans and dragons, I think. To answer your question, I know nothing of Haven, for while I've traveled far, I've never gotten that far. Nor have I known anyone else who has. I can only tell you that the most tempting beliefs are those that can cut your heart deepest. Beware of those."

Kiata's eyes searched Harlan's face, then mine. "Why are you two here? Speak no lies to me."

I had no intention of lying to her, but I wasn't sure if Harlan's words had made any impact upon her. Even if they had, it was a long way from accepting that Aragor's so-called *jing* no longer inhabited his body to being okay with letting ghastrays consume him.

"Can you show us Aragor?"

"You haven't answered my question. You are hiding something."

I sighed, resigned to the situation. In truth, I already had a pretty good idea where the former ruler of Ni-Yota lay: the ground beneath that white-wrapped Mizu warrior didn't smell right. The body was underground in some kind of tomb, I presumed to keep predators at bay until Gia had a chance to burn it to ashes. I just needed to find the entrance. Or make my own.

"I already told you about the failed attack on the hollowing tower-bridges. Legao's magic has delayed their advance, but the hollowings will eventually reach the river. We need to stop them from crossing."

"How can Aragor help you now? You don't even believe his *jing* exists."

"The ghastrays can help us." Kiata's eyes lit with horror as soon as I said it. "They are not what you think. They are different than us, but there is much more to them than many suspect. They could hold the river for us."

"You are mad." She nearly choked on her words. I could tell she was upset to learn her brother was possibly insane.

I could've told her then that we needed allies. I could've told her about Vengeance, about what he'd asked, and what I hoped the ghastrays could do to aid us. But I knew I couldn't persuade her. Not with my words. Kiata was intelligent, but young. Too young for reason to triumph with her. I turned to Harlan, once again, to save me.

"Harlan, I think you must share with Kiata the lore of your people so she might understand."

He rubbed his head. "Those tales are long ones. Longer than the light we have left to us, not to mention that we have been flying for nearly two days."

"I shall have food brought to my tower," Kiata told us. "Let us meet there when the sun has finished settling below the horizon."

My sister flew off, not to her own tower, but to the smaller one beside the late Protector's spire—the windowed construction where the glasswing had arrived and departed. Kiata disappeared inside. Sure enough, a short time later, two of the birds flew from the window of the tower as Harlan and I watched.

"She sends a message to Gia," I concluded sadly. "It will take time for the glasswings to reach the river. Until then, you are a fine storyteller, Harlan. Tell her all you told me, and more."

Harlan dipped his chin slowly, guessing my plot. "There will be a price to pay for all this, my friend."

I knew he was right. "I listened to your legends. I believe there is some truth in the lore of your people. In time, I think Kiata will understand that as well."

Harlan sighed with regret that matched my own. "As you wish."

At sunset, Harlan strode over the bridges to Kiata's tower in the middle of the great lake of Trishan. There, he told Kiata that I would join them shortly, and began his story. Harlan was a gifted weaver of words. That night, he spun the histories of his people, all he had been told by Tellers, plus some more embellishment. Harlan had such charm, such wit. It was easy to become immersed in his tales, to lose track of time as one contemplated his magnificent mysteries and legends. Kiata, a mere child, with a child's curious mind, no doubt feasted on Harlan's stories.

In the meantime, I broke into Aragor's tomb and dragged out the late Protector's corpse. He was heavy, but his time as a corpse had robbed his body of liquids and left him with an empty stomach. With difficulty and an unfortunate lack of dignity for both of us, I dragged Aragor's remains to the river, then I pulled him along the water into the great gulf upon which Trishan was situated. I intended to drag him to some shoals, but I couldn't fly high enough to do a proper reconnoiter while still holding onto the corpse. So, with an even more unfortunate lack of dignity, I ripped off Aragor's neck. I kept the top half with his head in my grasp, but let the body slide into the depths of the salty gulf waters.

Then I flew off to find some ghastrays.

SIXTEEN

I dropped Aragor's head into the sea.

It fell like a stone, made a little splash, and sank. If the forces of Haven were offended, there was no immediate indication of such—the skies were unchanged, the sea indifferent.

I didn't have the time to fly all the way to Harlan's island where we had fed Drasu's remains to the other ghastray. Instead, I found some white-capped waves lapping against rocks near the mouth of the bay and dropped the head of the late Skyking there. I was pretty sure I saw a ghastray's tail emerge from the waves as the neck disappeared. There was no visible sign of any *jing* leaving the remains. It was just a dead piece of flesh as far as I could determine. I did a few more circles, then headed back south. I knew better than to expect Vengeance to just pop up to speak with me. If all ghastrays somehow communicated, he knew what we needed to know. The question was if he and his deadly pals were going to help or not. In either case, there was a battle to fight in the west.

I didn't fly back to Trishan to pick up Harlan. He probably expected me to do so, but I'd never promised him that. I needed to get back to the Tayo River as soon as possible to help defend against the inevitable hollowing attack. Legao's rain had delayed the attack, but the behemoths would eventually slog their way through the mud. Also, I didn't want to face Kiata, not so soon after betraying her to steal Aragor's corpse. I wanted to consider myself brave for doing what I had done—tricking my sister for what I believed to be the greater good—but I couldn't quite shake the feeling that this time, I had truly broken the fragile bond that existed between us.

I had plenty of time on my journey west to doubt my actions. I rested little, flying deep into the night. My foremost worry was that all this would be for nothing. Ghastrays were a species totally apart, their minds different, their decisions incomprehensible. I knew Gia would think I was crazy for putting any faith in such a thing. Of course, I suspected he'd tried to get me killed by hollowings a few days ago, so I wasn't tremendously concerned about further loss of his esteem. I flew on the roof of a waystation to sleep for a bit at the tail end of the night, but resumed my journey as soon as the sun rose.

The next day, I reached the Narrows of the Tayo. As the river and the Mizu army came into view, I saw that Gia and the knight-lords had not been idle. Additional trenches had been dug behind the river. Several raised platforms had been hastily assembled on which catapults had been placed, increasing their view and range. Cavalry massed behind the lines. Paths had been smoothed and strewn with dry pebbles to ease their eventual charge. It wouldn't be enough.

The hollowings had seemingly multiplied, their numbers now uncountable. Whatever commanded them had some understanding of military organization, albeit a different one than the Mizu knight-lords. The hollowing forces were packed together in an organized fashion, each soldier, man or wolf, in the proper position within crisp rectangular formations. Most made no obvious movements or noise as they waited. The exception were the toiling masses of humans who strained alongside the behemoths to move the great bridge-towers.

Rain no longer fell on the western side of the river, but the ground was still an absolute mess. An army that size couldn't help but take a toll on its surroundings. The towers and behemoths were desperately heavy. I counted eight of the giant armored beasts trying to drag the massive towers through the slushy mud, their footing constantly failing. All were covered in an ugly mix of wet mud and rust. Legions of humans scrambled about them like worker ants, laying wood boards along paths to the river, but the towers were too large, the ground too uneven, for even that to be successful.

Their progress was slow, but they were still making progress. It was only a matter of time before the bridges reached the river.

Distracted by the scene below, I only belatedly noticed the silvery flash rising upward in my direction. The object moved with grace and speed and I knew immediately it had to be Rinxia. My hearts stretched toward her, rejoicing that she was alive and well enough to fly. At the same time, she was here, again, and in peril.

As Rinxia came closer, her beauty made the tip of my tail tingle. The partially healed hole in her side made my own flank ache. She would be vulnerable there. It would take a few days longer for the scales to fully form again. During that time, combat would be an extreme risk. I changed my direction to meet her, the distance between us quickly banished by the combined beating of our wings.

As we neared, Rinxia's eyes glowed with puzzlement rather than the joy that mine reflected. "Where have you been? Gia is furious with you."

It wasn't the conversation I hoped to have with her. "He's not my favorite dragon, either." I wondered how much to tell her about Aragor and the ghastrays. Gliding through the air above the Mizu army wasn't the best place for a chat, but I decided I wanted her to hear the plan from me, rather than someone worse, like Gia.

"We need help if we are to keep the hollowings from overwhelming us. To gain help, there is a price to be paid." I told her about Drasu becoming fish food. I saw the revulsion in her eyes, but she took it reasonably well. Then came the bit about Aragor. When she spoke, Rinxia's voice trembled, even though I left out the part where I'd snapped his neck in half and delivered only the head to the ghastrays.

"Bayloo...no...please tell me otherwise ..."

"You should look at this as Aragor's last act as Protector of Ni-Yota. A final sacrifice for his people. Surely, a true Protector would've wanted me to do as I did."

"You fed the *jing* of a dragon—the Skyking, no less—to the most hideous of creatures. It is a sacred thing. The priests...the people... they will never forgive you."

"I accept paying a grievous price." I didn't care about the opinions of the priests or the humans of this place. I wasn't looking for friends or adoration. Rinxia's opinion was a different matter, though.

"It's worse than that." She didn't hide her annoyance. "You've... you've damaged the office of Protector of Ni-Yota itself. The *jing* of one Protector is released to Haven, its energy to then to be passed to the next. That cannot happen if the body is inside the belly of a shallowing—a ghastray, as you call them. People will lose faith when we need it the most. Why do you think the Mizu warriors fight with such passion? They *believe*, Bayloo. Even if you don't, our people believe. Elasu's domain is still restive, the tigris still fight. We must have the humans united with us. You may have ruined that. Forever."

Her rebuke stung. Still, I put on my brave face. "None of that matters if the hollowings cross the river. They are the enemy of all. You are the one who helped me realize that."

Rinxia was quiet for a time, gliding easily on the air as she thought. She was too intelligent to not realize I was correct. Or at least that I was partially correct. "Gia will use this against you as well. Whether you want the title of Protector or not, he sees you as a threat."

"I'm well aware Gia is not my friend and that he doesn't play fair. Maybe he'd prefer I was dead."

I told her about the raid on the bridge-towers and Gia's suspiciously late arrival.

Rinxia nearly hissed as I finished speaking. "I've known Gia all my life. He can be rash, even stupid. I've never known him to be dishonorable. That is not of the Way." She hesitated before adding, more to herself than me, "Never dishonorable."

"You sound like you may have a doubt about him."

"No, nothing like that. Something happened a long time ago. Rumors. He has always shown himself to be true to us. He is more emotional than most, but still he keeps to the Way."

"Well, I doubt his honor. He wants me dead." I looked at the horde across the river. "He may yet get his wish."

"We've strengthened our defenses. We have a few other surprises for them. This won't be an easy fight for the hollowings."

"They are too many. If they can all cross, it won't matter what fortifications you have constructed."

"Your plan is madness as well."

I couldn't really dispute that. "How is Legao? We only have this precious time to prepare because of her magic."

"She is still with us," Rinxia assured me. "There are whispers you aided in this magic as well."

Rinxia sounded hopeful, and I wished the rumors were true, but I did not think so. "I tried, but it was Legao that brought the rain, despite the effort it cost her. How is she?"

"She has been summoning more rain to slow them," Rinxia assured me.

"Take me to her."

Rinxia answered by breaking into a steep dive toward the camps of Mizu soldiers below. Our presence drew stares from hundreds. Even among the soldiers of Ni-Yota, where dragons frequented the sky, we were a sight to behold. Rinxia leveled her course, streaking over several encampments. Cheers broke out as we passed overhead. I'm not sure the reason. Perhaps it was reassuring to know we were on their side. I admit it made me feel a bit giddy. No one had ever cheered for me in Rolm.

We landed outside a pavilion tent near a staging area for Tia's mounted troops. A single soldier stood watch at the tent flap that served as an entrance. The stench of horse crap was pervasive.

"Seems like a cozy spot."

The tent was too small for dragons. My head might have fit inside, but my torso would have to wait under the sky. Rinxia addressed the guard.

"Can you ask Legao if we might have a word with her?"

The soldier shuffled uncomfortably. I got the impression that he might have refused the request from another human, maybe even a knight-lord. But seeing as we were giant dragons, he disappeared inside the tent. Legao emerged a short time later. She looked terrible. Her face was gaunt, circles of exhaustion radiated from her eyes, and, of course, she was still human.

"Maybe someone should bring you a seat," I suggested helpfully. "You look as though a stiff wind might topple you."

Legao's back stiffened. "I'm fine, or I will be if I'm left alone to get a meal and some sleep. The clouds and the rain don't just come when I whistle like some tame hound. They are like willful children, forever resisting, forever wanting to run free."

"You have done well with your magic." I considered the progress of the bridge-towers through the mud her magic had created. "At their current pace, you have gotten us probably another day to prepare, perhaps more."

"Telling me what I already know isn't a reason to drag me from my tent. What do you want?"

"I want to talk to you about magic." I spoke hesitantly, almost embarrassed.

"You've seen me at work. Do you still doubt my power?"

"Not your magic—my magic. Or more specifically, I wish to understand the nature of magic itself. I've never had a teacher, but I must learn."

Legao's weary eyes widened. "I know nothing of dragon magic. I learned at the foot of Drasu, as did all humans of the Conclave of Magi, be they wizard, binder, or windmaster. I follow the path of Eranna, the first magi. Dragons ..." She shook her head. "Dragon do not learn magic from humans."

"How were the ember dragons taught to use their power?"

The wizard looked baffled. She looked at Rinxia for help, and it was my fellow dragon who answered. "I'm not of the ember blood—your mother was the last of the ember dragons until Kiata and you. But to answer your question, I don't know of anyone teaching her. There are no decade-long apprenticeships among ember dragons, no Conclave to teach and weed out those who cannot survive the power. It is the dragon Way, the thought, the conduct that is passed from one dragon to another. Not the magic itself. And certainly we cannot... We cannot learn from humans." Rinxia seemed rather certain of that last part.

"I learned from Legao," I told them. "Just sensing her magic opened new doors for my own."

Legao's chin dropped. I thought I paid her a compliment, but she was visibly upset. When Legao picked her chin back up, she managed to ask, "You could see... sense my magic at work?"

I thought back to the storm Legao had summoned. "No," I admitted. "Not directly. But I can sense the Latticework—that is what it is called, yes? I could sense the changes to redirect the clouds, to pull in the rain."

Legao's breathing became erratic. "It cannot be that." But the statement was a whisper of uncertainty.

I was afraid Legao would faint given her weakened condition, and she didn't seem able to provide me with answers anyway, except that human and dragon magic was somehow different.

"Rinxia, how did Aragor truly never intend for Kiata to learn from Drasu? Surely the most powerful wizard in the world, a man who had lived for so many years, was not to just stand aside and play no part in the coming of age of a returned ember dragon?"

"Drasu said there would be no need." Uncertainty crept into Rinxia's voice. "He said ember dragons are born with an innate connection to magic, instinctual like flying. For humans, magic is unnatural, something they can learn only with talent and through struggle—like learning to play music—for magic was something not truly meant for humans."

I looked at Legao, who confirmed the sentiment. "I was taught the same, and it is true. Human magic... is a force of will. It takes strength, and emotion, channeled to create Grafts on what we call the Ar-Shadow. From what I understand, dragon magic is innate, an act of harmony and concentration. Ember dragons are born to come into their power, just as ash dragons are born to belch flame. Drasu rarely spoke of dragon magic, save this. When asked, Drasu would merely say that humans must travel a different path of magic."

I mused at those words. "It seems an odd thing to say, coming from the powerful human wizard. And he was wrong: magic certainly doesn't come naturally to me."

"You were enslaved from a young age," Rinxia pointed out, a bit more coldly than I would've hoped. "You never had a chance to learn anything or develop naturally. You are very odd. Your Way... it is not that of other dragons. Within you is a great deal of emotion. It is almost... human." I hoped the last bit was meant in jest.

I grunted at the memories of my early years on DragonPeak, at the Keepers' clumsy teaching and contemptuous bearing. "There is nothing natural about being a slave."

"For us, magic is a terrible struggle," Legao told me. "Those rare humans with the talent for magic begin their training with the Conclave of Magi no later than their eighth year. I began at six. Many never make it. Most pupils die, or go mad during the long years of training. Indeed, madness is a constant danger for human wizards, such that only a very few are allowed to continue in the craft. For years we do nothing but listen and train. I spent an entire winter on the peaks of the Pillar Mountains listening to the howl of blizzard gusts, then all the spring comparing that to the winds off the plain of Lita. And I would've not had an inkling of what to do with that knowledge had Drasu not been there to show me. He taught me to direct the raw emotion within me, to master it, use it. I wouldn't know where to start trying to teach a dragon magic."

Legao had meant her words to illustrate how different the process of human magic was from that of dragons, but she had actually told me the opposite. "Perhaps all that humans must spend years trying to learn and acquire, dragons are indeed born knowing. At least on some level. Even me. Your tiny ears—sorry, but they are tiny—they hear so much less, and your weak eyes, and all your other senses, they are less than those of dragons. There are other senses as well, those related to magic. It makes sense it takes years for humans to reach the sensory level to which dragons are born."

Rinxia flicked her tail about, impatient and uncomfortable with the talk of magic. "I hear, see, and fly better than you, Bayloo, and certainly better than any human. Yet I cannot do magic. I wouldn't even know where to start."

My mind raced. I was close to something important. "There is far more to wielding magic than merely being able to sense the world. That heightened perception is a prerequisite, but it does not by itself confer the ability to perform magic." Saying the words out aloud made me even more certain of their truth.

Legao reluctantly nodded at my words. "Drasu said that the woodmaster must be able to see his creation in his mind before he begins to work. He must know the materials with which he crafts, how they react to force, their strength, their texture. It takes decades of constant practice for a magi to do the same with the elements of the world, with the wind, the clouds. Even then we are little more than bumbling apprentices. Drasu taught me to use what we call Grafts, to manipulate forces that we cannot see and can barely sense. But I merely follow what I was taught. He was more. An archmaster of magic. He was an artist who could develop new spells, new powers. Like the great shield that protected the Tayo River. That is the greater power that separated Drasu from the rest of human magi."

"I know the wind, the sky; they are my home. Dragons know this at birth or with their first flight." I thought of Harlan. He lived his life on the sea. He knew water the way I knew the domain above. It partially explained his special talent for all things associated with water. It all fit.

Legao wasn't done. The weariness on her faded as she stared at me. "Yet that too is not enough. There is also... the other. The unknowable that must somehow be known. The unseeable that is there. The framework that links it all but cannot be comprehended by mortals."

My hearts pounded in unison at hearing what I had always known spoken aloud. "I know it." My blood surged faster as I thought of the silver threads. My voice became urgent. "What is it?"

"Drasu once called it the true world. One forever hidden from humans."

Only it wasn't hidden for dragons. That was the difference in the two branches of magic. One of the differences, at least.

"Yes, but what is it? How is it used?"

Legao's lips formed into a troubled grimace. "It is here that Drasu's teachings ended. He would go no further. He told me and the few others that reached my level over his long life that each wizard must find their own truth, their own perception of magic. I pressed him on this countless times over the years. I'm certain he knew something, understood something deeper, but feared... or did not wish to share it, for some reason."

"He never told you more than this?"

Her eyes gazed into the past. She released a long breath. "When I was a much younger woman, Drasu still had a bound concubine. Her name was Vixi. People didn't understand his interest in her, for Drasu could've had almost any woman or man he desired, but had chosen a gaunt girl who was blind in one eye as his bound companion. Their relationship was no mystery to those few lucky enough to know her." A hint of a smile played on Legao's face. "Vixi had poor sight, but her tongue was sharp as the finest blade, and she had a mind to match. They were together for decades, until she took ill."

"I remember Vixi," Rinxia said. "Although she had but one heart, it beat as strong as two. Yet no magic could save her when the sickness came."

"Drasu toiled like never before to cure her. The sky trembled, the spires of the palace swayed as he wrought his magic. All for naught. She died. For a week Drasu eased his sorrow with shoajiu. I joined him on one of those nights, trying to bring him back to us, for he was needed. Drasu was bitter with loss, cursing magic, speaking of strange things I'd not heard before. But in his ramblings, he spoke of that which we both sense, Bayloo. The magic that makes our power possible. The *Ar-Shadow,* he named it."

"*Ar-Shadow?* What is it?"

"When Drasu finally ended his mourning, I asked him about it. I'll never forget the flash of power in his eyes—it was anger tinged with concern. He answered with a tone that carried both warning and threat. He told me: "It is the limit of human magic. But every wizard must find their own understanding of the true world. If you try to follow my path, you will lose your way, your magic, and eventually, your life."

Legao's words quelled my premature excitement. "So magic—the real source of magic—cannot be taught, even to other humans? Is that what Drasu was saying?"

"I do not know for certain. At least among humans, he seemed to believe we had to take the final steps ourselves if we were able...My best guess is he believed the nature of the *Ar-Shadow* was that each magi had to find his or her own way of utilizing it, form their own relationship with magic. To some extent, we could merely copy what a master like Drasu told us, but only by actually perceiving and having some understanding of the *Ar-Shadow* could a human become a true archmaster—a forger of magic like Drasu."

"Is the *Ar-Shadow* the same as the Latticework?" I asked, my hearts beating. "Do you feel the power of it, the vast, dazzling complexity?" I remembered the magnificence of the weaves which formed the Latticework. "It is the true world, an intricate web that links everything."

Legao shook her head sadly. "There is no Latticework for humans. Perhaps we do not have the senses for it, as you say. So, our magic must work differently. I cannot help you utilize something I have never perceived."

I growled unhappily. I knew I had learned something important here, but I could not yet put it all together. Worse, Legao could not serve as the teacher I needed. If ember dragons were usually born with this knowledge, my time as a slave had robbed me of my birthright. I was alone in this journey—a freak even among my own kind.

Legao sensed my frustration. "I am sorry, Bayloo. You must find your own path."

"There isn't time for that. The hollowings come."

SEVENTEEN

The horde was relentless.

Day and night the behemoths and humans toiled to move the bridge-towers into position. The hollowings spread their huge constructions evenly along the portion of the river that was fordable, thereby creating a wide front for us to defend. More blood raptors flew from the west, circling over the hollowing army as it prepared its onslaught. The Mizu dug more trenches, but there were no more human reinforcements to come from the east. Newly arrived glasswings from Trishan, instead of promising relief, told of more unrest in Elasu's domain, just as Jinu the spymaster had predicted. No more troops could be spared, and they wouldn't have arrived soon enough to matter anyway. We would have to manage with what we had: dragons, horses, and soldiers. Alone, we would lose. There was no sign of Vengeance or the ghastrays.

Word of what I had done to Aragor's corpse spread through the Mizu army, the original information carried by glasswings from Trishan, including the one sent by my own sister. I expected Gia to explode with rage. He didn't. Indeed, the first time I saw him after I arrived, he looked at me with something like amusement. He thought as Rinxia did: I'd made a failed bargain that would ensure I could never become the Protector of Ni-Yota.

When Gia called his next war council, I wasn't invited, but Rinxia insisted I come along anyway. I did, for her sake, and to irritate Gia. It was strange to be here without Harlan. I regretted leaving him, for his advice was valuable, as was his company, but my choice had been for the best. No matter what outcome tomorrow, he and Kiata would live another day.

Gia returned from a scouting mission along the river as the rest of us gathered. I'd been up in the sky doing much the same thing earlier in the day. There was no way to miss the sheer size of the force arrayed against us. Even Gia's questionable mind grasped that we faced an enemy we couldn't defeat in conventional combat.

"We'll destroy the bridges," Gia announced to the assembled as if he'd discovered a new way to prepare roasted black pig.

In addition to the dragons, Avix, Dianti, and Tia also gathered around a barely lit fire under the open air of the night. Legao had refused to attend, informing us that rest was more valuable than words. She wasn't wrong.

I held the snort that wanted to escape my nostrils at Gia's grand proclamation. "Trying to burn the bridge-towers didn't work so well the last time." *Not to mention, you probably tried to kill me as well.*

"If fire will not work, we'll tear the structures apart," Gia replied calmly, ever the voice of reason. "They are wood, assembled by human hands. They will crumble under the might of a dragon." He stared at me with challenge in his eyes. "Any dragon will do, I suppose."

Rinxia answered Gia. "Each bridge is protected by dozens of ballistae on the shore. We can expect swarms of blood raptors as well. Bayloo has told me of your first attack. The horde makes mistakes, but not the same one twice."

I quoted Harlan's wisdom. "The hollowings expect the expected." Harlan said it with more flair. "Dragons destroying the bridges is expected. It will fail."

Gia batted his tail in annoyance. "Perhaps you should've dumped Aragor's dead and desecrated body into the Tayo River instead, Bayloo. Perhaps that would have helped us by demonstrating what utter barbarians we are. It surely wouldn't be expected, just as I didn't expect you would fly off to become a grave robber."

I stayed calm. I hoped Rinxia was impressed with my aplomb. "That has as much chance of success as your plan, and it will result in fewer soldiers killed. If you wish to lead with original thoughts, now would be the time to start trying to do it, Gia." I looked at the humans of this august council. They squirmed uncomfortably at the terse exchange between dragons. I knew none of the bipeds well, but from our last council I got the impression that Avix seemed to think himself as a knowledgeable veteran of the battles with the hollowings. "What say you, Knight-Lord?"

Avix seemed startled that I'd asked for his opinion, but he recovered quickly enough. "I agree the bridges remain critical." He looked uneasily at Gia. "They will anticipate an attack by air to burn them. When one is outnumbered, surprise can be the equalizer."

Tia, the Master of Horses, found his voice. "If the dragons can clear a path with fire, my riders can charge and take those bridges as soon as they are placed on our side of the river."

Dianti's lips turned downward. "Your riders won't last long against the horde, Horsemaster. What good are swords and lances against behemoths?"

"We don't need to last long. If we can confine their forces to four narrow choke points—the four bridges—their numerical advantage will mean far less. We need only hold our ground on the bridges while the engineers rip them to shreds with axes, fire, and whatever else they can come up with."

Dianti shook his head. "What about the behemoths? They'll be in the vanguard. Your charges will be stopped cold, your men slaughtered along with their horses."

Tia looked at Gia, Rinxia, then me, his eyes heavy. "We must rely upon the lords of the sky to handle the behemoths."

It was more of a dream than an actual plan, but I still judged it better than Gia's idea of trying to burn the bridges. I kept silent, waiting for Gia's predictable reaction.

"I can kill any behemoth."

"There is still the matter of the ballistae," Rinxia noted. "I've never seen so many in one place. Dodging arc-bolts while being harried by thousands of blood raptors will not leave much time for engaging the horde."

Gia merely growled. Such wisdom he had. It was time for me to open my mouth.

"We must rely upon Legao's magic. Swirling wind and lightning can reduce the danger from the arc-bolts," I said.

Tia agreed immediately. I decided he was the smartest of the human portion of the council, despite his limited skull size and lack of ear hair.

More noises from Gia, but not words. He was grumpy at being forced to accept others' plans, but at least he wasn't angry. "Tell the wizard to be ready. The horde draws ever closer. Rinxia and I will take turns monitoring their progress so we are ready when they arrive. Go make your men ready for battle."

After the rest of the council had dispersed and it was only Rinxia beside me, I spoke more freely. "They'll be slaughtered."

Rinxia stiffened. "It's a better plan than Gia's initial instinct to just fly at the bridges. As you said, the hollowings will expect that."

"Using cavalry charges and magic will mean that the humans will be slaughtered slightly more slowly." I gazed about at the army that surrounded us. I thought of Kiata, back at Trishan, likely fuming at me. I hoped Harlan could calm her. I missed his counsel at this moment. "Harlan would tell us we must do the unexpected. We must anticipate what will come, then shock our enemy with what they cannot imagine. The hollowings behave with intelligence, but not creativity."

"You have an idea?"

I supposed I did. "Perhaps, but it will not save us from defeat."

She studied me closely, slowly. My neck tingled under the gaze of those eyes. "Yet you're still here."

"I'm not without fear," I confessed. I sensed Rinxia's disappointment. Lamely, I added, "That does not make me a coward."

"I never thought you were, but you are not from here. You act with passion and emotion, like a human. As you told me when you adamantly rejected the notion of ever becoming Protector, this is not your fight. Why do you now risk your life and take the risks you take for a place that is not your home?"

I looked inside myself for the answer. Why did I feel this way? My insides weren't completely settled. It could've been too much dinner or something else. My answer wasn't complete, but I had an answer, at least. I met Rinxia's eyes. "Those that I care about are here. So this is my home. I will fight to protect my home."

EIGHTEEN

By the following morning, the hollowing horde's mighty towers loomed like mountains newly sprouted from the ground.

The great machines had stopped just out of range of the Mizu archers and catapults, letting our army gaze up at the massive constructions as well as the sprawling army that would utilize them. Unease coursed through my body. If I, a dragon, felt trepidation even though I had scales and could fly away whenever I wished (assuming I had been devoid of conscience), I could only imagine what a flightless, fleshy human experienced upon gazing at such a daunting sight. Gia and Rinxia could've swept in to attack, but we already knew the results of that. I suspected the horde wanted the dragons to come to their side of the river. That was what they expected. Peril undoubtedly awaited. We didn't give them what they wanted. Instead, we waited. Even Legao held onto her strength, waiting for the proper time. The morning grew long with a fleeting calm as we awaited the maelstrom that would surely come. Only once the hollowing intellect realized no dragon would be lured into whatever trap they had set for us did they begin their attack.

Without any audible signal or beacon, the hollowings began to stir all at once. The bridge-towers rolled the final distance toward the river's edge, pulled by the great behemoths beneath the burning rays of the late morning sun. The Mizu responded. Archers rained their arrows upon the horde while catapults hurled rocks dipped in burning pitch into the sky. The horde answered with a fusillade of arrows so thick they nearly blotted out the azure of the sky.

Gia, Rinxia, and I spread ourselves out at intervals along the length of the river, our spacing putting all four of the hollowing tower-bridges within easy striking distance of at least one of us. We hovered in the sky, out of range of the horde's weapons, waiting for the right moment to attack. Tia's mounted soldiers had formed themselves into two large formations. Tia himself led the southern group, the one closest to me. Dianti was among his soldiers closer to the river —those humans who would bear the brunt of the initial wave. Avix had command of the largest of the reserve forces, stationed just behind the Mizu trenches. I didn't care for most humans, including these Mizu, but they weren't cowards.

I gazed at the waters of the Tayo. The river rushed fast and wild, without a care for the slaughter that was to come. There was no sign of any ghastrays. Indeed, I'd never heard of ghastrays traveling into a river where the water was fresh rather than salt laden like the sea. Perhaps my plan had been as foolish as Gia contended.

The massive bridge-towers each arrived at the far bank of the Tayo within a few moments of each other, as if even the strides of the behemoths that pulled them were connected. Mizu arrows coated the constructions as if they were a porcupine's coat, but no real damage had been done to the towers. The horde would cross. I waited for the bridges to fall and extend across the river. The blood raptors came first.

They came not in an immense cloud, as they had in the past, but in a stream, narrow and purposeful. I knew where they were headed. The horde behaved with its usual logic. But understanding their objective was different than being able to do anything about it.

The blood raptors flew over our army, ignoring the soldiers, the horses, the catapults, and even the dragons. A few archers took aim at the interlopers, but their arrows were pebbles thrown at an ocean. Hawks were unleashed from their cages, but they were too few. The raptors came with purpose, seeking the person who had thwarted their advance these past days. They came for Legao. She was our most effective weapon, even more so than Gia or I, for she could attack at a distance. Unlike me, she could use her magic. Without Legao, this battle would be lost, as well as those that might come after, for she had no true replacement among the humans. She was the last of the master magi. We needed Legao.

At the back of our lines stood the robed figure of a wizard, stoic and unmoving even as the enemy flew at speed to our side of the river. I moved to intercept, as did Rinxia, but even as I beat my wings, I knew we'd be too late, and we weren't enough anyway. There must've been a thousand blood raptors in that black stream of death. The wizard did not meekly accept her intended fate.

The winds came at Legao's command. A breeze morphed into a torrent within moments. The tempest smashed into the leading edge of the blood raptor formation, sending the birds hurtling into each other, the violent gusts tearing dozens of the blood seekers to pieces. Feathers and mutilated flesh exploded in all directions. But still, they came. The single stream split into three, each moving as fast as the original. The new raptor formations flew around Legao's summoned storm like river water around a new boulder, barely skirting the edges of the twisting winds.

Dark clouds arrived like charging cavalry. They rumbled from within, the sound echoing through the sky. Then lightning struck. The bolt came not as a single great streak of light, but as a dozen splinters of fantastic energy, their passage cracking the air. The flashes ripped into the raptors, turning feather to ash upon contact. One bolt followed another in rapid succession. The stink of roasting raptor permeated the air along with their ashy remains. The ranks of birds thinned, but certain death was no deterrent to the hollowings.

They sought a mere human. Rinxia's speed got her closest to the attacking flock, allowing her to unleash her fire before I arrived.

She spewed flame far and wide. The inferno collided with one of the blood raptor streams. The birds didn't bother to scatter or evade the danger. The raptors flew through the flame, the urge to reach the lone wizard on her raised platform unshakable. Rinxia continued to close the distance between her and the blood raptors. I approached from the opposite direction, but I had no fire. I wished again for the magic that was just out of my reach. Rinxia unleashed another wave of fire. More lightning flashed through the sky. I came within moments of reaching the raptors. I let loose a roar that shook the air like thunder.

It was all futile.

A blood raptor reached its target, the bird's talons anxiously outstretched. A hundred more followed, then another hundred, until a statue of black feathers stood on the platform overlooking the field of battle. They attacked, furious and desperate. No human could survive that. The clouds that Legao had summoned dispersed. The wind ceased. Rinxia bathed the clustered blood raptors in her fire, ending any hope of survival for any creature of flesh on the platform. The enemy had lost a thousand or more of its raptors, but it was a price the hollowings were willing to pay.

The towers at the River Tayo dropped their bridges. The river was breached.

NINETEEN

Behemoths led the attack.

Four bridges. Two huge brutes per bridge. Eight walking piles of armored crap.

Hollowing foot soldiers followed the behemoth vanguard, their forces packed together in four orderly columns as they marched across each of the bridges. The wolf packs were held back in reserve. But that wasn't the worst of it. On the far shore of the Tayo, I counted ten more behemoths, the beasts waiting with unnatural stillness as their fellows tested the bridges and our defenses. The hollowing horde had learned something else from their prior battles: caution. They kept the most lethal part of their force in reserve, lest we have some new trick ready to defeat their mobile bridges.

Gia was already on his way to the northernmost crossing. Rinxia and I turned about and headed for two bridges to the south. We wore our *sai*. The largest contingent of Tia's riders charged at the final bridgehead, but it didn't change the ugly fact that there were more bridges than dragons.

The Mizu-mounted horses bolted through pre-determined lanes cleared for them by the foot soldiers, the ground laid with dry gravel to ease their passage on damp ground. The cavalry carried heavy lances and javelins, some tipped with metal. A rain of hollowing arrows from the far bank of the Tayo fell on the chargers, extracting a heavy toll even before the first horse got a hoof on one of the bridges. Dozen died—horses and men in equal numbers—but no one stopped. The behemoths increased their pace as the cavalry came, but Tia and his riders were quicker. On each bridge crossing, the Mizu soldiers bravely met the vanguard behemoths. It wasn't a pleasant affair to watch.

On my bridge, the lead behemoth swept a quartet of soldiers off the bridge's expanse with a single flail of its giant head. After that, it snatched both a man and a horse with its spiked tail, then hurled them into the next wave of Mizu advancing on the bridge. The initial carnage complete, the monster resumed its advance across the bridge, a second behemoth trailing close behind. I glanced at the waters of the Tayo in vain. The dead humans floated away in the current. The ghastrays hadn't come. They weren't going to save us. We were going to have to win this fight with blood and wit and mad courage.

I swooped down to attack the hollowing vanguard before the next group of humans arrived to throw their lives away. I stared down the behemoth on the south side of the bridge, then swerved at the last movement to rack my *sai*-tipped claws across the back of the other creature. A satisfying crunch followed my efforts. As I came out of my pass, I saw Rinxia sweep a leg out from a behemoth with her tail as she executed a reckless but elegant pass in front of her adversaries.

"A little caution!" I roared. If Rinxia heard me, she ignored me.

I made a sharp turn, coming back at the behemoth I'd recently wounded. The bleeding beast halted, turning to face me, while its ugly brother continued crossing. The Mizu came again. Horsemen died as they futilely attempted to halt the creature's advance, their lances shattering upon contact with the behemoth's thick armor.

On my next pass, I kept high enough to be just out of reach of the behemoth's tail spikes. I wanted it to try to strike me and miss so I had an opportunity to swoop down to grab the shaft of its tail from behind. I got half of what I'd intended. The beast swiped its pointy spikes at me, but it knew its range better than I. The thing understood it would miss me. So it leapt—the massive thing actually lifted itself into the air. I should've anticipated that, but I didn't. The behemoth's spikes struck my underside. If it had been on the ground with the full force of its weight behind the strike, I might've been impaled. As it was, it merely cracked a scale and sent me for an unpleasant spin. I missed my chance to grab its tail in my jaws as I'd intended. I righted myself, intending to attack again, when Rinxia's voice rang out.

"Dive!"

I didn't look, I just obeyed. A ballistae arc-bolt zipped past me. I beat my wings, gaining altitude, as two more projectiles failed to find their target. From my perch in the sky, I circled above just long enough to be certain that we were losing the battle.

The first two behemoths made their way across my bridge. Neither infantry nor cavalry charge could stop the beasts—the Mizu just kept dying as they tried to protect the eastern bank. The engineers that had dared to follow the initial horsemen's charge were gone and dead. The bridge was intact. To the north, Rinxia had done a better job at delaying the hollowings, holding them about three-quarters of the way from the eastern bank. Unfortunately, her success had drawn a swarm of blood raptors to her. As the dark cloud pursued Rinxia through the sky, the behemoths resumed their advance. The human engineers on that bridge abandoned their work in the shadow of advancing behemoths, but not before they had hacked away half the span and ignited a smoldering fire. Gia was furthest away from me, but he appeared to be engaged in close combat with the behemoths, with still more blood raptors swarming around him. On the final bridge—the one without a dragon to defend it—the hollowings had crossed with ease, endangering the flank of the force trying to hold Rinxia's area.

I continued my climb into the sky, then dove, this time coming down on the hollowing side of the river. They saw me coming, but arrows don't really bother me and ballistae are large, hulking machines that are ponderous to turn and difficult to aim. I had reached my target before I faced any real danger from arc-bolts, and the blood raptors were already engaged with Gia and Rinxia, leaving me with an opportunity to wreak some havoc. I took it.

I snatched the largest ballista I could find, grabbing it with my hind claws and dragging it along the riverbank into two other machines. I knocked a third ballista, along with a few hollowings, into the river with a swipe of my tail. Still carrying the massive contraption, I beat my wings, gaining speed and altitude, then dropped it in the midst of the columns of hollowings crossing the river. In addition to the hollowings that the machine crushed, the ballista's wooden structure shattered nicely, with the jagged shards killing several more of the enemy. It didn't stop the advance. The rest didn't even bother pausing to clear the bridge. They just stepped over the dead and the debris.

While I'd been taking out a few ballistae on one side of the river, the hollowings had been busy killing humans on the other. They controlled a bridgehead that stretched from Gia's location in the north down to mine in the south. Rinxia's bridge had been damaged such that only about half as many hollowings could traverse its span as the others, but we'd all failed to destroy any bridge or keep the hollowings from crossing over to our side of the river in numbers.

Avix had already committed the last of his reserve forces to the same bridge where Tia fought, and pitch-coated projectiles from the Mizu catapults still fired, but it was a losing effort. A single behemoth had been caught in a hidden pit trap, but I still counted six beasts that had already reached the eastern shore, along with several thousand hollowing warriors. For now, the Mizu fought on, clashing with the advanced elements, but it was clear they held their ground only because the hollowings had not yet begun a concerted push to crush the rest of the defenses. I guessed that the enemy was waiting for sufficient numbers to cross the river. Once the rest of the behemoths reached our side, the situation would be hopeless.

Rinxia came to the same realization. She flew toward me, still harried by a cloud of blood raptors, although the birds' numbers were much diminished. Rinxia's fire was lethal.

"We need to take out the bridges. Fire doesn't work. They don't stay lit."

"Then how?"

"We tip them. Together."

I didn't bother to debate the merits of her idea. We both knew staying in any one place would make us vulnerable to ballistae arc-bolts and blood raptors. If Rinxia was willing to risk it, I would as well.

We came about in a tight loop, with Rinxia leading. I hung back, just off her tail. A hundred blood raptors followed, talons longingly stretched at us. Rinxia headed for her bridge, since it was already damaged. Two ballistae fired, both at me. The operators must have learned that fast, sleek Rinxia was a difficult target—at least while she was moving. I wasn't a sloth either. I maneuvered under the first shot and batted the second away by striking its shaft with my tail. Rinxia gave me a disapproving look even as she continued toward our target. When she drew close enough, Rinxia bathed the hollowings on the bridge in fire, clearing a bit of space for us. She grabbed the bottom of the bridge's edge with her hind claws. I did the same, taking care to position myself between her and the hollowing side of the river. If a ballista found its mark, I wanted to be the one that took the bolt.

She noticed what I'd done. "I'm smaller and quicker, you fool." She said it through gritted teeth.

We beat our wings, straining with the bridge, trying to move it. The wood wasn't normal. Something had been done to it. It was cold like metal and hard as stone. But we didn't stop—I'd lifted heavier things. The bridge creaked. It cracked. It began to flip (a little). The blood raptors reached us, their talons and beaks immediately digging into my wings and backside. Just before the black storm came at my eyes, I saw the ballistae adjusting their aim.

Rinxia saw the danger as well. "Bayloo, go!"

"Almost got it."

It was true. The bridge was crying out as we twisted it apart. The hollowings on its surface slid toward the water on the opposite side. I heard a ballista snap its firing mechanism, then another. I didn't have time to do anything about it. I had to trust others. I intended to take out this bridge.

Rinxia cried out, "Bayloo!"

The arc-bolts never reached me. The sky opened to save me—a splintered bolt of lightning flashed down to incinerate both of the projectiles just a moment before they perforated me. We might be losing this battle, but we hadn't lost yet.

"Once more!" I yelled.

Powered by the elation of being alive and whole, I beat my wings harder. I pushed with my hearts and my will. It would not be enough. I would fail. That was my fate, and it did not bother me as much as it should, because I was on the path that I must travel, whatever the cost. In that moment of acceptance, somewhere in my mind, I touched that place that I had been born to know, but had lost in my years as a slave. My hearts pumped. I heard the wind, the air, and the water. They spoke in their own way, babbling to the world around them. Within the commotion, I found clarity. I was part of this. Suddenly, I understood how these forces of the world fit together— the weaves of the bridge, the water of the river, the wind blowing from the shore, the cloud looming overhead. It was a grand mosaic, a sculpture with countless bindings—Chords of Making—that joined everything into a cohesive whole greater than its parts. As sure as I knew I had wings, I knew these Chords were mine to command.

In that singular moment of clarity, where I wasn't conscious of precisely what I did, I made the water move. I willed it, I changed the pattern, and in response the river rose up. Not into some gigantic tidal wave, but enough to give Rinxia and I the extra help we needed. The wind pushed at our backs. The bridge rose further, its supporting beams twisting, then snapping. Finally, one section tore loose, flipped into the river, and broke away from the rest. We had done it.

I had done it. This was what they called magic.

Rinxia and I both headed for the sky, twirling madly to shake the blood raptors that harried us. She burned another dozen. Their numbers had thinned, but they were still dangerous. I saw Gia's flames ignite beneath us, near the ground. I circled above the heart of the Mizu army, watching them fight vainly to hold the shore. I was elated at my success, but the tide of the battle tempered my joy. Even with one bridge destroyed, we were losing.

"That got their attention." Rinxia flew past me. "They come with their strength."

She was correct. While we'd been tangling with the bridge, the rest of the behemoths had begun their crossing. They were huge. Ten more. That was too many.

The remaining blood raptors abandoned their pursuit of Rinxia and Gia. They quickly reformed, hovering like a protective cloud over the three remaining bridges, covering the crossing of the massive behemoths. If they crossed, Ni-Yota was doomed. The rest of the enemy ballistae remained similarly poised, a hundred eyes fixed upon the three dragons in the sky. It was a grim sight, but Rinxia didn't sound distraught as she glided around me.

"We must go again. We must destroy the rest of the bridges."

I kept watching. The last behemoth stepped on the southernmost of the three remaining crossings. It wouldn't take them long to traverse the river. We didn't have enough time to destroy the rest of the bridges, even if we could've somehow done that. It looked hopeless.

"They'll be ready the next time," I warned. "The hollowings adapt quickly. The behemoths will tear us to bits if the arc-bolts and raptors don't get us before then."

Rinxia knew I was correct. She was too intelligent not to see the same things I did. "Is it better to die today or over the coming weeks? Once they cross, once the hollowings control the river, they will overwhelm us. Avix cannot hold them, no matter how many men and horses he might deploy. They will come and they will bring the rust with them."

She wanted to make her stand now, here. I didn't. I would've retreated, kept fighting. I'd seen many battles. The tides of war change at unexpected moments. Better to fight another day. Better to savor a few more days (and nights) together. I didn't say any of those things. There wasn't time. Rinxia dove without me.

I followed her into the gauntlet of death that waited below.

TWENTY

Blood raptors rose to meet us.

They came like a blanket of night, spread thin and wide. There were just enough to block our view of the ballistae firing at us from the shore. The arc-bolts punched through the black curtain of bird feathers, giving us almost no time to adjust course or defend ourselves. Only luck (or something more divine) preserved us through the first three shots.

Rinxia released her fire. It punched a hole in the blood raptor formation, but only briefly. The gap closed as quickly as it had opened, but I saw at least a dozen arc-bolts headed for us through the fleeting window. There was something else as well.

"Break off, Rinxia."

She grunted. "We have to do this."

"We don't," I pleaded. "I promise. Do it."

Rinxia hesitated. I waited for her, unwilling to leave if she would not. I would not let Rinxia continue the attack on her own. I'd been left alone far too many times for that. It didn't take her long to decide, but any delay was still too long. As Rinxia pulled out of her dive, three arc-bolts punctured the curtain beneath us. I tried to swerve, but that just made my trajectory worse, because I hadn't accounted for the fourth projectile. One bolt grazed my tail, but another struck me directly in my wing—hard and fast. The tip must've been metal; it punched right through the membrane, and the whole damn thing passed through me. I had a hole in my wing. Chicken piss.

Rinxia saw it. She slowed, positioning herself beneath me, putting herself in the line of fire. "To our side of the river, Bayloo. Now."

I glided, not wanting to make the damage worse before I had a chance to inspect it. Rinxia circled back to throw some more flame on the blood raptors that pursued us. They broke off as soon as I reached the eastern edge of the Tayo, but it wasn't because of Rinxia's fire. Despite the injury to my wing, I lingered in the air to watch what was going to happen. I needed to see it.

Rinxia didn't understand yet. "Land, Bayloo. What are you waiting for?"

"Watch the bridges."

We both did that. My wing hurt, but some pain was worth it for the view.

It started with a vine, thick and gray, rising from the river. Only it wasn't a vine. If I hadn't been looking for it, I wouldn't have seen it in the din of battle. The behemoths crossing nearby didn't notice. Another tail appeared, then a dozen, followed by fifty more. They came at the bridges, at the behemoths, at the hollowing footmen. In three rapid heartbeats, the first behemoth had been whisked off the bridge. It happened so quickly it was as if the beast had been merely some horrid nightmare immediately banished with the flutter of an opening eye. The remaining bridges shook—all of them. The hollowings lost their balance, falling to the ground. As the tremors shaking the crossings grew more violent, men and beasts were hurled into the surging water of the Tayo. The current grabbed them, but that wasn't the greatest peril. Ghastray stingers struck, while tentacles rose to suck the fallen into the depths of the river to be consumed.

The hollowings collectively recognized the danger. They all

stopped for several quick moments—an entire army halted instantly by some unseen, unspoken command. When they moved again, it was with new purpose. The behemoths ran for the eastern bank of the river, struggling to join their fellows already across, while the hollowing footmen scurried to the edges of the bridges, beating at the water and the deadly tails that harried them. Blood raptors plunged from the air, diving into the bloody water as if hunting for fish.

The ghastrays were no less decisive than the hollowings. They swarmed the bridges from all sides, attacking the hollowings, but also the structures themselves. I'd never seen so many ghastrays in a single place. The Tayo was thick with their tails and eyes. Even a ship wrecked on the shoals wouldn't have drawn so many of the creatures. I shivered at the sight—this was more than mere payment for the head of a dragon.

"What took them so long?" Rinxia asked with surprise and relief.

"They were always there. They merely were waiting for the main behemoth force to begin crossing, so they could strike and do the greatest possible damage."

"How do you know?"

"It's what I would've done."

One of the remaining bridges fell into the water, every behemoth that had tried to cross there falling with it. The moment the massive creatures hit the water, stingers came from every side. Behemoth and human alike disappeared under the stained water like stones. Occasionally, one of the ghastrays' frightening eyes would emerge from beneath the current, but for the most part, we only saw their stingers. Much of the slaughter occurred beneath the surface. Even the skies cleared as the last of the blood raptors perished in the river, vainly trying to attack the ghastray host below. After the shock passed, a great cheer, one laden with both relief and elation, rose from the Mizu army. The humans fighting on the western bank surged forth with renewed purpose.

The next bridge fell. A single behemoth had made it across. That made seven on our side of the river. One more made it from the final bridge before the ghastrays destroyed that one as well. Eight behemoths and over a thousand hollowing soldiers still held a salient on the wrong side of the river. It was a formidable force, and under normal circumstances it would've been an intimidating one. However, we had just watched the impossible, as the greater part of the hollowing force was consumed by our mysterious allies with breathtaking speed; no one considered defeat a possibility. Just to make sure, Legao chose that moment to step out from the underground trench in which she had concealed herself from the start of the battle. She wore the clothes of a Mizu soldier, but her hair revealed her identity to me and the others who knew our plan. Her robes had been sacrificed in Rinxia's flames, along with the propped-up corpse that had baited the hollowings to begin their attack.

Clouds began racing toward the sky above the hollowing army. Rinxia glanced at my wing as I glided awkwardly in a circle beside her. "Show's over, Bayloo. Land and guard Legao. I'll help Gia to finish off the remains of the invaders."

I wanted to argue with her, but I couldn't. I couldn't fly well enough to execute precision maneuvers, and I couldn't breathe fire. But that didn't mean I'd be useless. I glided to the ground not far from Legao. She paid me no mind, the whole of her concentration remaining focused on her summoning.

Gia streaked across the sky on a course parallel to the river, flames pouring from his mouth. His tail looked to be missing a few scales, but there wasn't anything wrong with his flying. Rinxia executed a similar maneuver from the opposite direction while Legao called lightning, this time in single massive bolts that tore through the air. They all had the wrong idea. The path to victory was right in front of us. We just needed to use it.

I reached out for that place of equanimity I had somehow found even as I had struggled to tip the first bridge with Rinxia, a place that had existed beside the exertions of a perilous struggle. I needed to find it again. There, in that part of my mind, I sensed the Latticework. From that oasis, I had performed my first work of magic. Now, the calm once again eluded me. I tried again, this time more anxious, with the same frustrating result.

My head filled with the throbbing ache of my wing. There was a hole in it that didn't belong. I tried ignoring the pain, but that didn't quite work. Rinxia dove toward the enemy, and I worried for her until she reappeared higher in the sky. I needed to focus. I looked at Legao. Her eyes had faded to a dull silver, her body fixed in position. But her face was determined. Her lips moved, the sounds coming forth unintelligible, but unmistakably harsh and commanding.

That was the human path of magic. I needed to look elsewhere for dragon magic.

The answer for my previous failures came to me: I had wanted it too badly. I was demanding it. With Aragor, to heal Rinxia. I had been desperate in those moments. I was emotional, like a human. At the bridge, I had sensed the Latticework only once I accepted my fate. Perhaps that was what other dragons referred to as the Way—an acceptance of what must happen. Legao had told me human magic was a constant struggle, a battle to command a force larger than they. Dragons did not walk that path. Our magic was instinctive to us. It merely required us to accept who we were and our place in the greater pattern of the Latticework.

I was an ember dragon, and my fate would inevitably unfold. I shut my eyes. I sucked in wind, trying to push the sounds of the battle away. That brought me closer, but I still could not sense the Latticework. I needed to forget my past, forget the slavery, the death. I focused on the moment only, looking inward. I needed to fly my path in this world. I felt the wind, its beauty, its pattern, how it interacted with the water, the sky, the clouds, and with me. At the end of that journey was the impossible structure of the Latticework. I connected to it, feeling the energy in the Chords that connected all things, seen and unseen. I didn't understand it all—I did not dare try. Something within me knew that was the way to madness. I had merely to grasp the workings of the forces around me. The Chords of Making linked all things, and they could be tugged, pushed, even severed. Maybe even created or destroyed, but I was not ready for that. For the first time, I also sensed something else: the Latticework was not all it should be. There was a void, a place near its very heart where the Chords were black, or severed, or gone entirely. But I had no need of that broken place now. In this moment, I needed the elements of the sky.

I called the wind, pulling it through the Latticework's structure. I didn't direct the gusts at the hollowings, though. Not yet. Mere gusts, no matter how powerful they might be, wouldn't be enough for what I intended. I commanded a storm to gather in the distance, at the very edge of even a dragon's sight. I ordered swirling twisters, mimicking the patterns of the worst torrent I'd seen back in Rolm.

When my summoning was insufficient, I drew upon still more of the power of the Latticework itself. It answered as if it understood me, as if it wanted to answer me. There was no struggle here—it was an experience quite unlike what Legao had described. My storm grew, split, and grew more. The ferocious winds sucked in every bit of loose debris within the radius of its horizon. I'd deliberately chosen a barren stretch of plains, a place filled with sand and rock and common detritus that easily lifted from the ground. When I had enough, and my family of storms had become a wall of spinning projectiles, I called my creation toward me, tugging at the Chords of the Latticework. My summoning marched as fast as a dragon in flight, flowing across the landscape. As it moved, the storm system ached to fall apart—what I'd created was terribly unnatural, the winds wrong, the direction wrong. Somehow, the Latticework itself sensed my need, showing me what I must do. Hints of pain tugged at the edge of my consciousness. I ignored it. There was only the storm, only its path. I coaxed it onward.

I became vaguely aware of the startled reaction of the Mizu soldiers as the dark wall of swirling debris came upon them from the east like a massive wave. Some recognized it as magic, intended to aid it, but most gave in to their base instincts to flee from the massive summoning that had no natural place in this world. They were the wiser. I didn't have full control over my creation. Mizu died as it moved through our lines, some sucked into the clutches of the storm, their screams penetrating my cocoon of concentration. Within the Latticework, the impossibly complex weavings that linked humans to the greater structure dimmed with their death. I felt nothing. This was my Way. There was no other way to do what needed to be done. They and thousands more would die without my storm.

The torrent reached the edge of the hollowing bridgehead, where the hollowings and behemoths did battle with soldiers and dragons. Rinxia and Gia had the sense to fly clear of the storm. I unleashed my summoning, sending forth countless bits of rock and sand, flinging it at the hollowing force lining the eastern bank at fantastic speeds. Each projectile struck like an arrow, propelled by a wind force greater than any natural storm could've mustered. I commanded the winds to blow still harder. I urged and pushed until my insides felt like they were being torn apart. My hearts thundered inside me. Other storms appeared—not my work, but Legao's. I could not sense her magic being worked, but I could perceive the result within the Latticework. Together, we unleashed gusts stronger than the force of a dragon's tail. The hollowing soldiers were the first to lose their footing. One fell off his feet, caught in the wind. The river and its deadly occupants waited. The first of the hollowings fell into the water. Hundreds more hollowings joined him in the hungry waters. Even the behemoths struggled to hold their ground. They were huge, strong, heavy.

I had no more will left to expend. My legs trembled with exhaustion. I couldn't grasp enough air to fill my chest. The power of the storm was unsustainable. I'd done all I could. Rinxia didn't squander the chance I had given her.

She swooped down, striking a distracted behemoth in the torso, shoving it toward the water. Gia followed her attack, flying even more boldly, riding the wind I'd created to grab the behemoth and toss it to the waiting ghastrays.

Once the two flying dragons had a successful tactic, they were ruthless about putting it to work. Four more behemoths fell. Gia and Rinxia worked quickly, but not quickly enough. As my strength faded, so did the winds. I opened my eyes. Debris still infested the air. I saw Legao's lightning flash through the sky, followed by the fire of the circling dragons. Gia engaged one of the behemoths at close quarters, pitting claw and tail against its armored body, deadly spikes, and horrible triangular jaw. Rinxia knew the limits of her own abilities—she kept aloft, continuing to harry the enemy from above with her fire. The Mizu horsemen rallied, with Tia leading his forces around the distracted and unsupported behemoths. The Mizu charged the hollowing remnant from all sides, human and dragon fighting together. It was a worthy sight. I really wanted to see how it all ended. But I lacked the strength to keep my eyes open.

Blackness snatched me.

TWENTY-ONE

I awoke to victory.

By that I mean I awoke to the odor of roasted pig. It wasn't one of the delicious black pigs from Changsha, but it definitely smelled delectable. Also, if I was alive (I seemed to be) and someone had taken the time to prepare a meal for me, I was relatively certain we had won the battle. The hollowing horde didn't seem like the pig-roasting type. They probably liked chicken feet.

I lay where I had collapsed during the later stages of the battle. A large tent had been erected around and above me. The hole in my wing had been stitched together, and a stinky salve had been applied to a few places on my scales where I'd suffered other minor nicks in the fighting. A whole pig had been placed on a platter within easy reach. I considered this the work of a true healer.

While I ate, a human stuck his head into my tent, watched me chomp on some roasted pig, then scurried off. I chewed faster, figuring he'd gone off to find someone to bother me.

To my surprise, Legao appeared shortly afterward. Reservoirs of darkness radiated under her eyes. Her shoulders slumped and she shuffled more than walked into my presence, as if the effort of lifting her feet was too great. She looked like she could use some pig. I greeted her with the greatest courtesy a dragon could offer: "Would you like some?"

Legao stared at the mangled carcass scattered before me.

"Uh...it is kind of you to leave me some bones, but I must refuse."

"The bones aren't for you." I pointed with my claw to the corner of the tent. "I don't like the hooves. Too dry. I tossed them over there."

Legao's eyes darkened. "I don't care for pig feet, either. Indeed, meat makes my stomach turn."

I didn't understand what she was talking about. "You mean you don't like pig."

"I don't eat animal flesh."

She was speaking nonsense. The implications disturbed me. I changed the subject. "We won the battle, I presume."

"Remarkably, we did indeed. We won, and more. For the first time in a decade, the hollowings have withdrawn even from the west bank of the Tayo, their forces sliding back into their wasteland."

That part surprised me. They still had tens of thousands of foot soldiers and wolves arrayed in the west. Everyone was so certain the hollowings never gave up. "They retreat?"

"Rinxia has taken to the sky to keep a watch on them. At the very least, they have moved away from the fordable area near the riverbank, creating more distance from the shallowings—which I understand you refer to as ghastrays—and their horde."

I spat out a jagged bone. "Ghastrays are unpleasant enemies. Long stingers. Big appetites."

"How did you summon them here?" Legao wondered. "Is it some type of binding magic?"

I didn't get it. "Binding?" Even the word tasted sour.

"As I understand their particular magic, using those runes the binders can get the sha—the ghastrays to pull waveships, yes...but to fight. Not to come when summoned. Not to kill our enemies. And never to command so many. Even Drasu did not have magic that could do such a thing. Not even the other ember dragons could—"

I cut her off. "You think magic brought them here?" I snorted my annoyance through my nostrils. Legao ducked away from a bit of mucus that flew out with my displeasure. "You think that I somehow *enslaved* these ghastrays, as your binders would do?"

Legao tilted her head, unsure of the anger in my words. "If not magic, why did the ghastrays come to our aid? They do not normally dwell in rivers. I've never heard of one of those creatures coming into fresh water, not in the history of Ni-Yota. Their kind are certainly no friends of humans. These creatures are born killers, the ultimate predators of the sea."

I spat out a bone. "A human dares to call another creature a born killer?" I was disappointed in Legao. She was a better thinker than most of her kind, but she was still human. "Your race *enslaves* ghastrays. You collar them, chain them to your boats, take away their will, their lives. Do you expect their affection for such treatment?"

"The ghastrays were killers long before there were waveships. They are the scourge of the seas. They decimated fishing fleets, slaughtered seaside villages, consumed the bounty of the sea."

"Wolves feed upon sheep. Horned eagles upon mice. Dragons upon delicious pigs and everything else delicious. Do not expect creatures of great hunger to join you in your meatless life of vegetable eating. Take this lesson from a former slave: death is preferable to being forced to serve. Nothing is worse than having your will stripped from you and given to another. It is as if you are dead but forced to live anyway for the purposes of another. A slave's first thought upon winning his freedom is vengeance. You humans would be wise to heed that lesson. You hold slaves at your peril. You hold your greatest enemy at bay. You should think about that."

Legao's jaw dropped a bit. "You are suggesting we free the ghastrays?"

Actually, I hadn't thought that far ahead. But she wasn't wrong. "What your binders have done is an abomination."

Legao's eyes widened as she considered the implications. "Ni-Yota is vast. The other lands it trades with for silk, for metal, are distant. Without the waveships...commerce would come to a near halt. Trade would near cease. People might starve. The merchants, the nobles...well, no one would accept it."

"If the ghastrays do it themselves, it will be far worse. Revolts are bloody."

Legao's head shook, but not in denial of my words. She seemed to be struggling with the implications of her way of life. I could tell she resisted my notion, but at least she had listened. Better than I could've expected from many humans.

"But why did they help us now?" Legao pressed. "Because of you?"

I looked over the bare bones of my meal as I considered Legao's question. There wasn't anything left worth going after. I was still hungry. "It isn't completely clear why the ghastrays do something or nothing. But they are intelligent and they communicate in some strange way, as we see through their ability for collective action, which may not be so different than the hollowings. I asked for their help. We needed their help."

Legao's dark eyes squeezed together. "Word came by glasswing that you dumped Drasu's body in the sea and Aragor in the gulf near Trishan. Was this the ghastrays' price? Are they mercenaries who crave the flesh of the powerful?"

"They aren't mercenaries." I thought on my conversation with Vengeance and the patchwork lore of Harlan's people. "It may be the rust is not new. Even the ghastrays may have some history with it. They spoke of a greater Purpose."

"What do you mean?" Legao's voice had dropped to a near whisper.

"I don't know. I spent most of my life in Rolm as a slave. You are the wizard, someone who has dedicated your life to study. Is there no record of the ghastrays among the stores of knowledge of your people?"

"None that I know of."

"Do you have knowledge of the time before the Cataclysm?"

"Before the Cataclysm ..." Legao rubbed her temples. "Not within the Conclave of Magi. Not that I know of. The archivists of Oracles of Silla kept many records."

I recognized the name. "My mother once sought counsel in that place. Rinxia told me my mother once spent nearly a year on the Peak of Silla not long before her final exile."

"Silla is a mysterious place. It is said that only the worthiest are granted entrance, and even then they must pay the price."

"The price?"

"Supposedly, to enter, a newcomer has to come with a piece of knowledge not previously part of the archive. Only by adding to its knowledge could one gain permission to study what is already there. But the records kept at Silla are said to be vast, ancient."

"Who built it?"

"I do not know. Drasu said it was a trove of the knowledge held against the day when the world again wished to understand its past. The Archive of Oracles, it is sometimes called."

"Where is this archive?"

"No place you wish to travel."

"You could say that about almost everywhere that isn't a cozy cave filled with black pigs and a tub of shaojiu. I ask again: Where is it?"

Legao swept a hand westward. "At the very edge of the world. Across the Tayo River, across all of Illium, on the tip of a peninsula in the far west known as Haven's Finger, for it protrudes from the rest of the land like a broken pinky. On the Silla Peak, at the end of the Finger, you will find it. Even for a dragon, it would be many days of flight. No one has traveled there since your mother's time, before the hollowings came. To make such a journey now...even for a dragon, it would be perilous. The archive may not have survived. Even the mountaintops are not safe from the hollowings and the rust."

Legao certainly knew how to make a place sound unappealing.

However, from what I'd been told, my mother had spent considerable time on that peak. Whatever she'd learned had prompted her to risk exile, to leave Ni-Yota, maybe even to give birth to my sister and I, in search of something. Perhaps it held the secret of aurathorn as well. My mother had thought there were answers at the Silla Peak. Or at least, there had been at one time in the past. It could indeed be gone, and I had no doubt that Legao spoke true about the perils of journeying there. To take such a risk and find only more devastation was unappealing.

I felt the wizard's eyes boring into me, questions waiting on her lips.

"What else is there you wish to know, Legao?"

"You came from past the Edge, from a place few in Ni-Yota even know exists. In that short time, you have seen the death of two rulers, as well as a great victory over the hollowings. You claim a lack of magic yet manage to conjure a storm of a power unrivaled by any seen in a hundred years. And you seem to have forged some kind of alliance with the ghastrays, whose freedom you now champion. Who are you, truly?"

It was one of those moments that made me rejoice that dragons get to choose their names as their lives change.

"I am Bayloo, He Who Was A Slave. I will always be Bayloo. But I have become more. I am the Son of She Who Was Dawn. I am the Seeker of the Lost Truth."

TWENTY-TWO

I knocked down the tent trying to leave.

There might've been some trick to the entrance flap. Maybe my wings were too big, or I shouldn't have hit the sides with my tail. Whoever put the tent up would presumably fix it. Not that I required a tent to sleep in.

Almost two days had passed since the battle had ended. A healer had come and taken out my stitches. My left wing, while still damaged, had mended enough to allow me to fly, as long as I didn't push it too hard. It was great to be a dragon.

The Mizu army had redeployed into a more defensive formation, dispersing into various positions along the river. Much of Tia's cavalry was already on its way back to the east. The horsemaster came to see me before he departed.

"We are recalled already. Every soldier is needed to deal with the unrest on the other side of the mountains. Barely enough time to get drunk and sober before we must ride again."

"Your withdrawal does feel hasty. Are you so sure the hollowings will not return?"

Tia crinkled his nose, a gesture I was unfamiliar with. "In the whole course of the war, the hollowings never lost as many as they did in the Battle of the Bridges, as it is being called. We had never seen so many behemoths, much less defeated them. They have no way to cross the river so long as those terrifying creatures swim in the waters of the Tayo. Even if they left, I'd think the hollowings would still be wary. I hope, finally, we struck a blow that was decisive."

I grunted a long, deep grunt from my belly, because I knew in my gut Tia was wrong. "Despite your time with these horses, you still think very human. This enemy is not like you or I. Whatever they are, they do not exist to merely sit still on their side of this river."

"Rinxia reported that the hollowings march westward without stopping," he answered. "Every single one of them. There are no more behemoths or bridge-towers among them. There isn't a tree left for twenty leagues to the west—they've consumed every resource in the area to sustain a force so large. Even the blood raptors have gone. Still, you are probably correct. They will return one day. But it will not be to cross the river with bridges."

"When they come again, your riders will be needed. They fought with uncommon bravery." It wasn't very smart to charge a behemoth, but I didn't point that out.

Tia inclined his head, pleased at the compliment. "I have my orders. We are to ride east to help against the tigris and the traitorous lords who have joined their cause."

"What cause is that? Elasu is very dead, I assure you."

"The land is without a Protector. The will of Haven has been shattered. The tigris proclaim a new revolution. They claim the dragons have betrayed Ni-Yota. Only when the land is cleansed of Aragor's tainted followers will Haven again bestow its grace upon Ni-Yota."

I gave a double snort.

Tia's face betrayed nothing. "Even if one does not believe in such things, the tigris are fierce fighters and deal with defectors viciously. Lord Hito was skinned alive and left in his farmers' pen for the hogs to consume when he renounced his allegiance."

"It is unfortunate for the pigs. Humans taste terrible."

Tia sucked in a sharp breath of revulsion. I understood. Such a waste of good pig meat, tainting them in such a way.

The soldier shifted on his feet. "Should the hollowings show any sign of returning, word can be sent by glasswing. Gia has sent orders that new fortresses are to be raised along the river, great fortifications that can withstand even the charge of behemoths, although they will take years to build."

I looked around at the wasted ground, at the depleted soldiers. Castles seemed like a fantasy. "I see no sign of Gia. Or Rinxia, either."

"Gia flew east this morning." With some distaste, Tia added, "I heard that a glasswing came with a message from Jinu, the Master of Shadows."

"Gia flew back to Trishan?"

"He did not tell me his destination, but that would be logical."

"And Rinxia, did she go back as well?" Somehow that hurt, that she'd leave before I'd awoken without saying farewell.

"Rinxia flew west."

I jerked my head so close that Tia jumped backward. "What?"

"Like you, she feared the return of the hollowings. And what they might attempt next."

I searched the horizon for her immediately, in vain.

Tia looked as well, but he knew we both would not see anything. "She left at first light, flying at great speed, as she can. A silver streak in the sky."

I wanted to lift myself into the air at that moment, to rip through the open air, to follow Rinxia into the west. Imagining that for a fleeting moment made my hearts lighter. It would've been stupid, though. I'd never find her. I reminded myself that Rinxia was the swiftest dragon in the skies. She was an unrivaled scout. Nothing could catch her so long as she didn't land. She'd be safe.

I tried to sound unconcerned. "Did she say when she expected to return?"

"She did not. It is not the way of dragons ..." He paused, hesitant at first. Tia shrugged. "In matters where humans are not deemed to be of use, we are not consulted by dragons."

I gave him a kindly sniff. "The reverse was true in Rolm, where I come from. There, humans made decisions about the life or death of dragons as they would with livestock." Tia's eyes widened. "Perhaps we can all do better. This victory was a shared sacrifice by all."

Tia bowed his head. "Your words...honor me and my men. I know that we all would be dead but for your bringing the shallowings to our aid. But..." Tia pursed his lips, his eyes flicking at the ground.

"What?"

"Word has spread that it was Legao's magic that pushed the behemoths into the river. That she even had control of those creatures in the river through a binding. Perhaps she is the next Drasu."

"Is. That. So?"

"Indeed," Tia confirmed. "I thought it proper that you know."

"And who says this?"

"I am but a soldier, sworn to serve Aragor, who is dead."

I wasn't as good at this as Harlan, but I got the impression that Tia wanted me to get more from him, so I asked. "If you had to guess, being an experienced soldier, how do stories like these begin?"

"This one spread so rapidly. It is unusual that a tale so obviously false moves with such swiftness." He shrugged. "I suppose, even within the Mizu army, there are men in the employ of those who work in shadows." He inclined his head.

Shadows, indeed. Did he refer to Jinu? The man was far away in the safety of Trishan, but that didn't mean those in his employ were not here. I supposed that a Master of Shadow would have spies everywhere. Did he serve Gia in this? Or did he have other motives?

"I fought with the great wizard Drasu, and have known a dozen other magi besides, although none as great as he or Legao. None could've conjured such a storm. Not even the greatest binder could command shallowings in such a manner. I know we owe it to you. I have never seen you belch fire." Tia hesitated, then asked his question. "You are of the ember blood, are you not?"

It had not occurred to me that my heritage was not widely known, but it made sense. I was a new ally, and not a trusted one. "I am."

Tia's chin dipped slowly. "Then we shall win this war."

I bent my neck so that my eyes became level with his. This too surprised him. "Safe journey, Tia."

The horsemaster rode off with his men a short time later. I waited impatiently for Rinxia's return. Several times I took to the sky for a better view, but I didn't cross the river boundary, even though I saw no enemy lurking on the other side. There was no reason to do so. I could see as well from the safety of the eastern bank as I could on the far side of the river. Soldiers stared at me when I flew, and when I landed. I flew north on one of my reconnoiter flights, over a large formation of soldiers. They raised their blades in the air as I passed. It took me a moment to realize it was no challenge: they cheered me. Jinu's spies might spread rumors, but plenty of humans knew the truth. I had come a long way from being a slave dragon in Rolm.

As the daylight faded without any sign of Rinxia, my anxiety increased. I understood the need for her flight into Illium. I would've done it myself, had I been asked and conscious of what was happening. But staying in the land of the hollowings past nightfall seemed unnecessary. Rinxia could travel a vast distance in a single day. She only would've gone deeper and stayed later if she'd found something important to investigate. Or something bad had happened to her.

I flew yet again to watch the sun sink below the horizon. Several scattered formations of hollowings still dotted the landscape far to the west as they retreated inward in neat columns, like ants marching back to their queen. The ballistae had also been moved inland. The sky was perilously empty as the sun dipped below the ground.

I stayed a lot longer than I should have with my injured wing. Below, fires of the Mizu army dotted the land. The smell of roasting meat filled the air, mixing with the boisterous shouts of soldiers drunk on shaojiu and victory. I wished I could share the booze and joy, but I was too worried about Rinxia for celebration.

I skirted the edge of the river, flying far to the north then back to the south, scouting for signs of movement in the water. There was no sign of Vengeance or the ghastrays. Perhaps their actions spoke more clearly than any words. For one reason or another, they were with us against the hollowings.

As the sky darkened, I convinced myself the far side of the river no longer posed any danger. I was accomplishing nothing by staying in the Mizu camp. I hated being powerless. I hated sitting still. Finally, I succumbed to my anxiousness, worry, and reckless stupidity. I crossed the Tayo.

It was hotter on the other side of the river, the air heavier. It wasn't my imagination—dragons were sensitive to such things, as they affect our flight. I flew deep into Illium, over nothing but rust-encrusted dirt. Eventually, the ground began to stir. Not humans—wolves. Their lupine eyes glinted in the starlight. They were covered by the rust. With my night vision, I spotted several ballistae as well, hidden in ditches and covered by the crimson rust. That likely meant human hollowings still lurked somewhere. Not all of them had left. Two arc-bolts fired at me. Despite the darkness, their aim wasn't bad. I was too high to hit, and the projectiles fell harmlessly to the ground. I realized that even though the humans operating the machines could barely see me, that wasn't the case with the wolves. Somehow they could communicate—the wolves were spotters. I needed to be cautious.

There was still no sign of Rinxia. I turned back toward the Mizu lines. I saw no more hollowings on my way back.

I crossed the river to Ni-Yota, vowing to force myself to eat even if my stomach wasn't in the mood. Before I landed, I turned for one last look toward Illium. There, I caught sight of a glint of silver out in the west. I fixed my eyes on that patch of sky until I saw it again. Some of the tension in my body eased. It had to be her.

I thought Rinxia saw me as well. She seemed to be taking her time flying to my side of the river. She was torturing me. That had to be it.

As Rinxia drew still nearer, I noticed the odd cadence as she beat her wings. Our eyes met. Neither of us spoke with words—that would be idiotic until she had crossed onto my side of the river. But I saw in her eyes that Rinxia wasn't toying with me. She flew slowly because she was exhausted. She must've flown further and deeper than even I had suspected. That was Rinxia—everything for her cause.

Finally, she crossed over to the comparative safety of Ni-Yota. My hearts pounded and I smiled with my eyes, dragon-style. Rinxia stared back with warmth, but nothing equal to what I'd shown her. I tried to remind myself that extreme emotion was not the Way of dragons. But still...ouch.

She didn't speak until we were both on the ground. I asked a nearby human for water and food to be sent to us as we huddled away from the human encampment.

"How long were you up there waiting for me?"

I hesitated, so she answered for me. "Too long." She didn't approve. "I can take care of myself, Bayloo. Don't waste your strength. The hollowings could come back any time. To act as you did...it is very human."

Ouch.

I tried to ignore the insult. "Are they coming back?"

"Undoubtedly."

"What did you find out there?"

Rinxia snorted in frustration. "Nothing of note, which is why I am worried."

I waited for her to explain. I could hear her hearts pounding. She had pushed herself hard over there.

"I followed the main body of hollowings as they pulled back from the river. Some stayed behind, but not many. There are some wolves lurking about. They are faster, nimbler. I intended to follow the human host west, or at least get a sense of their direction and follow it further so that I might know where they travel."

I guessed where this was going. "That didn't work."

"They split. Not just into one or two columns. But into ten different groupings. They moved in every possible direction. I couldn't follow all those paths, although I tried, hoping to get lucky."

I had a low opinion on the reliability of luck. Like bowel movements, luck never seemed to arrive at convenient moments.

"I held the course west. It is wasteland as far as my eyes can see. On the old maps, areas that were once marked as forest are gone. Everywhere, the ground is coated with the same tainted rust. The hills are bare, but for the same growth. Villages are empty. I flew over a city—a big one—completely abandoned. The same with the old fortress keeps of Illium. The buildings of their cities have either fallen or are covered by the rust. Eventually, I turned north, flying toward the coast. It was more of the same—except for one thing: roads. I saw at least two—long, straight, and seemingly well-maintained. They led north and east. I followed the northern route. For leagues, I saw only emptiness, but as light faded, the blood raptors came."

"So we are not rid of them all."

"I think their numbers are diminished. They harried me, flying across my path. Wave after wave. But none tried to attack. They sought only to delay me, I think. To slow my journey north or get me to turn to a different route."

I knew that would've had the opposite effect on Rinxia. Trying to deny her would only make her more determined.

"I flew harder and tried to move faster. Small waves continued to rise up, twenty birds. Just enough to force me to be cautious. To slow. It was nightfall by the time I reached the north coast. There was nothing. The road ended at what looked to have once been a trading town. The quays still stood. Some buildings and warehouses were still there, although covered in rust in most places. But no life, not even hollowing life. On the sea, I saw nothing but the waves."

Servants arrived carrying troughs filled with fresh water, along with platters of fresh meat. For once, I was more interested in the story than the food (there wasn't any roasted pig, anyway).

Rinxia drank deeply, greedy for the water. I watched her, taking pleasure in just being near her, listening to her, even if she had no glad tidings to share. Even if her feelings for me were not as strong as mine for her. When she finished, she looked back up at me, her eyes troubled.

"The hollowings plot something new, but I have no idea what it might be."

TWENTY-THREE

A glasswing arrived the next morning.

To my surprise, it was for me, from Harlan. The message was neither lengthy nor subtle: teturn to Trishan.

I was hesitant to go. Rinxia hadn't yet said it aloud to me, but I sensed she wanted to return to Illium, to understand better the intentions of our enemy there. I wanted to accompany her. However, she didn't need me. Indeed, she could move faster, with less chance of detection, without me. She told me just that as soon as she learned of Harlan's message.

"Gia has had several days in Trishan. There, he confers with Jinu and the council. If you are correct about him trying to see you killed when you attacked those bridge-towers, you have become a greater threat as your magic emerges. You would be wise to heed the human's advice to return."

"I do not wish to leave you, even though I know you will call me a fool."

Rinxia favored me with a flash of indulgence in her eyes, but disappointment as well. "My Way leads me to serve Ni-Yota before all else. You should strive for the same." I tried to hide my disappointment as she would expect, but didn't succeed. Yet her next words delighted me. "But the Way does not command me back to Illium, as you fear."

Understanding came to me slower than I would've hoped. "You'll come back with me to Trishan?"

"There is no imminent danger here. You are a blind babe as far as the politics of Ni-Yota are concerned. I cannot have you stumbling about in Trishan by yourself. This would not benefit Ni-Yota."

I should have been insulted, but instead I was glad that Rinxia would be traveling with me.

I bid farewell to Legao before we left. The wizard still looked exhausted—it seemed it took humans far longer to recover than dragons. I offered her a ride back to Trishan if she wanted it.

"I will remain here for several more days to recover. If there is no sign of the hollowings, no further danger, I will return by horseback." Her eyes looked me over. "It seems you have found your path to magic."

I wished that were true. "I have begun the journey. I have far more questions than answers."

"That is the nature of the pursuit of magic. So much of it is hidden, at least from us." She moved her lips to form something like a smile. "Beware of Gia."

"I am not his rival," I protested immediately.

"Are you not?" She seemed skeptical. "You do not seek to be Protector?"

"No."

Legao didn't seem to quite believe me. "Ni-Yota seems to be running out of dragons to serve, then." Her lips tightened. "I hope you will keep yourself safe until my return to Trishan."

"Gia will do nothing to me," I assured her.

"Listen to Rinxia. She is worthy of your trust."

After a final meal, Rinxia and I departed for Trishan. I knew that trouble awaited us there, but I didn't see how it could be worse than what we'd just faced. Our pace was swift, but not panicked. Flying beside Rinxia gave me a sense of purpose and determination. We spoke mostly of small things, of wind, of hunting, the oddities of humans. She told me about her mother, a great silver dragon with a roar like a song who had been slain by Elasu in the first year of Aragor's reign. Rinxia's sire had succumbed to the great plague from Illium many years before that, when she had been little more than a hatchling. She told the tale without sadness or remorse, in dragon fashion. I felt sorrow as a human would. And a bit of jealousy—at least she had known her parents.

I, in turn, told her my own sorry story of my mother and of our first and last meeting on the island of Maricopa. I spoke of slavers and my ryders, of Bethy Rann, Prince Dayne the Dark Fool, and Brindisi, and finally my mother's murderer. Somehow, I lost track of time as I rambled on. Before I knew it, night had fallen and we had stopped at a waystation to eat and rest.

I asked for shaojiu. I'd earned it. Rinxia didn't refuse a bowl either.

"You've had a life stolen. It is made worse by the emotion you inherited through your link with the humans. I hear the sorrow in you, Bayloo. For that, I feel pity."

I didn't want her sympathy. Nor was it merited. "Save any pity, Rinxia. You were taught by your parents, shown values, put on a path in this world, taught the Way. Slavery was my teacher, even if I didn't know it until recently. My ryders, too, were teachers in their own manner, their lessons harsher than any parent, but no less effective. Hardship has forged me. Emotion tempers me. The loss of so many years makes the present precious." I thought of my mother, the memory of her song tightening my throat. I banished the image. "The losses of my past have given me the strength to follow the path to a different future. I may not follow the Way as you do, but I have no regret for that. I am the beast who has tasted blood. I know the value of that for which I must fight."

Rinxia's eyes glowed. Her eyes lingered on my chest before rising to match my gaze. "I hadn't expected to find a philosopher's hearts beating in there as well."

It *had* been a pretty good speech. Even more so because I meant every word.

"The night is warm," Rinxia observed. "Let us make it warmer."

We did.

WE RESUMED our journey to Trishan the following day.

While the countryside seemed peaceful, there was an unusual amount of boat traffic on the rivers and canals. I'd never seen so many ships.

"These are watercraft of the great human lords," Rinxia told me. "Look at their size, the banners. They journey to Trishan."

The sprawling city and adjacent palace came into view late in the afternoon. Even from a distance high in the clouds, the lake palace was a picture of harmony beside the nearby chaos of the massive city of Trishan. The port bustled with the huge rivercraft of the eastern human lords, while several dozen others remained in transit. The boats came in all shapes and colors; some were trimmed with metal, others had elaborate carvings of animals on their bows. All flew huge banners. My attention was drawn to only one craft, however. This vessel was little more than a raft that plied a narrow canal neglected by the other craft, for it led away from the city to a derelict shipyard. On it was a crudely painted image of a goat. My eyes glowed with a dragon's smile as I remembered Harlan's signal.

I flicked a wing to draw Rinxia's attention away from the city far ahead. "Harlan would like to speak before we arrive at the palace."

"How do you know?"

"Look down at the small raft on the side canal with the strange painting. He used an image of a Rolman goat to get my attention once before, back at Elasu's palace in Changsha. He'll be waiting for us near the raft."

"If Jinu or Gia is watching, they'll have spotted us by now."

"No matter. I presume they won't be able to get spies there faster than we can fly. Let us find out what Harlan has to say and why he sent that glasswing message."

We changed our course, setting down at the edge of the canal near Harlan's message raft.

The man himself appeared to be snoozing in the grass when we landed. A single eye opened as the massive presence of Rinxia and I glared down at him.

"The beds in the palace aren't good enough for you?" I asked.

Harlan sat up, a hand on his back. "Now that you mention it, they are too soft. All my life I've slept in a ship's bunk, even after I became a captain. That mushy stuff the people in the palace fill their mattresses with is unhealthy."

"Is that why you summoned us back from the west? To lodge a complaint about your sleeping arrangements?" I huffed. "Your human needs are like your stinking breath—forever returning to your lips."

Harlan got back onto his feet. "Gia has called for a meeting of the nobles. There, the servants whisper that he intends to burn some of Aragor's personal effects since he lacks a body, and then declare himself Protector of Ni-Yota should none stand to oppose his right."

Rinxia made a noise similar to a human sigh. "It's called a Kai-Moot. I'm not surprised. Gia likes to take the most direct route to his goals. Open declaration and physical combat." She gazed at me. "You could beat him, if you wished. With your magic awakened, it would not be so difficult."

I knew Gia wanted to rule Ni-Yota. I didn't. The only reason I might even consider putting myself forward in that contest was to spite Gia. After all, the dark-hearted fiend had likely tried to get me killed fighting the hollowings. His Shadowmaster, Jinu, likely undermined my role in the battle (not that I care about glory). But I'd have to fight Gia to the death. I didn't want to kill another dragon, and I didn't want to be killed. Winning meant being the Protector. As I saw it, if I fought, I lost no matter the outcome.

"You expect I've changed my mind about challenging him? I haven't."

I sensed Rinxia's disappointment at my answer. "You are already acting like a Protector, Bayloo. You have risked your life for Ni-Yota. Your magic, your actions with the ghastrays, saved us. The warriors who fought with you already love you. You could help unite this land, keep it safe."

My past protests about just wanting to get Kiata and leave would no longer suffice. I burned that relationship and that excuse when I'd chosen to win Vengeance and his kind to our cause at the price of my tenuous bond with my sister.

"I will not kill another dragon." It sounded inadequate. Killing Gia would be more like self-defense.

"That may be true, although we both know you kill when you must." Harlan's annoying smirk crept back onto his face. "But your hesitation is because you are afraid."

"I don't fear Gia."

Harlan nodded knowingly. "That isn't your fear. You don't want the responsibility. You don't want to give others the chance to rely upon you, for fear you might fail them."

"You are like an itch between my scales," I told him. "Humans enslaved me. I want no part of ruling or protecting them." I dipped my head toward Harlan. "You've proven yourself a valued ally, for which I'm grateful. Maybe there are other humans of worth. But that is not enough. This is a waste of all our breath. I will not challenge Gia. I do not wish to be the Protector of Ni-Yota."

Harlan showed no disappointment, no surprise. "Yes, I knew that would be your answer."

I sensed trouble. "Then why bother to send for me? I have no desire to watch Gia start some more fires or put a crown on his head or whatever else he wants to make him feel good about himself. There is no need for me to be a witness to this."

Harlan frowned. "You may not have a choice."

Uh-oh. "Explain yourself."

Rinxia understood immediately. "No one chooses to be Protector. Haven decides."

"Are you trying to say some higher power calls me forth? As I sit here, I hear nothing but the wind and the subtle farts of an overfed human."

"Haven does not speak in the language of mortals, not human nor dragon. The will of Haven must be divined through events, through actions, through the world beneath its Light." I could've sworn there was a hint of smugness in Rinxia's voice, but it was Harlan who finally hit me with the point of all this.

"People see the favor of Haven upon you, Bayloo."

"Upon me? I've still got a scar when I had a hole punched through my wing. I'm lucky if I manage to get a decent meal every couple of days."

Harlan pretended that I was jesting. "You can understand why people think this way. You slew Elasu, ending the Schism."

"Aragor was locked in combat with her. I barely did anything."

Harlan kept going. "Then you slew Aragor, without consequence from Haven. Indeed, quite the opposite. You helped Ni-Yota win two great victories at the Tayo without the magic of Drasu. Even Aragor could not claim such favor in battle. The Light of Haven shines upon you."

"I fed his head to the ghastrays." I looked at Rinxia with something like desperation. "I thought this affront would all but disqualify me as an unworthy heretic."

"If we'd lost, that would've been true," she replied. "Your horrific disrespect likely would've been seen as an affront to Haven. Gia and Jinu would've encouraged this. But we won. That cannot be denied. They've tried to credit Legao for the great feat of magic that was decisive, but those with knowledge of such matters are unlikely to believe it. The soldiers closest to the battle do not. Then there is the matter of the ghastrays. Our enemies, the scourge of the seas, coming to aid us?

There could be no clearer sign of the favor of Haven than such an unnatural thing."

"There was no favor of Haven involved with ghastrays, as you well know! People must understand the lore of Harlan's people, the tales of the *Iraliss*..." I didn't need Harlan's dubious look to understand. I would never be able to explain what had happened with the ghastrays. Even I didn't completely understand it. I blew an unhappy snort out of my nostrils. "So what happens now?"

Rinxia answered, her voice determined. "You should accept the mantle that Haven wishes to bestow upon you."

For the first time, Rinxia's voice had become grating to me rather than pleasant. "Harlan, you brought me here for a reason. Surely, you have a plan to handle this."

"I sent that message because I feared that Gia would fly out to the Tayo River and try to kill you in full sight of the Mizu army and the hollowings. In such a case, no matter who won, Ni-Yota would be doomed."

"You brought me here because it's a better place to fight Gia than at the river? Are you mad?"

Harlan shifted on his feet. "If there is to be a fight to the death between dragons to determine who is to rule Ni-Yota, it is best it takes place in Trishan, before the eyes of the Kai- Moot."

Rinxia didn't bother to hide the approval in her eyes at this notion.

I had been betrayed.

TWENTY-FOUR

"I didn't betray you, Bayloo."

Harlan's mouth was moving, but I barely heard the words. The implications of being forced to fight Gia *and* forced to become Protector of Ni-Yota were still banging around inside my head. They could not make me be Protector, could they? I'd just fly off. Of course, then I'd lose Rinxia and Kiata forever as the hollowings destroyed Ni-Yota.

The smuggler kept talking to me. "Bayloo, are you listening? If you need to pee, please go in the river, not here. I'm wearing new sandals."

"Now you're trying to tell me where to relieve myself too?"

"I asked you to come back here so you'd have a chance to avoid unnecessary conflict. I have a plan if you will but listen—I'm trying to fix this. I haven't abandoned you, my good dragon. Even if you did leave me here with your furious sister when you flew west without me."

Oh. That. I'd forgotten. This was Harlan's revenge. My actions had been necessary. I'd known Kiata would be angry with my deception, but I hadn't expected Harlan to still be bitter, considering how well things had turned out with the hollowings.

"How are things with my sister?"

"Bad, for you deceived her. I've tried to make her understand your greater purpose, without much success." Even though I'd known the price, it didn't make hearing it any better. "I have a plan to fix that as well."

"If you know a way to get Gia off my back and help me regain Kiata's trust, I will do it. Just tell me."

Harlan took a careful step back, away from me, as if concerned that I'd react poorly to something. "You will pledge your allegiance to Gia publicly, credit his wisdom and leadership for your actions in helping to defeat the hollowings."

I nearly choked. Rinxia wretched in horror—she sounded as if she were trying to cough up a mistakenly swallowed cat.

"That giant lizard tried to get me killed."

Harlan pretended not to hear me even though I'd spoken loud enough to wake the dead. "There's more. To make it work, you'll need to become one of his Sworn."

I tried another tactic—I spoke slowly, so Harlan got it. "Gia tried to make me dead."

The human merely shrugged with infuriating nonchalance. "The past cannot change, but the future can. I've given you a way to avoid a fight with Gia, ensure stability in Ni-Yota, and get yourself back into your sister's good graces. There is no need to thank me, but it would be gracious to do so."

I stared as hard as I could. The weight of my gaze alone should've crushed him, but Harlan didn't disappear. His words still echoed in my head. I turned to Rinxia. She didn't look pleased, but neither did she share my utter revulsion at Harlan's suggestion. She released a thought-laden breath. "If you will not become Protector, this is the best alternative. It keeps the peace. Kiata will be pleased. Isn't that all that matters to you?"

I twisted my neck back in the direction of the palace spires. My hearts still beat at an outraged pace. I sucked in the wind, willing my head to clear. Anger was for fools. "When would all this happen?"

"The Kai-Moot gathers even now. But it is a long journey for the eastern lords, and Gia won't wait for most of them. He's sent glass-wings to inform more distant lords that because of the lingering attacks by the tigris and their allies, those lords should stay at their keeps. I'd guess Gia will wait no more than a few days to begin the ceremony, perhaps less if his mood becomes too foul. But each day the whispers that you should ascend grow. As more soldiers return from the battle, the stories about you will grow."

I ground my teeth. Swearing loyalty to Gia shouldn't have bothered me as much as it did. It wasn't like I couldn't lie. I did it all the time. "I would like to speak to Kiata. Is that possible?"

Harlan's hesitation stung. "Not sure how well that might go... seems a bit like sailing in a tempest. Without a sail. Over shoals."

Rinxia walked beside me, her body close. "Let me try to speak to her. Perhaps if she realizes you have acted in the interests of Ni-Yota, indeed, you have come back for that purpose, her anger may soften. She is still very young, driven more by hearts than head, her Way still uncertain."

Rinxia did seem the best choice of an intermediary. As charming as Harlan could be, Kiata doubtlessly associated him with my deception to her. He was also a human. Rinxia was the only other female dragon in Ni-Yota. If anyone could reach my little sister, it would be her.

"My thanks, Rinxia. I appreciate anything you can do for me."

"Given all this, perhaps it would be better if you waited until dark before arriving at the palace. I'll go on ahead to speak to Kiata. When night comes, fly directly to her tower."

"Gia can see as well as you or I in the dark."

Rinxia flicked her tail in the dirt. "But the city and the rest of the palace are less likely to see you. There will be less commotion. If all Harlan has told us is true, your presence could merely provoke Gia to do something rash. He loses his path on the Way."

"I will do as you ask."

She looked up toward the sun, gauging the coming of night. "Where will you wait? A dragon sitting alone near the river is going to attract some attention."

"I'll go visit a friend."

Rinxia stared at me a long while, trying to determine if I was serious. I was. Harlan's lips twitched. I guessed he had a request.

"You want to come, Harlan?" I wasn't sure that I cared to have him there. He had a habit of complicating my life.

Harlan's smirk slipped from his face. "I should like to speak to Vengeance again. I may be of some help in understanding their actions."

It had been Harlan's knowledge that got the ghastrays into this fight for us. It would be foolish to refuse him.

Rinxia nudged Harlan with her tail. "Keep Bayloo out of trouble."

He grinned wide. I didn't like it.

To me, Rinxia said, "And you keep Harlan out of trouble."

I flashed a smile with my eyes.

"Take care, both of you. I will speak with Kiata." Our eyes met once more before Rinxia returned to the sky.

I watched her silvery form fly off toward Trishan. Harlan climbed onto my back and once again we flew. I turned north, away from Rinxia and Kiata. Why do I do things like this?

It was dark by the time we reached the shoreline of the great gulf near Trishan. I chose a location well north of the city and also far away from the area where I had deposited Aragor's head several days ago. Harlan dismounted. I walked toward the gentle waters of the great bay until the low waves lapped onto my claws. Harlan lingered further up the beach. Even with my superior sight, there was only dark water out there. I stuck a claw into my jaw and bit until the tip of one of my teeth wedged through my scales, piercing the flesh beneath. I dipped my bloody claw into the water. The salt of the sea stung, but only for a moment. A wave, larger than the rest, crashed beneath me, splashing cold water over my neck. I backed out of the water and wiggled my body into the sand to wait. Harlan took a seat beside me. He kept digging into the sand, repeatedly running it through his fingers.

"You like the sand here? Is it good for magic?" I asked him.

Harlan let the grains pass through his fingers again. "It's just sand, but everything has its use." He put some in the pocket of his tunic.

I listened to the waves to pass the time. Some evening gulls hunted in the shallow water, their disembodied eyes glowing a dim scarlet. At first they avoided coming too close to me, but as the night wore on, they became bolder. I'd never eaten a gull. I worried they'd taste like chicken, but I wasn't so worried that I wouldn't give it a try. I rolled out in the comfy indentation I'd made in the beach, but when I scanned the sea for a nearby snack, not a single gull remained. The chilling call of a ghastray followed.

I didn't see it at first, but the sound was unmistakable. No other creature produced such a horrible combination of moan and shriek. I walked toward the water, wary. This was still a ghastray. I'd killed more than my fair share and I'd given them a taste of dragon flesh. They might've enjoyed it—we probably taste fantastic, because everything about dragons is fantastic.

An aberrant voice spoke from the waves. "You are He."

The words were garbled, even more difficult to understand than usual.

"Vengeance?"

The noise that followed wasn't one made by human or dragon. It reminded me of ice being crushed underfoot. "I am to speak to He. Are you He?"

I took that to mean this wasn't Vengeance. This ghastray sounded different, its harrowing voice even colder and more alien that its brethren. Also, its Avian was lousy. That made sense; Vengeance had been a slave. He'd had far more contact with humans than those of his kind who escaped that fate.

"I am he who gave you Drasu. I am he who gave you Aragor, the dragon."

"Then you are He Who Revealed the Return, yes?"

This conversation was already getting tedious. I gave the answer the creature probably wanted. "Yes."

"Then we offer this: the Purpose is remembered." A wave crashed into the beach. "For now."

I felt Harlan tense behind me. He wanted to speak. I poked him with my tail so that he would remain quiet—this creature couldn't handle multiple voices. "What is the Purpose?"

The strange crunching sound resumed. I didn't really expect a reply. This one had even less to say than Vengeance. But it did finally speak again: "None shall pass through the waters."

I had begun to suspect this species learned to speak only to piss me off with their vague talk.

"Pass where? Do you mean the Tayo River?"

"It is done. But this one...the *human*." It screeched out the last word.

Harlan took a tentative step toward the waves. I could still barely see the ghastray. It was shy compared to Vengeance. Harlan didn't seem as afraid as he should've been. "I am the human."

"We...remember the Purpose. Your kind must also remember. We are not *slaves*. Tell the other land walkers they are warned."

The ghastray's words were unclear; his intention was not.

"I will tell them," was all Harlan could offer.

The ghastray was silent, but still I sensed his presence, something uneasy in the ocean breeze. Again, it spoke. "Dragon, seek your own Purpose."

Another wave broke onto the beach, its water rolling up the sand. It left an animal bone on the beach. A moment later, everything felt different. Tension left my body.

"What is my Purpose?"

I asked the question, but I knew the ghastray had already gone, back to his dark, cold waters. He had come to deliver his messages and they had been delivered. One part of his message was heartening: none shall pass. Despite being a bit vague, I took it as welcome news. I'd requested the Tayo River be protected, and it now seemed that the ghastrays agreed. Perhaps their assistance was not a one-time event. Perhaps the river was now their domain. That would explain the hollowings' retreat better than a single defeat in battle. The hollowings recognized the prowess of their horrific enemy. They might even understand the ghastray better than I did. But there was a catch.

"It seems they don't appreciate being tethered to the ships of Ni-Yota."

Harlan grunted. "Power and commerce flow from the speed of those craft. Legao warned me that it will not be easy to convince the people of Ni-Yota otherwise."

"Better that than lose their allies in a war for their very survival." I grunted with frustration. "I do not understand humans."

Harlan actually chuckled. "You overthink us. We, too, are slaves: to the dark greed of our heart. Only very few of us manage to gain a degree of freedom from those shackles."

I considered those words. The dragon I'd been when I came here from Rolm would've accepted them. But I knew the truth was more complicated. I still didn't understand humans. I didn't want to understand ghastrays.

"It is time to return. To deal with Gia and deliver the message of the ghastray."

Harlan climbed onto my back. I beat my wings, headed back to the lake palace of Trishan. A difficult meeting with my sister awaited me.

TWENTY-FIVE

A flickering light burned in Kiata's tower.

We arrived back at Trishan far later than I'd anticipated. The night was more than half over. I took it as an auspicious sign that Kiata had remained awake to wait for me. I really shouldn't have been so presumptuous.

I wanted to speak to my sister without Harlan. "I will leave you on the shore near the palace."

"I understand your desire for privacy, but if I may be the fish that wants to stay hooked, Kiata and I have had some good conversations in your absence. I suggest we land at her tower together. Let me first ensure she isn't going to eat you." I snorted my dislike of that idea, but Harlan didn't relent. "Don't worry, I also know when to make for the open waters. Walking down some steps in the middle of the night won't kill me. Probably. But I really think I can help smooth things between you two. Trust me on this."

I didn't answer immediately, but I did trust Harlan. He possessed a more delicate touch in conversations than I. After a few moments of circling over Trishan, I flew to Kiata's tower, landing softly on a stone balcony built for such a purpose. The twin dragon-sized doors leading inside were closed, but the same soft light visible through the tower's windows also crept through the slit beneath the doors. Since dragons didn't need light to see, I took the flame as an invitation.

Harlan slid off my back. "I'll give it a nice soft knock."

The reply came before he reached the doors. "You may enter."

Kiata awaited us inside a chamber far more ornate than those favored by Aragor or even Elasu. Lush rugs of white bear skin covered all of the floor, while tapestries depicting various landscapes—some familiar, some bizarre—hung from the walls. Glittering pedestals of crystal circled the chamber. My sister sat nestled among her rugs, a square table of cream-stained wood before her. On it lay a great parchment and a ceramic bowl filled with a black goo that resembled ink, some of which also covered one of Kiata's claws.

"Is that a dragon you are drawing?" I asked, astounded at the half-formed collection of lines. Did dragons create art?

My sister tilted her head as she evaluated her work. "It is a picture of our mother. Well, almost. I am still learning."

"Our mother? But how can you ..."

Kiata's eyes flashed a regret-tinged smile. "It is how I imagine her, or how I should wish to imagine her. That is the wonderful thing about drawing: I can create that which I desire. It is a form of magic."

I looked again at what Kiata had drawn. The partial picture bore no superficial resemblance to our mother. Even allowing for the lack of color, the snout was too long, the jaw too narrow, the scales all wrong. But there was something in the eyes—a noble sadness that did recall her.

"I'm no expert, but you have captured something ..." I stared at the ink on my sister's claw. "I didn't know dragons could make such things. In Rolm, this was unheard of."

Kiata dipped her black claw into a pot of clean water, polluting it with the ink residue. "It was Harlan's idea. The ink does not stain our claws, for I do not wish to have black claws."

Always, it was Harlan. "Our friend whose casual smirk hides the surprising depth of his knowledge and innovation."

The man himself shrugged. "There was no special lore involved. I merely spoke to the curator of the Hall of Glass while he was overseeing its repairs. The palace is filled with works by dragons. Paintings, but also sculptures, magnificent works of glass wrought by both fire and claw. Aragor had many of them put away, out of sight. He did not care for the creations of other dragons in the past. But they are still in the archives beneath the Hall of Glass."

I felt embarrassed at being so ignorant of my own kind, even if that mostly wasn't my fault. I hadn't exactly had a lot of leisure time since I'd arrived in Ni-Yota. "I'm glad to see you adding to the works of our kind."

"This is nothing—a sketch to pass the time, something to occupy me so I can keep my thoughts at bay."

"Which thoughts?"

Kiata's eyes flashed. "My anger at your betrayal. Your lies. Your condescension." She took a deep breath. "To let emotion dominate, to cloud judgment, is not the Way. Still, actions must have consequences. That is proper. You have committed wrong against me, your sister."

No words of reply came to me. The cold pain in my hearts was too great. Harlan's silent footsteps retreated toward the door, a coward making his exit as the battle was joined. I didn't really see what help he had been. I hoped it was a long, cold walk down to the ground.

Kiata noticed his attempt to leave. "Harlan, we shall speak again later." I couldn't fail to notice how much warmer her voice was when she spoke to him. It was terribly unfair. Plenty of my treacherous ideas had come from Harlan's devious mind.

I steadied myself beneath my sister's cross gaze. "I'm sorry I deceived you. I did what I thought needed to be done."

She flicked her tail several times. "If you had to do it over again, would you once again lie to me?"

Chicken piss. No easy questions were asked today. Answering the ghastray had been easier, and the stakes lower, than dealing with

Kiata. I had come here to make amends, so my instinct was to tell her of course not. I even opened my mouth. Then I closed it again.

"What is it that you have to say? More cute words to please me?" Her voice was level—and that level was "pissed-off." Way or not, Kiata was angry. It might not be the uncontrolled rage of a young human, but there was strong emotion within her.

I tried a different tactic. "I've changed since coming to Ni-Yota."

She answered with ice. "You lied less in Rolm?"

Actually, no. I'd been lying since I was granted the free will to do so. It had all been necessary, of course, but I didn't think I currently had a sympathetic audience for my excuses.

"I lied in Rolm, for the purpose of freeing our kind. I lied to you because I deemed it necessary to fight a greater threat. Without the ghastrays to aid us, the hollowings would've crossed the river, Ni-Yota would've fallen, leading to an even worse fate for the world." I swallowed hard. "To answer your questions: I would do it again."

I could hear the air Kiata blew from her flaring nostrils. Even though she wasn't a fire breather (for which I was currently thankful) I could feel the heat of her breath. "At least you have told me one truth this night."

"I cannot fix the past. That bitter vegetable has already been consumed. I can only try to choose better in the future."

"You said you came here to Ni-Yota to save me. Has that changed as well?"

My sister should be a teacher—one for errant dragons who needed to be punished—because her questions were impossible and unfair. I looked at the table again, at Kiata's incomplete rendering of our mother. "You captured a bit of Mother in that drawing. It looks nothing like her, but even so, even without having laid eyes upon her since your first days as a hatchling, you caught some of the essence of her. How did you do that?"

"I sense you wish to tell me."

I ignored her hostility. "Because that same mettle that she had is in you too. You drew eyes, heavy with regret. I remember those eyes as well. I think our mother had them because she felt regret with choices that had to be made, even if her Way compelled them. Our mother cared about something more than herself; she made terrible decisions. That strength is within you, or else you'd not have been able to render such a work without ever seeing our mother but for a few precious days before the humans came." I raised my head toward her again. "To my surprise, I've come to suspect some of this strength from our mother is within me, as well. Somehow, her quest is becoming mine." I readied myself to answer Kiata's question. The hard part. "It's true I came here originally to find you, to save you. But you already did that by yourself. You have your own mind. I'm no longer here for that."

"Why are you here, then?" Kiata sounded slightly less hostile.

It wasn't an easy question. I still didn't completely know the answer, but I tried my best. "Those that I care about are here."

Kiata sniffed with disapproval.

"I know, it is not the Way of dragons to make decisions based on emotion. I do not stay only for that. I sense the greater threat that is the rust, just as I believe our mother once did. It is vast and still unknown to me, but in my hearts, I know that it will envelope this land, just as it did Illium."

The spikes on Kiata's still-soft mane twitched as she digested my words. "Why should that matter to you? You are free. You seem to think I no longer need you. Why risk your life fighting behemoths and befriending the creatures you call ghastrays? What now drives you if not my interests or your own?"

I knew that question was coming, and I dreaded it. "I don't know." I said it, but I didn't like the answer, and it wasn't the whole truth. When I spoke again, it was in a voice that was not quite my own. "There is something within me...I feel a need to fight against this. It is the purpose within me. Within us. We are connected to the greater whole of existence, as are all living things. But we dragons, and we ember dragons in particular, most of all."

Some of the angry tension faded from Kiata's face, replaced by relief, even happiness. "You have sensed the Latticework!"

I was shocked. "Already you perceive it?"

"Bayloo, I was born to this, as were you. It has always been a part of me. We are connected to the fabric of existence. We must find our Way, to be a part of it. If yours is to protect that very existence... perhaps that is your Way."

The notion that I had a unique place even among dragons when it came to the rust unnerved me. "There is also the matter of our fellow dragons, who are slaves in Rolm. They are a part of this, and I shall not forget them. Mother sought my freedom for a greater purpose. Something connected to the rust...I do not know what, but I must find out. And doing that requires me to do things I do not wish to do, to those I care about. Even though it is very human of me, I am sorry for the pain I inflicted."

For a precious moment, I thought Kiata understood. Then her gaze sharpened. Her eyes widened in alarm. She roared.

"Gia, noooo—"

Gia?

Fire erupted along my mane and backside, bathing me in an inferno of petty hate. Kiata's table and the drawing of our mother turned to ash before my eyes. I shot upward toward the open space in the attic over Kiata's chamber. Even there, I had limited room to maneuver, but my position forced Gia to venture in through the doors of the tower to keep his fire on me. Finally, the flames ceased. I looked around. These were tight quarters—a bad place for me to do battle with a dragon who was larger and stronger than I. Gia advanced toward me, as angry as I'd ever seen him.

Kiata roared at him. "Gia, what are you doing here?"

Gia had eyes only for me. "I see you, spinner of clever lies. I see what you are." The dragon's eyes smoldered. "You shall not destroy Ni-Yota."

Kiata roared again. "Gia, this is my brother. Fire is not the answer."

The giant dragon still didn't look at her. He was here for me. "The deceiver seeks to ensnare you in his web of lies. His magic addles the mind of the people, of you even, dear Kiata. In time you will understand this."

I snorted at him without fear. "You are haunted by delusion. I'm not the source of that."

"Did I imagine the tigris assassin in my tower, this very night?"

"Gia, I—"

His fire interrupted me. I leapt to a different wall, but there wasn't any place to escape his attack. Heat covered me, mostly deflected and absorbed by my scales, but not all. Being bathed in flame hurt, but the worst part was that the heat made my scales brittle, further adding to my disadvantage if I had to engage Gia in close combat. I didn't want to do that. Gia was bigger and stronger. But I couldn't keep taking his fire in close quarters like this. I was about to charge him when Kiata placed herself in the path of Gia's fire.

I called to her. "Kiata, no—your scales aren't strong enough."

My sister knew that as well, as did Gia. His flame cut off abruptly. He wasn't completely out of control.

"I know you think him kin, Kiata, but it is not so. He's like Elasu; inside he has given over to the darkness which he claims to fight. It is all but a lie."

I growled at him. "I killed Elasu, you giant oaf."

Gia's roar shook the tower. "You took her place. Her dark powers are yours, as are her dreams of taking Ni-Yota. Even her servants are now yours, or perhaps you are the servant of the darkness that ruled her."

Now he had pissed me off. "I serve no one."

A snort of contempt. "You have the runes on your chest still. The runes of a slave. All this time, the truth stared us in the face. But finally I understand what must be done. Haven has shown me the way."

Gia launched himself at me, swerving at the last possible moment to avoid crushing Kiata. That gave me plenty of time to evade his clumsy assault. Folding my wings upward, I dropped beneath Gia. That gave him an advantageous attack position to slam me from above or bathe me in fire again if I didn't act fast. I needed to either engage him or flee. Kiata would want me to flee, but I wasn't done with Gia. He'd tried to kill me at least twice. His mind was failing him. The next time he might come with an army, or when I was in an even worse position. Time to finish this.

Harlan's arrival changed my decision. He appeared at the doorway, out of breath, his hands clenched into fists.

"Bayloo, let's go."

There wasn't any time to think. Gia's roar tore through the tower at me as I hurled myself at the doorway with a mixture of leg strength and awkward wing power. Harlan positioned himself as if he intended to leap onto my back. No way we had time for that. Gia would crush us both if I slowed. He knew that. Harlan took a step further into the tower, then tossed two fistfuls of gray sand in the air. I guessed it was the same sand he'd taken from the beach with the ghastray. The tiny crystals glowed red with heat. At the same moment, a fortuitous gust of wind burst into the tower. The gust caught the sand at precisely the correct moment, dispersing the grains wide and hard—right into Gia's face. It happened faster than his lids could react. Gia flew uncontrolled into the floor, foreclaws over his eyes.

"Neat trick," I said to Harlan as he climbed onto my back.

"Let's discuss it away from Trishan."

Harlan's advice was sound. I beat my wings, soaring into the night, unsure of my destination. I expected pursuit shortly. "Even for Gia, that attack was...unexpectedly direct."

Harlan sounded grim. "We beat the hollowings at the river, but Ni-Yota has many enemies. And they aren't going to give up."

"Then let us destroy them."

"We must understand our adversary first. That cannot be done with fire, nor even with magic, Bayloo. Until we know the menace we face, there can be no hope of victory."

"I know where to find answers," I told him.

"Where?"

"We have merely to follow my mother's path. We need to know what she knew, to understand the truth of the enemy we face. I think it is more vast and even darker than we suspect. But that is the path that took her eventually to Rolm, to freeing me, and to the precious aurathorn, which we both seek."

I didn't wait for Harlan to agree. I already knew he would. If I could leave Rinxia and Kiata to do this, Harlan could put everything else on hold as well. Rinxia had her Way and I had mine.

I turned west, to Illium, to find the so-called Archive of Oracles, and there to learn the secrets that had sent my mother to Rolm.

TWENTY-SIX

We escaped to the west.

I looked behind me as I flew away from Trishan, expecting to see Gia's dark silhouette against the brightening sky of the coming dawn. But in the east was just a horizon, just another sunrise. The landscape below was still, as if frozen, and disconcertingly peaceful. The inhabitants of Ni-Yota were just beginning to stir as the new light called them to another day, blissfully unaware of the dragon over their heads.

"Gia did not seem in the mood to relent. Why does he not come after us?" I asked Harlan. "I am slower carrying you. He might have a chance to catch me."

"Perhaps your sister stayed his anger."

Oh, Kiata. If there was a bright part of Gia attacking me, it had allowed my sister to see the menace that lived within the black dragon who had served as her guardian. I hoped her eyes could persuade her to be wary of him in a way that my words never would. Or would it be the opposite? Would she believe Gia's increasingly mad ravings that I was in league with Elasu? Gia's accusation that I was still a slave particularly grated upon me. But I also understood where his delusion originated. Slavery had been Elasu's fate, and I pitied her for it. It was not me.

Harlan seemed far less worried about Gia than I. His heart beat normally. He might even have been enjoying himself up on my back. "Do you think Gia has finally gone mad?"

"Who are we to say what is madness, my friend? We fly across Ni-Yota, across the cursed land of Illium, in search of a place more myth than real. Gia attacking you may not mean his mind has failed him. It may be that he has succumbed to his fears—he wants something so badly he sees threats in the shadows."

"For the hundredth time, I don't want to be Protector of Ni-Yota. It's a worse job than chicken coop cleaner, with a shorter life expectancy. I hope that someone will finally take me at my word at this."

"Gia does not hear your words; he fears your actions. With every success you achieve, with every person who cheers your name, he feels he becomes less, regardless of whether you covet something as he does. Then there is the matter of the tigris attempting to kill him. That may, indeed, have been real. He sees your hand—claw—in that. You were with Elasu for a time. He might think you forged a bond with her tigris as well. Perhaps this is even their work. Ni-Yota has many enemies."

I snorted as I thought of the giant cats who'd taken me prisoner, muzzled me, tricked me. "They have some kind of magic, those beasts. They made even Elasu their slave, although I never saw them use their power, even when they faced Aragor in battle. I will admit they are able fighters, but they did not have the strength to defeat Aragor directly, even with Elasu."

Harlan was about to answer when I hit a patch of rough wind, forcing me to adjust to a higher altitude. "Not too cold?"

"It's fine. You're rather warm. It is quite cozy up here, actually." He chuckled, then quieted quickly.

"You were about to speak of the tigris, I think."

Harlan grimaced. "I asked about them during the time you left me at the palace. Their story is a strange one. Throughout the long history of Ni-Yota, these creatures existed only in fantastic stories, as creatures of myth who appear to serve justice for the downtrodden or to act as protectors emerging for a single battle, only to disappear again. They are the kind of stories that no one truly believes, but repeat because they make them feel better about an unseen justice watching over the world. Until one day, when the kingdom's peril is at its height, the tigris suddenly appear in the flesh to bolster the claim of a pretender."

"I told you, Elasu was their slave. She had the runes of control carved into her. If that magic worked as it did in Rolm, somewhere, one of those overgrown cats had connected markings. Elasu had always been their slave." I looked down at my own ugly markings. "I do not believe the tigris emerged from their dark forest because of the Schism. I think they were the cause of it to begin with. Elasu acted at their behest. The young dragon Windlore who was killed in the tower I once inhabited in Changsha must've discovered that, so they murdered him as well. I found the claw marks on the stone. And all those events—the emergence of the tigris and the Schism—coincide with the hollowing invasion. I do not believe in coincidence. It may be that these many battles were somehow connected to the other."

"You believe the tigris to be allied with the hollowings?" Harlan asked, seemingly surprised at the notion.

I had wondered that myself. "If they are, I do not see how. The rust and the hollowings...it seems difficult to believe they are aligned with anything as mundane and alive as the tigris."

"Aye, the giant cats, they are like predators. They want something. But the hollowings...they are like a great storm. A thing apart from the living, yet giant and terrifying. I prefer to face the tigris, for at least they are flesh."

I wouldn't mind killing some tigris. I'd never liked them—any of them. But I had a feeling learning their secrets would be more important than defeating them in battle. "Let us hope there is some lore that tells of the giant cats at this archive as well."

I turned toward the north coast of Ni-Yota, flying along a path on the Ni-Yota side of the Tayo River. For the rest of the day we flew, sometimes speaking but mostly in silence. I landed near a small fishing village, where Harlan bought both fresh fish to fill our stomachs and several smoked ones he kept in his pack for the journey ahead. I stayed on the outskirts, in the fields, to avoid alarming anyone, but to my surprise, a group of nearly ten humans approached me anyway, following in Harlan's wake. There were human children among the group, their heads too large for their boney bodies, their eyes wide as they looked at me. I drew myself upright, puzzled. I expected humans would keep their distance from a strange dragon, but Ni-Yota was a different land than Rolm. My kind was revered rather than feared here.

The oldest among the arrivals had hair the color of gray ash and skin like a raisin. "Welcome, Bayloo the Chosen." He fell to his knees. The others did the same, pulling the children in their midst down to the field with them. The scene made me think of Prince Dayne. His covetous heart would've taken pleasure at this sight of people kneeling. It just made my neck twist even more awkwardly to look at them.

"Rise, all of you. You owe me no homage, no fealty."

They got up, not because they wished it, but because I'd asked it. Still, if I had to speak to humans, I preferred to speak to ones who weren't on their knees.

"You honor us by coming to us here," the old leader said. "It has been many years since one of the winged lords visited our village. That was before the war. The children have never seen one of you. They thought the great dragon protectors only stories told by old men like me." He managed a smile, showing a mouth with no more than seven or eight teeth inside. "I am Li, elder of the village." He motioned to one of the boys, as gaunt a specimen as I'd seen. No one was going to bother eating him. "Might young Eral have your blessing?"

I didn't get it. My what?

At the urging of the Elder Li, the stick-like boy moved forward, his eyes downcast. Each hand grabbed the elbow of the opposite arm. I noticed one of the boy's hands was more clubbish than usual for a human, the fingers having grown together in a single mass.

Harlan whispered to me, "He wants to touch your scales. He believes that it would heal his hand."

"Is there something wrong with his hand?" I asked loudly (I don't really whisper well). "It's different than some humans, but it could be useful in a fight."

Elder Li looked horrified. Harlan chimed in again. "They are fishermen, not brawlers."

I understood. Fingers were probably better for fishing. Unfortunately, I didn't really see what I could do about it. Touching my scales wasn't going to make that boy grow fingers. Even if I knew how to heal, this human's hand wasn't an injury. It was part of him.

"May he approach?" the elder asked.

It seemed I was to disappoint yet another person. "Come, if it matters to you."

Elder Li nearly shoved the young Eral into me. Only when the boy stood beneath my shadow did he finally look up. His legs shook.

"Touch him with your deformed hand and receive the dragon lord's blessing. See if the chosen of the Light of Haven deems you worthy of being healed."

The boy laid his trembling club-hand upon my chest. Nothing happened. Water brimmed in his cavernous eyes, and in that moment I actually felt pity for the little human. Water began leaking from his eyes in tiny drops. Humans do leak sometimes.

"Look upon my chest, young Eral," I told him.

The shock of my speech made his eyes widen. His chin dropped.

"Look at the brutal carvings made upon my scales by evil Sculptors from long ago, wielders of a stolen magic."

The boy didn't look. He kept his neck craned upwards. I'm not even sure if he understood Avian. I told my story anyway.

"I was born on an isle of lost dragons, taken as a slave before I had anything to remember of the place of my birth. For decades I was held, used as a weapon, accorded about as much respect as a sword. I was useful only for my killing, and I was to be used by my masters until I broke. A chance came to me—an opportunity to live a different life. I chose to be free, no matter the cost. Perhaps there was a reason for that. I came here, and perhaps there was a reason for that as well." I reached for his head with my foreclaw and pointed the boy gently toward that which I wished him to see—my runes. "These markings are a part of who I am. They aren't beautiful. They make me different than any other living dragon in Ni-Yota. Yet I would not change them even if I could."

Eral seemed to shake a bit less.

"Your birth is not your destiny. You require no healing from me or any other. Once you accept who you are, you are already healed. Your destiny is yours to make."

I left the child with those words.

"That was handled well," Harlan told me as we resumed our flight.

"You don't need to sound so surprised."

"You've changed, if you don't mind my saying."

I snorted with derision. I hadn't changed. I was just never meant to be a slave. Now, I just needed to discover what I was meant to become. I flew faster, so fast the wind screamed off my back. Speed was better than talking to Harlan more on this subject.

While daylight reigned, I made the most of it. I beat my wings, propelling us along the rocky coast of northern Ni-Yota. The Tayo River terminated in a great delta dotted with patches of grass-covered land surrounded by murky, almost still water. I saw no signs of men or any other creature of note, including hollowings. Further west were rugged mountains that hugged the River Tayo, the wide waters and the peaks impassable to man or beast. Beyond the river, the Mizu lands ended and Illium began.

I made for the open sea rather than fly across the river itself. Only once I had left the land behind did I turn full west, passing an invisible line into Illium's waters. I waited for something terrible to mark my passage—a clap of thunder, the sudden appearance of a flock of blood raptors, a dark cloud—but there was nothing.

Day fell to night, as each of them always do. Inevitably, my wings began to ache, followed by a low burn in the muscles of my chest. I pushed onward, flying over the water but always keeping the coast within sight. I wanted to cover as much distance as possible, but even I must rest. Twilight filled the sky.

"Harlan, I've seen nothing but heaving waves in the water since we crossed the border. Have you some sailor's trick to find a patch of land in your vast sea?"

"As you mention it, yes, but it only works when I ride upon the waves. There must be a physical connection to the water, but before you go drop me into the sea, I need to tell you that it's not as effective as just having an uninterrupted view from up here. I too have spotted nothing but some barren spikes of rock in the shallow of the beaches, none big enough to fit a horse much less a dragon."

"When the veil of darkness falls, I will turn inland. I cannot fly much farther without injuring myself."

The night came, forcing me to fly to Illium. The land there was flat and dead, its surface mostly covered by tenacious weeds and the strange rust that reminded me of dead, spoiled algae baked by the sun. I dropped my altitude to confirm nothing hid within the thick patches or even beneath the layer of taint upon the land. I saw nothing. I smelled nothing alive, only the sickly-sweet odor of the rust.

Harlan couldn't see as well as I in the dark, but he could see enough. "Is there any place clear of the filth?"

"No."

Harlan let go of an uneven breath. "Then we must camp on a

narrow beach, where the sea washes the taint from the sand." By his tone, he was hoping I had an alternative. I didn't.

I agreed with him. "Better to risk the dangers of the coast than spend a night atop the rust."

"Spoken like someone who has never spent a night at sea."

Harlan was correct, and his tone dubious, but I had to land somewhere soon. I returned to shore, searching for a decently wide stretch of beach. Harlan stopped me as I went to land.

"Not here. The water is too deep."

I disagreed. "It's shallow. Too shallow for a leviathan. I may not be a sailor, but I'm not a fool. As for the ghastrays...they seem to have taken our side."

"The water is shallow, but only close to shore. Leviathans prefer the deep, but they'll shove themselves through the shallows if it suits them or if they are hungry enough. Besides, the sea holds more dangers than leviathans and ghastrays. These waters are cold enough for nightcrawlers."

Rather than argue, I found a different beach that met with Harlan's grudging approval. It was a pathetic stretch of sand, backed by jagged boulders, abused by the sea over countless years. But it was free from the taint that infested the land beyond the near shore.

Harlan climbed off my back. He first inspected the sand, letting the particles run through his fingers, then he waded closer to the sea, stopping where the waves climbed on the beach. He placed a finger onto the wet sand, letting the sea's dark water come to him. Three waves crashed into the shore as he just sat there, crouched in the dirt. There were any number of comments I might have made, but I was exhausted and I got the impression Harlan actually had some purpose. When he finally finished with the water, he climbed upon a nearby rock. From atop the mound, he spoke like some prophet of the sea.

"The tide will come well before daylight returns. When it does, the waves will reach well over these rocks. This whole beach will be underwater. That is the reason it is free of rust. The sea comes frequently to cleanse this place."

It wasn't what I wanted to hear. "I need not sleep long or deep. So long as I rest my wings and eat, it will be sufficient."

So we ate smoked fish, mostly in silence. Harlan had the impressive ability to place an entire hunk of fish in his mouth and then spit out the fleshless bones a few moments later. I just ate it all, although fish bones can be a bit sharp, even for a dragon.

"Do you wish me to take first watch?" he asked.

"Sleep, Harlan. You humans need far more of it at regular intervals than do my kind. It may be that alertness is needed later in our journey."

"Do you mind if I ..." He indicated my belly. "It's cold. You're warm."

"You wish to mate with me?"

Harlan raised his brows. "Not so much, but I'll do what I must to keep warm."

I snorted but I didn't refuse him (the warmth, that is). Of course, the human snored. I tried to concentrate on the waves to tune out the horrible ruckus coming from Harlan's nostrils, but without complete success. It was remarkable that human couples willingly chose to cohabitate. Harlan's wife might miss him, but she was probably sleeping better.

Harlan awoke in the middle of the night, as if he had a sense of such things the way we dragons do. Rima had appeared at that moment, a shattered moon over a shattered land. Harlan took a long gaze at the sea, perhaps seeing something in the faintly reflecting light that even I could not, before he turned to me.

"I knew you wouldn't sleep. The turmoil of the waves grows. Soon enough, water will lap at our feet, and I think we'll have a storm tomorrow. I'll keep watch. Take this time to rest."

I should've just done that. Instead, I asked a question. "You've not spoken of your quest since the destruction of that bit of aurathorn and the death of Aragor."

I watched Harlan's face grow tense. It was rare for him to show emotion. Perhaps he let his guard down in the darkness. Or this question truly bothered him.

"I haven't spoken of it to you, that's true."

Had he discussed it with someone else?

"Will you return to your wife without it, then?"

"No, I will find aurathorn."

"There is no more here. The plant is extinct from Ni-Yota. Rinxia said as much. My mother thought the same."

Harlan shut his eyes as he drew a long breath. When his lids opened again, his expression was at peace. "It is still out there, somewhere. When you have been searching for something as long and hard as I have, you form a bond with it. Aurathron is woven into the fabric of the world. I would know if it was truly gone." He smirked, although I couldn't tell if his confidence was true or a ruse.

"I believe it still exists, on the other side of the Wall of Fire."

I expected more of a reaction than I got. Harlan must have been excellent at bluffing in his card games. "Why do you think that?"

"A human told me. But it must be so. My mother journeyed to Rolm to free me using aurathorn. She did not bring it from Ni-Yota. It is still there, somewhere."

"Then why do you fly west rather than east?" Harlan kept his tone flat, but I knew him well enough to know he was anxious.

"To find aurathorn, before she traversed the Wall of Fire, she came to this archive. She was seeking something. Knowledge that is connected to the rust. Knowledge we must have to beat the rust and free my kind. At least, that is what I believe."

Harlan was quiet for a time before he spoke once again in a low, near-whispered tone. "A quest is more than going to a place to find an object. Aurathorn is not something that can merely be found and dug up like gold or gems. It is ancient, a relic from the days of the Cataclysm that still clings to existence in a world where it does not belong. It is powerful. To find such an object, one must revere it and understand it. I have always known that I would find it, but only once I was ready to do so."

"That is wise," I told Harlan.

He chuckled more easily than I would have in his place. "It is particularly wise since there isn't any way back to Ni-Yota except on your back, much less across the Wall of Fire."

"Sleep while you can, Harlan Dor. Your quest is far from over, as is mine. Tomorrow will doubtless bring another chance to gain knowledge, and also a chance to die along the way."

TWENTY-SEVEN

Water woke me.

It was the cold, unwelcoming water of the sea. The tide had decided my rest was at an end. The sun had not yet risen. The air swirled with an angry chill.

I got to my feet, stretching my neck and sniffing the air. My nose told me that Harlan had been correct in predicting a forthcoming storm. I flew quickly to get ahead of it. That didn't work.

When the morning light arrived, it revealed a cloud wall of ominous darkness to the north. Lightning flashed in the belly of the system, as if the coming torrent were hungry. Perhaps it was.

I flew as far as I was able, but I'm not faster than a lightning storm. The dark, laden clouds took position above me before the morning was old. The tempest began its tantrum with a hard, driving rain, the drops coming like projectiles. Harlan's grip tightened. The wind picked up.

"Use both arms to grab me. Pretend I'm your wife."

"You don't want me doing that, dragon or not. Don't worry—this isn't my first storm."

The sky heard the challenge. It answered with gashes of light that singed the air. The clouds were too thick to attempt to rise above the storm. Instead, I was forced to a lower altitude, where the wind swirled with a terrible confusion, its gusts switching direction like a lost child. The sea nearly matched the anger of the storm above it, the waves lurching to heights as they battered the shore. I scanned the land, but saw no place where I might take shelter along the devastated, rust-coated flatlands. So I continued to fly, as if that were my choice.

A curtain of hard water surged toward me, carried on furious gusts. The sky had its way with me, pushing me downward and in any other direction its mood required. To fight would've been futile. I worried for Harlan, but I need not have bothered.

"Eat the storm, Bayloo! Devour its winds!" He sounded to be on the edge of madness, but joyous at dancing on that edge.

I didn't share the sailor's delight. This was perhaps the mightiest torrent I could remember, and the seas around Rolm could conjure mighty gusts in the winter. There, I would've sought shelter. In Illium, the land itself might well be poisoned. But even with the rust, I was about to turn inland in search of shelter or better weather when something unexpected in the sea drew my attention: a ship. Or part of one. The construction appeared to be some kind of hybrid between a raft and a sea-faring vessel, with a low bow but twin hulls.

I called behind me. "Look there, off the shore ahead, caught in high waves."

Harlan didn't answer immediately, but I knew his sharp eyes would quickly locate the strange vessel. I wasn't wrong. "It looks like some kind of outrigger, like those used on the Kanal Islands, except larger. It runs low in the water."

"It has been battered," I observed.

I dropped closer to the water. I knew Harlan's eyes were still fixed on the craft. "I see no sign of splintered masts. This vessel may not have them, or they hadn't been attached yet. Her timber is fresh. I think she's a babe of a vessel, washed out to sea before she was ready."

"A new ship? Who would be building..." I didn't need to finish my sentence. "Rinxia told me she'd followed a well-maintained road to a port of some kind on the north shore of Illium. But she saw no signs of a ship." But she also said that blood raptors had harassed and delayed her. Was this what the hollowings were hiding?

I came even closer, flying a tight circle around the debris. I had sharper sight than Harlan, but he knew ships and the sea far better. Still, it took me only a few moments to realize he'd been correct about the recent construction of the ship. Its battered hull was free of barnacles or the regular wear of a veteran vessel.

"Long and narrow," Harlan commented, more to himself than me. "Couldn't carry much cargo in that shallow hull, and she doesn't seem fitted to carry ballistae, so neither a trader nor a warship. She's built for speed."

"A scout?"

"Maybe." Harlan didn't sound convinced.

Another gust hit, spraying drops of seawater high enough to graze my belly.

Harlan tapped his hand against the scales of my back. "Nothing more to see here. Let's see if her shipyard is further up the coast."

The storm came at me even harder as I pressed forward. My wing muscles burned as if I'd been flying for a full day without rest, rather than a single morning. Not that there was much evidence in the sky that it was morning—only gloom punctuated by echoing thunder. It was as if the wind tried to hold me back. It couldn't, of course. I located the strange port that must have been the same one that Rinxia had described, not far beyond the derelict ship. I saw the buildings Rinxia described, all well-maintained and mostly free from the rust, as if they'd been recently constructed. The road that led to the coast from Illium's interior was similarly maintained and also completely empty.

"Those warehouses are big enough for a dragon," Harlan suggested as I flew over the deserted port. "Can you get a bit closer?"

Instead of answering, I got closer, dropping my altitude.

"No need to slow down," Harlan assured me. "I just need a better look at the buildings near the quay."

I obliged, passing low over the rain-soaked port. There were no homes, and the only roads led between the large wood structures, their roofs tilted and downward-sloping to protect against water accumulation. Nothing stirred as I flew past.

Harlan apparently got a pretty good look, despite the rain. "I think two of the buildings are built over the water. They are hiding slips for vessels beneath the roof. The water-facing side can open to allow a ship to depart. I think this place could be some kind of shipyard."

"The hollowings seek to hide their activities. That is new for them. Do they seek to sail an armada to Ni-Yota?"

Harlan made a grunting noise. "Two ship slips aren't a fleet. Those ships couldn't possibly match the Mizu navy, not to mention deal with fire-breathing dragons."

"There may be more such places as we travel the coast. Rinxia scouted only a small portion of Illium."

Harlan didn't seem convinced. "We shall see. Fly on, Bayloo."

He made it sound so easy, but Harlan wasn't the one pushing against the wind while carrying a noisy, hairy human on his back. I pushed into the formidable wind, still flying along the coast. Heavy gusts continued to come at us from the north, but as the day passed, so did the worst of the storm's anger. My speed increased as the rain and wind relented. By the early afternoon I had put the storm behind us. Clear skies had returned, but I was sufficiently exhausted that continuing much further wasn't an option.

I landed on a cluster of craggy rocks just off the coast that were high enough to avoid most of the waves that crashed below. Harlan sucked in long, deep breaths.

"You snort the salt air with such relish, as if it were the steam of a roasted pig," I observed.

"It's the smell of my youth, my life. My first memory isn't the sound of my mother's voice—it's the knocking of the waves against the hull of our cabin on our ship. The sea put me to sleep every night and woke me each morning. I fell in love with the noises of the water in the background, like music in a fine concert. But always there is the scent of the sea. There is nothing else like it. When I suck in the salt, all that I miss flashes before me. The best memories are linked to smell."

"As I said, you treat it like it's the steam of a roasted pig."

"You play the innocent, Bayloo, but you hide something deeper within you." I couldn't see Harlan on my back, but I imagined his dark brow furrowing. "I understand you better than you think. You know, I once thought I desired only the sea, a ship of my own, and a full belly."

"That sounds rather pleasing, except the sea and the ship."

He answered me with a single barked laugh. "Too simple. To live that life wouldn't be living at all compared to what I know now. The world opened my eyes. I heard the stories of my people. I began to see hints of the truth in the places I visited—the wall of an ancient fortress still standing, its structure stronger than the hardest steel. In a market I've seen a forgotten artifact of the Cataclysm, its surface so smooth and shining one cannot look on it for more than a few moments. In the depth of night in the deepest waters, I've seen creatures that glow like the sun beneath the waves, humming a tune so soothing I thought I was dreaming. Then I met my wife, and she opened my mind as the world had opened my eyes. She taught me to think about what I saw, rather than stop at mere amazement. Suddenly, I realized that all that I'd seen hinted at the greatest tale of all, a puzzle to be solved. There is something that ties it all together, the past, the present, and perhaps the future." Harlan's voice grew thick as he spoke. "Finally, reluctantly, I accepted that I had a part to play in what would unfold, this great tapestry of a story for all the inhabitants of our world."

"You'd live a longer life with your wife on a ship in calm seas."

"You cannot unsee what you have seen, Bayloo. You and I are not traveling such different paths. We're going to the same place. I've had longer to accept it, but you are catching up quickly. Or else you would not be here."

I held my contemptuous snort, because the fact was, I was indeed here, tenuously perched on some rocks on the shore of hollowing-infested Illium, listening to fish-stories from a human, while my sister was back in Trishan and the rest of my kind were still slaves in Rolm. Some of what Harlan said rang true, but I was too tired for self-reflection. And he didn't understand me as well as he thought.

"Dragons are not humans, Harlan Dor." A truth sprang to my mind unbidden. "We were created differently. Our destiny is not yours. This all may be part of one great tapestry of a story, as you say, but do not suppose our roles or our endings are the same."

Harlan was wise enough not to press me further. He gave me time to rest. I ate another smoked fish and counted the waves, letting my mind wander. Harlan grew bored, removed his shoes, and climbed down to a precarious perch just above the tidal line. I don't know how long he stared at the water. I thought perhaps it spoke to him, that he was meditating in some way. Then, as quick as a viper, his arm shot into the water and pulled out a long, silver-scaled fish, its tail wriggling, furious at being snared in such a manner. Harlan tossed his catch over his head without even looking at me. I obligingly scooped it out of the air with my mouth, swallowing the fish whole.

I belched my appreciation.

Harlan climbed onto my back and we resumed our journey. For two days and nights we hugged the coast, resting on rocks, sleeping on the edge of the sand. We shared watches. I slept little, and poorly. The sense of wrongness in this land pervaded the air. Even the beach, mostly free of the rusted taint, made me feel uneasy. But at least we could rest beside the relative safety of the sea.

That was about to change. A great scar on the land—a ditch that looked like a huge claw from Haven had reached down and pulled a chunk of ground out sometime in the distant past—marked the end of the first part of our journey.

"Rinxia told me of this place—the Wound of the North. The

people of Illium, the real ones who lived before they became hollowings, believed that this was the place where the rulers of Haven had reached down to strike Yanis, one of the great enemies of humanity."

"I've seen similar formations. Different lands explain these places differently, but all seem to agree they were made by some great power from the sky."

I slowed to a glide, gazing at the sheer rock walls of the massive hole. It was large enough and deep enough to fit a thousand Trishans. No human nor dragon could've made such a thing, even if they'd ever had a desire to do so. That meant something else had. I didn't really care who, or what, at the moment. This was merely a landmark to me.

"According to Rinxia and the old maps, it will take another week to continue along the coast, passing through an area of permafrost with terrible blizzards and no food. The people of Illium referred to this area as the Stormlands. Even for dragons, these blizzards are dangerous. For humans, they are deadly. Nor do we have the time or supplies to dare that route."

Harlan knew what was coming. "It is time to cross into the wasteland of Illium."

TWENTY-EIGHT

The waste beckoned.

Refreshed by a bit of sleep and a bit of food (although smoked fish had become tiring), I faced the most daunting portion of our trip with the renewed determination that comes with terrible fear: I didn't want to land in Illium. Much of the ground was infected with the rust and there were hollowings lurking—and those were only the dangers I knew about. Unfortunately, based on the information I had, the distance to Silla Peak was further than I could travel in a single day. Fine. I would fly through the night as well. I wasn't going to land in Illium if I could help it.

The constant noise and energy of the coast tides turned quickly to the uncomfortable silence of a lifeless wasteland in the interior. Worse than a wasteland. In every direction, there was only the rust, its pervasive presence so monotonous that it was disorienting. It was like staring into a void of crimson-tinted blight, the only variation being changes in shade, presumably due to the thickness of the coating in any particular location. Only my shadow interrupted the horrible perfection of the rusty ground. As I passed, the land seemed to glint ever so slightly, as if reacting to my presence above. I flew higher, gliding whenever I found a pocket of warm air so that I might save my strength.

"Have you seen the likes of this in any of your travels, Harlan?"

"Even my weary eyes have not set themselves upon such a terrible sight before this day." His voice was heavy. "The view from across the Tayo does not capture the terrifying vastness of what is below us now. At a glance, it is like the blossoming of the amber wildflowers of Karak after the first of the spring rains, but only for a false moment. In the plains of Karak, the color is that of new life. This is something else. Not a pestilence, nor a fungus. It is ominous."

There could be no argument about that. Somehow, the rust, seemingly motionless, evoked a greater dread than the hollowing horde. Its sheer size—an expanse beyond the edges of my own vision—was chilling.

"I think this is not the first time the world has seen the rust," I speculated. "I think my mother knew of it as well. She did not come to Rolm just to free me. That was part of something bigger. She was searching for something in Rolm. The people who dwelled on Maricopa, where I met her, were refugees from Ni-Yota—a people with knowledge of enchantments driven from this land." I strained to recall what Bethy Rann had told me. It had been only weeks, but it felt like months. "The Ellugar, they were called."

"I have heard of them," Harlan admitted. "But they are usually only mentioned in passing, as a warning."

"A warning?"

"The Ellugar wished to stay apart from the Conclave of Magi. This was not permitted. Both the humans who governed the Conclave and ultimately their dragon masters could abide no independent wielders of magic within Ni-Yota. They ended badly, exterminated. Although, it seems, not all of them." I heard tentative hope creep into Harlan's voice as he asked, "These are the ones who have aurathorn?"

"Alas, no," I told him. "But they are a piece to the puzzle of finding it again."

"If we survive this journey."

Harlan said it as if I needed reminding. I didn't. My hearts weighed on me as we flew over Illium. The morning rolled into the afternoon. I spotted the remains of lost villages and even cities, the outlines of their buildings now covered by the rust, their inhabitants more than likely now part of the hollowing horde. I was sure Harlan noticed it all as well. Neither of us spoke of it. There was no need, and nothing could be done.

With the dusk came a new dark speck in the west, like a piece of dirt in the sky, the setting sun burning scarlet behind it. I flew toward it, and it came toward me. Even before my view confirmed it, I knew it was a blood raptor. We'd not encountered any direct hostility from the hollowings on this journey thus far, but they had to be aware of our presence. They had to be watching. I doubted a single bird would attack—more likely it was a scout of some kind. It continued to come at me. There was no point in taking any chances. I flew higher, but the raptor matched my maneuver. I could've risen well beyond the clouds had I been alone, but human lungs need far more air than dragons. For Harlan's sake, I faced the blood raptor rather than risk killing him in the thinnest of the high air above.

It came at me as if it were the dragon and I a puny feathered beast. "I will handle the little birdie," I told Harlan.

"Surely it does not intend to attack."

Surely, it did. The bird stretched its talons beneath spread wings of black. It made no attempt to maneuver, no attempt to deceive. The raptor flew toward me as if it were an arrow without a choice in the matter. As it neared, its mouth opened in a silent cry of defiance. I veered at the last moment, snatching the bird in one of my foreclaws and crushing it in a satisfying fist. I let the mangled remains fall from the sky to the endless expanse of rust-coated wasteland below us.

"I see no others," Harlan said. "What was the point of that encounter?"

"Must there be a point?"

"This is no mindless storm that opposes us. The hollowings may not think like us, but they do think. They are logical in their own way. It does not seem they would throw away even a single blood raptor without a reason."

I didn't disagree with the conclusion. I stared at the horizon from which the blood raptor had emerged, then at the ground beneath us. "Perhaps it was a message."

"An obscure one, then."

Maybe not so obscure. "The bird was sent as a marker, a trip wire even. The intellect of the blight below knows we have arrived. Look down, look at what lies beneath the fading sun: mountains."

"Haven's Finger." Harlan sounded impressed, a rare enough thing for his jaded eyes. "Not many men have traveled to the end of the world. Yet here I am, riding on a dragon, no less."

The great peninsula ahead extended from the end of the rest of the continent into the sea like the appendage for which it was named (obviously by humans). Here, the flatlands and rolling hills of northern Illium ended. The Finger was a place of jagged rocks and treacherous cliffs. There were no flatlands, no visible roads. The sea pounded the strip of land from the north and south, as if angered that it had dared to interrupt the desired path of the waves. Yet it gave me hope. Harlan saw it as well.

"The rust ends here. It hasn't crossed onto the Finger."

"You see with human eyes. And too much optimism, which, I suppose, is the same thing."

I beat my wings, flying westward. The sun disappeared behind the horizon, leaving only its residual light in the sky. Still, there was enough brightness remaining for even Harlan to see what I had already known: the blight had already spread throughout the narrow peninsula, just not with the same all-encompassing presence as elsewhere in Illium. As I dropped closer to the ground, the tide pools that marked the beginning of the Finger came into easy view. Harlan understood quickly. He was human, but not stupid.

"With each high tide, the salt water comes over the land bridge, severing the link between the peninsula and the mainland. Each time the water comes, it must wash away the rust that has clawed its way onto the Finger, much as the tides clear the beaches to the north."

He sounded almost excited. I didn't really see reason for optimism. "But still, the rust is here. Look at the rocks beyond; see the streaks that reflect the light at the wrong angle, their color different than the rest. It has spread all over the Finger, onto every mountain. The sea has not stopped its advance." I flew over the Finger to show him of what I spoke. As I passed over the first set of rocks, more rust revealed itself, the crimson blight plunging with narrow lines into steep crevices and climbing over crags of sand-ravaged rocks. It was the same stuff that had consumed the rest of Illium. The terrain and the sea posed more challenge for the rust, but it could not halt its advance.

Harlan's voice turned grimmer, but still determined. "It is here, but it's somehow less. On the continent, the rust is everywhere, covering whole cities, hills, and valleys. Only the water is free of the taint. But on the Finger, it is less pervasive. It only clings to the rocks. It snakes through this place, but it has not smothered it, not the way it has the rest of Illium."

I circled, studying the terrain below, watching the pounding of the sea, feeling the direction of the wind as it whipped off the water. "This place is beaten by the sea and wind the way a farmer beats a wayward oxen. The rocks speak of the harsh spray of salt air. And this place—a narrow strip of land daring to poke into the sea—must suffer powerful storms much of the year. Each day the land is scrubbed by the brute force of the elements. That is why no humans have settled here."

"Your eyes are better than mine in the dark, and I do not doubt your knowledge of the winds," Harlan said. "But I wonder if the tide also makes a difference. The rust here is cut off from the larger mass each day. Disconnected from the rest of its great host, it could be that it is somehow weaker."

"Weaker?" I wondered.

"Here the rust is a narrow sliver, like a fruit trying to grow on a slender, wayward vine. Here it may be slower to spread."

I grunted my skepticism. I tilted my wings, riding a gust of wind to a higher altitude and getting a better view of what lay ahead. I saw what I feared and expected. "I do not see a single mountain that is completely free of the rust, although I cannot see with clarity to the tip where the Silla Peak supposedly lies."

Harlan caught my glum assessment. "You are afraid we have come a long way for nothing. But there was the bird, as you say."

"It may be that the blood raptor merely mocked us. Our enemy's way of letting us know that we were on a pointless errand. Once again, we may have underestimated the rust. If the knowledge held at this archive is a threat, I believe the hollowings would eliminate that threat. What we seek may already have been consumed by the blight."

TWENTY-NINE

I told myself it wasn't much further.

The pale glow of the rust below mocked my efforts. The disconcerting light extended through the rocky terrain of the peninsula likes veins filled with contaminated blood, their sickness highlighted by the moonlight above. The path of the blight led ever west, toward the tip of the peninsula, toward the Silla Peak and the ancient archive once located there. It was far too late to beat my strange enemy to the destination, but I pushed forward as if I still had a chance to win an impossible race.

Dawn revealed the extent of the blight's infiltration. The new light splashed over the misshapen peaks of the Finger, each one adorned by streams of rust crisscrossing their face. As the polluted lines neared the tip of the peninsula, they merged, the twisting snakes of tainted crimson becoming a single great river of rust that drove with purpose at the last mountain that sprouted before the sea—that peak standing alone at the edge of the world like a forgotten child watching the endless water beyond for some sign he hadn't been forgotten. I flew at it, my hearts nearly empty of hope for what I might find.

Silla Peak itself was unlike its brethren. Nearly devoid of the weather-torn scars of the other mountains, the outcropping resembled a hatchling fresh from the egg, its sides as smooth as a paved road, its shape unnaturally symmetrical—more like something carved by a craftsman than naturally born from the depths of the world. It seemed to rise from the water below, its form separate and distinct from the land of the Finger that reached toward it. The rock of the peak differed as well—while the rest of the mountains of the Finger were a dull gray, polluted with streaks of brown, the final mountain was mostly white, the color of dirt-stained snow.

Harlan ably summed up the sight: "It is beautiful."

It was indeed. Perfect. Empty. Alone. But beauty could not defy the rust. Even through the deep green water of the sea that surrounded the mountain on every approach, the blight had still come. It began at the base of the rock nearest to the peak, just above the waterline. Then it spread upwards and around both sides of the peak, a gash of desecration on the otherwise pristine surface of the rock.

"Although we cannot see it now, at low tide, there must be a land bridge across the narrow channel," Harlan said. "Otherwise people could've only come by ship, and there is no moorage. Those waves seem vicious and unpredictable, as well. I'd not want to try to sail anywhere close to this place. It is a place of pilgrims, not sailors."

"Or the rust found another way across." My tone and hearts were grim. "It is relentless."

There was no sign of any structure on the landward side of the peak. I banked left and swooped around the mountain, mirroring the path of the rust as it wrapped itself around the white rock of the peak. I saw a treacherous pathway had been carved into the mountain's face which led from the landward face to the seaward side of the peak. However, I guessed that the journey would've deterred all but the most determined human travelers.

On the far side of the mountain, facing directly into the horizon where the sun came to rest each day, I found what had to be the entrance: it was a hole, a missing section of rock on the otherwise smooth surface of the mountain. The opening was rimmed by jagged teeth of stone, making it look as if a beast had reached into the peak with a massive claw and scooped out a piece of rock to chew upon. Despite the brightening light of morning, even my eyes couldn't penetrate the blackness beyond the portal's entrance. Neither the dark nor the perilous location of the entrance had stopped the rust, though. The crimson blight framed the edge of the portal, as if it had encircled a besieged keep before breaking inside. A switchback staircase had been carved into the rocky facade, the steps extending from the narrow pathway that circled the mountain. The workmanship of those stairs was meticulous, each identical to the last, and unmarred by the passage of time and the elements. I hovered outside the gap despite my fatigue, foreboding heavy in my chest.

Harlan was impatient at my hesitation. "We've come a long way to get cold feet now."

"Dragons don't get cold feet. We don't even have feet like humans."

I flew inside, cautiously. Dragons are not stupid either—usually. The opening was large enough that I could glide.

The reason I hadn't been able to see into the belly of the mountain was that there was nothing to see. The design was clever—a dead-end tunnel of midnight stone. The rust ran through the otherwise pitch-black rock in twin veins. Following its path led me to the great hole in the tunnel floor.

The rust's faint luminosity was just enough to make me uneasy. It felt like being trapped in a hole with a sleeping predator. Harlan spoke in the half-darkness. "The rust hasn't spread here. It is a narrow line, and that pattern cannot be random. It is directed, as if it seeks something within."

I went through the hole without answering because we both knew he was correct. We entered a carved corridor wide enough to accommodate two dragons side-by-side and high enough to allow me to fly if I was careful. Here, too, the rust ran in thin veins along walls of smoothly-cut stone on either side of me. I smelled fresh air tinged only slightly with the taste of salt from the sea nearby. At the end of the passage, I found the Archive of Oracles. I was impressed.

Another world, hidden from the light of the sun, existed inside the Silla Peak. This massive cavern had a ceiling of glowing azure stone that stretched in each direction, nearly to the walls of the mountain itself—essentially creating an artificial sky. Air from outside flowed through the chamber through hidden crevasses, while huge mushroom-like crops as high as corn stalks grew untamed in what I suspected had once been manicured fields. I had flown into a forgotten underground farm, which left no doubt that the builders of this place had terrible taste in food. So much trouble just for vegetables.

I saw no other creatures and sensed no other movement. The rows of fungus crops stood as if frozen in time. They were all covered by the rust, as was a portion of the walls and ceiling. Still, the sheer size of the place and the near absolute stillness within was impressive. Constructing this cavern had been no easy feat. The builders must've had a very good reason for doing so.

At the center of it all was a pit. One so massive it consumed almost a third of the surface area of the cavern's floor. A staircase circled its way downward into the portal, leading even deeper into the mountain.

"I've never seen a crop like that, but I don't think we want to walk through those fields to take a closer look," Harlan commented. "Perhaps they once fed the inhabitants of this place, but they are now poisoned by the rust. I suspect we'll find the archive below, through that great pit-like portal. Can you fly in here?"

The question was insulting. The opening was huge. I answered by tilting my wings, changing my direction toward the opening. I pulled up abruptly just before entering, beating my wings to change our direction. The gusts sent debris into the sky, and I brought us even higher to keep my distance from any unknown particles in the air. I saw evidence that there had been a battle here.

Human remains lined the stone stairway as it wound into the next chamber. I saw no flesh, but there were plenty of bones. Weapons lay scattered about. The rust had spread everywhere.

"The hollowings came down here," Harlan concluded. "By the look of it, that happened many years ago. Perhaps around the time the war started with Ni-Yota, perhaps even before that."

I studied the remains of the old battle. "The staircase has been destroyed further down. No humans can enter unless they can fly."

"I think it was done intentionally. The people who resided here tried to keep the hollowings out."

I studied the ugly crimson clawing its way relentlessly through the cavern. "I suspect they could not stop the rust."

I flew downward to find out. It was just as I suspected—the rust's advance had not been halted. It was everywhere.

Through the gaping hole was another cavern, this one larger and better lit, the ceiling glowing a blue so magnificent it truly could've been mistaken for the sky. Not even a human would need a lantern in this place. There were structures—impossibly high columns of translucent ivory that resembled marble—that extended from the floor to the ceiling. I entered through the portal with some speed, flying into the cavern, carefully maneuvering around the strange pillars. This subterranean chamber made the upper cavern look like a hovel. It was also scarred by tragedy.

The great soaring pillars touched both the floor and ceiling of the massive space, but I was fairly certain they had not been built to support the ceiling. Or at least that wasn't their primary purpose. They were like narrow spires—about as thick as my belly—but their height was nearly equal to the highest tower in Trishan. I noticed a few of the columns did not quite reach the chamber's glowing ceiling. The strange towers were clustered into groups of different sizes with large gaps of space between the clusters. Even with my limited knowledge of engineering, that didn't seem to make sense if their purpose was support of the roof. Yet, the columns had no doors, no windows, and no battlements. As I neared, I studied the spires: they were not made of a single piece of stone, but rather had been constructed of rectangular bricks of different sizes, all fitted perfectly together. Each individual piece of the tower was inscribed with some sort of writing. There were at least a hundred of the spires sprouting from within the cavern, like a stone forest buried within the bowels of the mountain. At the center of the various tower clusters was yet another portal in the ground that I presumed led even deeper into the mountain.

It occurred to me that the strange pillars would've been beautiful in the past. Not anymore. Now, they were dangerous: the rust had infected them as well.

The pestilence had seeped down the rock from the cavern above, passing into the chamber of soaring columns in eight thin lines of ugly crimson that resembled spider legs. Once the rust tentacles reached the cavern's ceiling, the blight spread directly onto the spires. Dozens and dozens of narrow veins of rust spread over every pillar, snaking downward like ivy on the side of an old building. Even the floor was infected.

I glided downward through one of the gaps between the clusters, wary of a collision with the blighted pillars. It was dangerous flying. I headed for the edge of the cavern, where there was more space. The rock walls were less infested, as if they were of less interest to the invading rust. I latched onto a clear section of mundane mountain stone, digging my claws into the rock. Harlan clung to the spike of my mane.

"I think they are books of some kind," Harlan marveled. "Those pillars are filled with countless books. These huge things...these towers, they are massive, soaring bookshelves. There must be more volumes stored here than in the rest of Ni-Yota combined."

I hadn't seen a lot of human books—it wasn't the kind of thing people shared with dragons—but knew enough to recognize them. I'd seen the ledgers that the Keepers of Rolm scribbled in from time to time, but I couldn't read human script. The markings on the books were gibberish to me.

"Are these the so-called Oracles?" I didn't bother to disguise my disappointment at the prospect. "Towers and towers of books?"

"Perhaps. The knowledge held within books could be seen that way, I suppose. Particularly if there was so much knowledge collected in one place. I want to take a closer look."

I scanned the ground. "There isn't any rust-free area on the ground large enough for me to land. Only the cavern walls are relatively free from the rust."

"As if it came here to destroy the books themselves." I sensed Harlan's anxiousness to explore. "I'll jump to the ground. Just get me close."

"Flying in the narrow spaces between these pillars isn't easy."

"I'm sure you can do it." He tried to sound flattering, but I knew immediately it wouldn't work. Harlan sensed my hesitation. "This is important, Bayloo. Books may not dazzle on the outside, but the contents can be far more valuable than diamonds."

He might be right, or not. I couldn't read, so I wouldn't know, and that annoyed me. Still, we had come a long way. My mother had apparently dwelled here for some time looking through the knowledge held here. Something within must be as valuable as Harlan suspected. "Call out to me when you need to be picked up. Don't touch any book that has been tainted by the rust. And don't trip over anything."

I pushed off the wall, choosing the widest path between the pillars I could find. I had to tuck in my wings slightly and tilt, but I could do it. I made as close a pass to the floor as possible, taking pains to slow myself. Harlan leapt off my back, landing easily on his feet with aplomb as if he'd executed the maneuver a dozen times before. He didn't even look at the floor, seemingly unconcerned with the patches of rust that lurked around him. He gave me a wave of encouragement as I climbed back upward and latched onto the cavern's outer wall. I craned my neck around, doing my best to keep my eyes on Harlan, although the forest of pillars partially obstructed my view.

Harlan began his investigation by circling several of the book-packed spires. He peered at the shelves of each, looking upwards, his eyes squinting. He took an inordinate time staring at several of the volumes. I wondered if he could read the writing. Harlan wasn't from Illium or Ni-Yota, although it wouldn't have surprised me if he'd learned some of their writing sometime during his travels. He reached his hand out, his fingers dancing, as if he intended to remove the book from its resting place. I thought that ill-advised. The rust spun a thorough web through the vast library, seemingly tainting a vast majority of the volumes. No book seemed worth the risk. I gripped the rock tightly with my claws, partly out of frustration with this place. I had expected to find more than this when I set out across Illium. Much more. Could my mother really have spent so much time in a repository of human books? I couldn't believe it. There must be more. The passage that led even deeper into the mountain beckoned. We couldn't have come here for nothing.

Harlan kept dancing between spires. At one point he jumped over a patch of rust. A stupid risk.

"Whatever knowledge these books held is lost to us." My voice, hardly quiet to begin with, echoed through the vast chamber. "Let us continue our search. Perhaps there is something below that the rust has not yet tainted."

Harlan kept circling one of the pillars, his eyes fixed on the volumes. Eventually, he called back at me. "The books are ordered by topic, I believe. They must come from every land on Inkra. I recognize Kalish, the symbol language of Cern, and even the tactile print of Silloss, yet I can only understand the language of one out of every twenty volumes. This is the greatest collection of knowledge in all of Inkra."

"It was," I reminded him. "Now it is a graveyard filled with the rust."

"Bayloo, I might be mistaken, but this pillar here...it seems some of these books...their titles suggest that they speak of the world before the Cataclysm."

I scoffed. "They would be dust by now."

"These are copies of copies of copies." Harlan kept circling, wary of his treasure. "It may be they only pass down old legends. But even that would be something. There are so many." He gazed upward.

The particular book spire that held Harlan's gaze of adoration was within a dense cluster of pillars. There was no way I could've flown inside such a tight space even if I was inclined to do so. "Too bad I can't fly up to inspect them." I wasn't the least bit sorry about it. It wasn't worth the risk.

Harlan did another full circle of the tower. He reminded me of a frustrated cat. Then, he took a step forward. He looked down at the floor. The odd movement made it seem like he was dancing for a moment. Until he started flying. Well, not flying really. After a moment I realized the section of the floor on which Harlan stood had risen off the ground. It was attached to the book pillar in some way, although it lacked wings or any obviously external pulley. The floor section accelerated as it moved ever higher. Harlan jumped off, falling hard back onto the ground. He lost his footing, barely bracing himself with his hands before he planted his face into the floor. A patch of rust was a nose length from his fingers—a human nose length.

I roared at him. "You fool."

Slowly, Harlan lifted himself upright. The platform that had lifted him returned to the ground. Like the stubborn idiot that I knew him to be, Harlan got back on it. This time it rose slower, moving him ever further up the spire. He seemed to have learned the knack of controlling it. Something to do with his feet, I supposed. A device built for humans.

Harlan played with his new toy as I hung on the wall mashing my teeth. I wondered who had built this place—likely humans, since it was filled with their books. But the spaces had also been made large enough for dragons...or something else. I wondered how it had been built. As impressive as the spires and buildings of Changsha and Trishan were, they were nothing compared to this place. Even a dozen dragons couldn't hollow out a mountain. I supposed magic had to be the answer.

Finally, Harlan called out, "Let's move on from here."

He'd taken his sweet time. "You've seen all the books?"

"Only in my dreams. This place is a treasure without equal, but our time here is dwindling. Look at the ceiling."

With dread, I did. I stared at the rust. It looked different, although I hadn't taken that close of a look when I entered. I kept staring, dread growing inside me, until I saw what had finally prompted Harlan to leave his books: the rust grew. A new branch of blight sprouted from an old one. It was stretching before my eyes. Moving. Another vein of death. I didn't believe it was a coincidence. The rust knew we were here.

"Look at the floor," Harlan warned.

Chicken piss.

The rust wasn't just growing above. It was expanding everywhere. Slowly, but it was growing.

"I'm coming to get you." Unfortunately, the area where Harlan now stood was too densely packed with spires to make it easy to fly there. "Ride your floating floor tile to the top of that great book spire."

"The top?"

"Stay just below the rust on the ceiling. And be ready."

"You want me to jump onto you?" He sounded excited rather than frightened by this idea.

"Too risky. Jumping off a dragon is quite a bit easier than jumping onto one. Just ride up and hold still."

I pushed off the wall, gliding carefully in the confines of the cavern. I didn't know how fast the rust could spread, but I suspected it would be far faster than we could afford. I still didn't have the answers I'd come to get. There had to be more to this place. I swooped past Harlan, grabbing him in my left foreclaw as he stood gaping at the ceiling. He wriggled in my grasp. "Try to relax," I told him. "I don't expect a long trip."

I circled around, gaining altitude, before plunging down toward the gap in the floor, flying ever deeper into the archive.

The next chamber was almost identical to the one we had just left: more spires, more rust, more disappointment. Another portal, this one considerably narrower than the previous two, led still deeper. At least this wasn't the end of the archive's secrets.

"Those aren't books on these spires," Harlan observed.

Upon a closer inspection, I realized he was correct. These pillars were also shelves of a sort, but they held cubes of glass—or something that looked like glass but probably wasn't, since glass didn't occasionally flash scarlet and azure like these things did.

"We should investigate these items," Harlan said. "You can drop me—gently—on the ground again."

I scanned the cavern. "The rust is already thick here. There are only a few spots on the floor where even you might stand."

"It is worth the risk. If the books held one store of knowledge, these spires likely hold another kind. This may be our last chance to find out."

"They are tainted, same as the books."

"Not all of them. I have in my hands—which are being crushed by your claws, by the way—a volume that may contain words from before the Cataclysm. There may be even older, more precious knowledge here. We must try. This is why we came."

Without replying, I slowed myself, almost hovering in place, as I searched for a section of floor relatively free from the rust. The best spot seemed to be a slender rectangle located between two clusters of spires. It would be like flying into a tight valley—I wouldn't even have enough space to fully extend my wings. The alley between the pillars was long, but not wide.

"You see it?" I asked as I began my approach.

"I'm ready."

I gave my wings a single flap, then tucked them back into my body as much as I dared. The canyon of spires beckoned. It was going to be tight, but I'd make it. I was moving faster than I'd hoped, but I needed the momentum to carry me through until I could make full use of my wings again. I dropped lower, concentrating on keeping my course straight and my forelegs steady. I dropped even lower. I wouldn't be able to set Harlan down. He had asked for it. I opened my grip. Harlan dropped, landing on his feet. He bent forward, using a hand to steady himself as he hit the ground. I knew immediately that I'd made a terrible mistake.

The landing area had been too clean. The rest of the cavern floor had been nearly covered by the rust. Only that one place had a long, contiguous stretch of seemingly safe space, and it was conveniently located close to a patch of tempting spires. It was the logical place to land. The only logical place. Which meant it was a trap.

THIRTY

Harlan's choice curses confirmed my suspicion a moment later.

This was a trap. His realization, like mine, came too late. I had no idea how fast the rust could spread. Faster than I could get back to Harlan.

I couldn't stop in mid-air. I couldn't turn around in the valley of spires. I had to continue along my original flight path, passing through the narrow space. Once I'd cleared the towers, I swung to my left, circling back for a second pass. It wasn't until I'd completed my wide, arcing turn that I had a clear view of what had happened.

The rectangle of clear floor was all but gone, except for a narrow, irregular strip that a mountain goat would've had trouble maneuvering along. There was no sign of Harlan.

I calmed myself. The rust could not have consumed him so quickly.

"On the spire!"

I saw him.

He had jumped onto one of the columns. He wasn't high off the ground. Apparently, the rising tiles didn't work in this chamber, or they'd been contaminated by the rust. Harlan shattered several of the glass receptacles on the spire to form handholds, which he'd used to scale the tower. Clever, but it wasn't a sanctuary. The rust was on the tower as well. It was moving toward him, albeit slowly. The strange glowing glass seemed to cause it some trouble. Still, I only needed a bit of time. I beat my wings again, picking up the necessary speed, before tucking my span in tight enough to fit in the close quarters.

"I can't grab you!" I warned. "The rust is everywhere on those towers. You'll have to jump."

That sucked worse than pig feet. I forced myself even closer to the ground. Far closer than was safe, prudent, or sane. But I needed to be beneath Harlan if he was to have any chance to grab onto my back. I felt the rust surging beneath me. It might have understood my plan and was trying to counter me. The blight rose from the ground, building upon itself, forming mounds, like anthills of pestilence. I held my course. Harlan twisted his body toward the inside of the valley, preparing to jump. My eyes met Harlan's. His held far less fear than mine. The only thing I could do now was fly straight.

I didn't see him jump. I had to keep my eyes straight, and there wasn't any room to crane my neck. But I felt him. I dipped ever so slightly from the new weight landing upon me. My hearts were seized with a fleeting moment of cold panic. I didn't hit the ground, though. I was still breathing. I was still flying.

I came out of the valley of soaring spires, gliding at speed. Relieved, I spread my wings, beating them to propel me, gaining altitude. I wasted no more time in this place. I had Harlan. I flew down toward the portal into the next, deeper chamber.

A chill passed through me at the threshold. My blood ran cold, as if I'd suddenly been injected with ice, before restoring itself a moment later.

"Did you feel that?" I asked Harlan.

"You mean did I feel terrified at almost being consumed by the rust?" He laughed like a madman. "Or was it my jumping onto a flying dragon that you are referring to? By the balls of a leviathan, you bet I felt that, Bayloo." He cackled.

Harlan didn't get it. If he had experienced the cold that I had, if he had felt his blood freeze and his bones turn to ice for a fleeting moment, he wouldn't have been speaking of the mere mundane fear of flying through the sky without wings. What I had felt hadn't been fear. It had been something far more ominous. But as terrible as the feeling was, as awful as the moment of despair had been, the sight before me pushed it from my mind as easily as I forgot yesterday's sunset.

The new chamber held no soaring spires and no books. There wasn't any portal leading deeper into the mountain. Indeed, this cavern—the final cavern—was mostly empty. Except for the rust, which seeped down the walls here, as it had elsewhere. And except for the small island in the very center. The circular plot of land wasn't huge, and the lake surrounding it hardly looked formidable—Harlan could've swum across the still, black water with ease, if endurance had been the only test. Yet there must've been more to it, because at the water's edge, the inexorable expanse of rust halted. Across the lake, safe from the corruption that had tainted all the rest of the archive, was what I hoped to be a worthwhile end for my quest: there, a dragon awaited.

The beast on the isle resembled no other dragon I'd seen or imagined. It was wingless, its skin devoid of scales, smooth and pale as that of a human too long away from the sun, except for clusters of black dots around its neck and left eye. The dragon's eyes were closed, but they opened as I flew near, two orbs of milky whiteness perched upon a stub of snout. There was no emotion in those eyes, no thought at all. To look upon a dragon's eyes was usually to look into a portal that led within us. Our eyes were all that the human face was, and more. Yet not with this dragon. It was as if I looked upon a statue of a fellow dragon, one resembling me in general form, but devoid of the life force that beat within me. Even its gaze was wrong. It seemed to look in my general direction, but it didn't track my movement as I circled above its island.

"She's blind," Harlan observed.

Again, the human saw the obvious when I did not. I'd never contemplated the possibility of a blind dragon, for I'd never known of one without sight. It was as strange as one of my kind being devoid of wings. I also had no idea how he'd arrived at the conclusion of the dragon's gender, yet I didn't disagree. Even though I smelled no scent from my uncanny cousin, she moved with the fluid grace that was more typical of the female of my species.

I wondered how she had gotten to the island, to this strange place on the edge of the world, even though she lacked the power of both sight and flight. How long had she been here? I intended to find out.

I floated down gently, choosing a spot of land as far away from the other dragon as was possible on the tiny land mass that had no more space than the inside of my tower back in Changsha. The other dragon didn't exactly watch me, but she turned in my direction. I had no idea if she was a fire breather, but I didn't detect any indication of hostility. The moment I landed on the island, I knew I wasn't standing on rock. The ground here was metal, cold and hard, but made to resemble rock.

The other dragon moved closer to me. She walked slowly, each footfall deliberate. She was very old—ancient. Her claws were yellow, two of them broken. After a few steps, she halted. "It is forbidden to land on the Core." The dragon spoke Avian, albeit stiffly, with a dry scratch of a voice that reminded me of the squeaking metal door of my cage-cave back on DragonPeak in Rolm. Not exactly the warm welcome I was hoping for.

"The Core?"

"The ground on which you are standing is part of the Core. Only Anjins are permitted to cross the boundary."

The boundary. I assumed that meant the lake.

Almost the entirety of the cavern was infested with the rust. Indeed, the entirety of Illium was infested. I'd flown day and night to arrive here. And this dragon was annoyed that I'd landed on the only safe place in the whole cavern.

I was about to complain about my cousin's lack of reasonable hospitality, but a fierce shriek interrupted my words. I spun as quickly as I was able, gazing at the water, but not quite believing the new peril that had emerged from the depths behind me. I really had absolutely no luck.

It was a ghastray.

THIRTY-ONE

How had a ghastray gotten in here?

That was only one of the thoughts that flashed through my mind. The others were more primal and less pleasant.

Two more ghastray tails appeared on either side of the first, each forked and covered with deadly spikes. The trio of appendages twirled in the air, thin and long and poised to kill me. Initially, I thought myself facing a small army of ghastrays, until several hideous eyes and a portion of slick gray fin poked above the surface of the surrounding moat. I realized that the three tails all belonged to a single, massive creature. Like the dragon, this ghastray was some other breed, resembling its fellow predators but with distinct differences. Unfortunately, the unusual ghastray seemed larger and more formidable.

I spread my wings and showed my teeth to the poised creature. "I am Bayloo, a friend of Vengeance and an ally of your kind."

It was an exaggeration, of course. Vengeance and I were hardly friends (he might have a taste for my hearts), but this ghastray was really big and I didn't want to fight it. Too bad for me.

The ghastray poked all eight of its eyes out of the water, blinked each one, then snapped two of its tails at me, one from either side. I beat my wings, intending to take to the air, but I went nowhere. A debilitating pain surged through my body, a stabbing cold that originated in my chest and spread from my nose to my tail. The sensation came and went quicker than a flap of a hummingbird's wings, but it was enough to startle me, and to slow me. Fortunately, the pain didn't afflict Harlan. He flicked his dagger at the ghastray stinger as it approached from the left, the blade catching the ghastray precisely in the spot where its whip-like tail forked. The beast convulsed in enough pain to disrupt the stinger attacks. The creature's tails rippled like sails losing their wind.

With the respite, I lifted from the ground, sluggish but airborne. The ghastray quickly rallied from Harlan's attack. It made a noise less pleasant than a rusty dagger tip dragging on glass, as three forked tails raced toward me. I didn't have enough altitude to evade the attack. My wings barely seemed to work. The stingers had me. Until they didn't.

The other dragon shrieked, an abrupt, emotionless scream loud enough to send tremors through the water and chills through my scales. The extreme sound shocked me, but the ghastray actually froze at the cry, its stingers coming to a halt. For a moment this creature of death was as still as a painting. The cavern quieted.

"Hold." I realized that the other dragon was addressing the ghastray. "Begin perimeter patrol. Secure the boundary."

The creature obeyed. The ghastray sank into the water, disappearing into the murk that I realized wasn't quite water. It was too thick, too viscous. I wondered what would've happened if someone tried to swim across.

I glided back down to the ground. Not because I felt I was safe now, but because each time I moved my wings, I ached with a bone-chilling cold. Something else was wrong with me besides almost getting killed by the ghastray.

"I am surprised that it attacked you." The strange dragon spoke without emotion, as if discussing the weather.

"Is that an apology?" I felt Harlan stir with unease at my pointed question.

The blind dragon tilted its head, seemingly puzzled. "I made a statement of my current thoughts. An apology would imply that I had erred. I am not aware of an error."

Dragons were few, so it hurt me to immediately dislike one of my own kind, but sometimes I didn't have a choice. This dragon spoke with a tone of obtuse snobbery that I associated with nobility. "That ghastray attacked me. It's apparently under your command in some way."

More head tilting from the dragon. "The water guardian is intended to protect the Core. It has performed that function admirably for considerably longer than ever intended. You believe it was in error in attacking you?"

She sounded so smug.

"Attacking me is always a mistake."

The strange dragon sniffed at me audibly, not once, but three times, as if she were a hound and I a piece of meat that might have gone rotten. Her head tilting stopped. She stretched her neck so that her blind eyes were level with mine. "There is a reason why it is forbidden to land on the Core. You did so anyway. You broke a command."

"The rest of this place is covered by the rust. This was the only place I could land."

The blind dragon closed its useless eyes. After several long moments, she spoke again. "The rust...ah, yes, this is what the invasive is called in the world now. The rust is not a bad name. The invasive grows upon what others have made, changing it, ruining it. The rust is not a bad name at all." The dragon sighed, a sound of resignation and sadness. "There is nothing to be done. Punishment is not a cure. I shall attempt to provide knowledge in the time that remains, using what remains. Have you brought a contribution to the Core?"

"A what?" I asked.

"Additional knowledge to add to the collective whole," the dragon said, seemingly exasperated.

"Uh...I don't know." I considered what information I possessed that would be unknown here. "Humans taste like chicken."

The dragon wasn't amused. "That is an opinion. In any case, given the destruction of much of the archive by the invasive, there is no longer a point in accumulation of additional knowledge. I will share what I can, if only to preserve some small portion of it. What information do you seek?"

Was she now offering me what I wanted? "Who are you?"

"Ah, yes, introductions." The dragon drew herself upright. Something about the stiffness of her movement made me suspect that it caused her some pain. "I am the Core, although for the last three hundred years, visitors to this archive have come to refer to me as Oracle."

A faint hope dared to spark within me. "You are a dragon. This place is known as the Archive of Oracles. Are you the only Oracle?"

"Humans began calling this place the Archive of Oracles several hundred years ago, when the people of the land that would come to be known as Illium stumbled upon this place. I don't precisely know why they chose the name Oracle. But to answer your question, there is only one of me. There has only ever been one of me."

Finally, some emotion revealed itself. She was proud.

"So you are known as Oracle. Does that mean you know everything? Do you know the future?"

"I do not know everything. No creature can claim that. I once had all the knowledge that was brought into this place. That information can be quite useful in understanding future possibilities, but I do not know the future with certainty."

"What do you mean that 'once you had all the knowledge?' What happened to it?"

One of the dragon's legs trembled slightly. "It is hard to describe in this language so you can understand the process. So much has been lost to the inhabitants of this world, and even more will be lost soon." That sounded ominous, but she didn't elaborate. "You might say, when knowledge in the form of writing or certain other devices enters this place, I gain that knowledge as well. It becomes part of me. A far more efficient process than reading books or viewing the storage cubes."

It was an amazing revelation, a magic unknown to me or any other. "So all those books and other things, you've read them all?"

"Reading is one way to think about it. The knowledge flows to me. From the book and from the cubes in the towers in the chamber directly above this one. I am a vast store of information, the greatest in the world."

"But you no longer have the knowledge?"

The old dragon hung her head. "The rust, as you call it—when it damages the contents of this cavern, that which was destroyed is lost to me as well. It is as if I have a hole in my mind. I know something was once there, but can no longer remember what has been lost."

Harlan chose that moment to slide down from my back. He took several tentative steps toward the dragon-oracle. He, too, must have many questions. He had a quest, related to my own, but distinct.

Oracle opened her eyes again, although she never bothered to turn her head in Harlan's direction. "Ah, a human of Farlight." She didn't sound pleased. "Although of course, you are not really the same as the ancient ones."

Harlan gaped. "Farlight is the ancient term for our lost homeland."

"I told you, I have all the knowledge that has ever been brought to this archive. I am the center of it all. Even with the gaps which the rust has created, my knowledge is still vast. As to how I know you are a descendant of that place, well, I cannot see anymore, but I can smell."

Harlan frowned, as if insulted. "Smell?"

"Indeed, smell. You can best understand my words in this way: the original founders of Farlight changed themselves. They altered the building blocks of who they are to enable themselves to do certain things. Think of it as using limestone mortar in a castle instead of mud. They altered the very fabric of who they are. Some might say they improved themselves. The exact process is lost to me, and I suspect you would not have understood it anyway. The important thing to know is that the changes they made were passed onto their descendants, generation after generation."

"We are taught this as well," Harlan confirmed.

"Your glinting skin, which takes sustenance from the sun, enables you to consume less traditional food and protects you from harmful rays from the sun. But it also emits a distinct odor that I can detect. Even though you have apparently not cleaned yourself in some time, I still know I am in the presence of a human with traits of the original Farlighters." With arrogance, Oracle added, "No one except me would notice the smell."

I disagreed about noticing how Harlan smelled, but didn't say so.

Harlan still looked offended, his face tense. "What else do you know about how my ancestors changed themselves?"

I heard the anxiousness creeping into Harlan's voice. But I was losing patience. I had questions.

"Many things, but among the most important were immunity to most illnesses and alterations to their skin to protect themselves from the deteriorating external environment of this world. And, of course, they sought to increase their own power. For example, they attempted to give themselves the ability to integrate themselves with their various creations." Oracle paused, seeming confused. "The exact details are now lost to me, but I can say—"

"What of the curse?" Harlan interrupted.

"What curse do you refer to?"

"Our children. Why must one of our children die before their first year?" Harlan's voice was tinged by anger.

"Visitors to this place have reported the existence of a reproduction defect among the pure-line Farlighters; however, you are the first to actually enter the archive and confirm this condition." The dragon's blind eyes blinked twice. "I do not have enough information to answer your question. I can only share the obvious lesson this world has shown: tampering with the natural order of existence leads to unforeseen consequences. Or perhaps there are other reasons that cannot be easily explained. That is why it is a curse."

Harlan digested this answer with disappointment. I could see his mind racing. But I had important questions.

"Where is aurathorn?"

Oracle turned her head so those blind eyes almost looked at me, but not quite. "You are related to the guidelight dragon that came to this place with a request for similar information. The answer is that I do not know, as I am unable to leave this archive. I can only tell you what I told her: Once such a creation existed and was utilized. I do not know its current status."

More disappointment, but I didn't need Oracle to find aurathorn. I already knew where to start looking for that. "What is a guidelight dragon?"

"You are," Oracle said. "I believe the current term for your kind is an ember dragon, which is quite appropriate as well. You are the last flames of fading magic."

It was time to learn if this journey had been in vain: "How can the rust be destroyed?"

"That question has been asked repeatedly since what you now refer to as 'the rust' first came into being, a fateful event that precedes my own existence. The question has been put to me by both humans and dragons in direct form fifty-seven times that I am able to recall, including your own inquiry. In each instance my answer is the same: based on the information available to me, it cannot be destroyed."

THIRTY-TWO

I'd flown so long and endured so much to be so disappointed.

If this was how my quest was to end, I'd have been better off staying in Rolm to perish among the last of my kind.

Oracle's words soured the air. Another chill swept through me, but I was too numb to focus on that. I didn't want to accept what I'd heard. Neither did Harlan.

"It's not invulnerable," Harlan insisted. "The rust isn't everywhere. We beat the hollowings back at the River Tayo. We've defeated its servants, outmaneuvered it. It doesn't even cover all of this peninsula. It did not manage to cross your boundary. It can be defeated."

"I did not say that portions of the rust cannot be...cleansed. I retain the record of this being accomplished in the past, of course. But, as you can see, this past cleansing somehow failed for unknown reasons. It appears that while sections of the rust can be destroyed, it is insidious. It adapts. And so long as any portion of it remains, it will change itself and return."

"How was the rust cleansed in the past?" I asked.

"You do not know?" Oracle was obviously surprised. "Dragons cleansed it from the surface."

My breath caught in my chest. "Dragons destroyed the rust previously? How?"

"Balefire," the blind dragon said.

I knew the word. It was a legend, but apparently more than that. "There are still fire breathers, but no living dragon can send forth balefire. It exists only in stories."

"The other dragon who came here said the same. If that information is accurate, if balefire has truly vanished from the world, the rust cannot be destroyed. Balefire is the only recorded method of successful cleansing. It is the original purpose of your kind."

I didn't like the sound of any of this. I shivered. Maybe from the words, maybe from some other ailment afflicting me. "The purpose of my kind?"

"Dragons. Dragons were created to destroy the rust."

This kept getting worse. Yet it also explained that feeling inside me, the compulsion to fight against the rust. "Who...how...how were we created?"

"Dragons were created by humans who had previously failed in their attempts to destroy the rust through all other means available. The same humans who created me, and this archive."

Humans created us? I wanted to puke. It was too much. I was having trouble focusing. Trouble seeing, even. "I don't understand."

"Time grows short," Oracle declared. "You should know that the rust, as you call it, arose before what you call the Cataclysm, during the time of the so-called Lost World. It was insidious."

"Did humans create the rust as well?" I asked.

"Yes," Oracle replied with emotionless certainty, her head moving between Harlan and I but not quite looking at either of us. "That is known. The details of its creation preceded my existence and are mostly lost to me now. But it is known that other humans also attempted to destroy the rust for many years before they finally had no choice but to attempt radical solutions."

Harlan's face was as cold as I'd ever seen it as he listened to Oracle. I wasn't feeling well myself.

The dragon spoke faster than it had before. "As you are no doubt aware, the rust has the ability to change itself to ensure its own survival, and it did so. In the Lost World, it killed anything that attempted to restrain its growth." Oracle paused, her blind eyes shaking again. After several moments, she resumed the narrative. "The humans of the time unleashed weapons of such power, there is no current equivalent. Simply put, these weapons were of a destructive magnitude you cannot imagine. They melted the ice caps that once existed on this planet, raising the water levels and poisoning the seas so that the rust could not cross between continents.

"The creatures you call ghastrays were created in powerful machines known as creation forges, their purpose to patrol the seas, to destroy any ship containing the rust that attempts to cross water. In the air, the humans used their forges to introduce an element called AragonNull-285. Its name doesn't matter, nor does its function, I will simply say that this molecule was intended to starve and kill the rust while being harmless to all other creatures. It was created with the ability to adapt as well, so it would remain deadly. The rust, of course, adapted to the newly poisonous air as best it could. It attached itself to the ground at all times, drawing on resources such as silicon to counteract the poison. This is the reason the rust does not travel through the air or across the sea. Then, the remaining humans set about trying to eradicate the rust, one land mass at time. At first, the humans used the weapons they had available; weapons humans had developed for fighting each other. I don't remember them all, and it doesn't matter anyway."

I could guess the next part. "But these weapons weren't enough."

"The human devices worked at first. But these were the same weapons that had been used since the emergence of the rust. Even when new machines were developed—bigger, faster, and more accurate weapons—they were still all based on the same basic principles.

The rust adapted to them, as it does. Worse, it adapted to their users. It found a way to turn the weapons against their masters."

"The hollowings," Harlan concluded.

"I had not heard that term before, but I believe you are referring to the rust's ability to extinguish the consciousness within a living creature while preserving its motor functions. Hollowing is a good description." Oracle sniffed at the air once again. "War raged and the humans were losing. A radical new approach was needed.

"Among the countless humans who inhabited the planet, a precious few recognized that time was running out and they needed something new, something that the rust would not be prepared for. They devised a plan so horrific, so dangerous, that they knew even many of their fellow humans would oppose it, for it meant fundamentally damaging the world. Yet they believed it was the only way. They kept much of their intentions secret, revealing only a small part, that portion that would be least objectionable, for they feared civil war among their fellow humans. These humans have different names, as they were united only by their common purpose, but may be referred to as the Archivists, simply because they created this place."

Harlan nearly whispered, "What did they do?"

"They destroyed the old world. They remade it. Using a new device, a machine of unprecedented power which they placed above the world itself, they changed the nature of this world that is now known as Inkra. This great machine changed the fundamental laws upon which the old world and all the creations within it functioned. That which was once worshiped by many in the Lost World"—the old dragon dipped its head ever so slightly toward Harlan—"was gone. In a single stroke, the Archivists made all the weapons of the past and almost everything else useless. Then they unleashed their latest creations, weapons based on a power totally different than anything that had existed in the past. They intended to cleanse the world of the taint of the rust once and for all. These humans believed they acted for the greater good, to preserve their species and prevent the rust from destroying everything, but I may be biased."

I was so cold I could barely speak. "What did they unleash?"

"Dragons."

Even through the fog that was consuming me, this revelation stung. I stared hard at Harlan, then turned back to Oracle. "So dragons were supposed to destroy the rust. That has always been our purpose. That is why I have this...feeling inside me. This compulsion to fight against the rust. But we failed."

"That failure is now obvious, given current information. However, at the time, it was believed that the desperate gamble was a success. The seas became prison walls that held the rust in check. The poison air kept it from taking to the skies and being unstoppable. The new dragons swept across every land, their breath not just incinerating the rust but actually setting it ablaze, unmaking it. Ten thousand dragons, infused with the power of the reformed world, using their breath as weapons. In the new world, the only energy was magic. The great fire that the dragons could unleash was designed such that rust itself became the fuel that accelerated the cleansing fire —an inferno of unmaking that would burn for as long as it was in contact with the rust."

I snorted with disappointment of what was lost to my kind. "Balefire."

"Yes. The rust adapts, but not to balefire. It is the fundamental energy of the new world—magic itself. It is order that reduces all else to chaos. This made it much more difficult for the rust to adapt. Perhaps, given centuries, the rust has become immune even to balefire. But at the time, the dragons, aided by other creatures—birds that could sense the rust, great worms that burrowed underground, even insects—the dragons led the new attack successfully. At their forefront were the so-called ember dragons. Creatures of great intelligence, designed to improvise in battle and created to act as conduits between the new magic and the other dragons. The ember dragons' power made the balefire unstoppable. Together, the dragons wielded a magic fire that was the greatest power of the new world. Your kind turned the tide of the war. The rust fought back, of course. It tried to adapt. It turned some of the dragons into its servants. But the dragons were stronger. After three years, the surviving humans finally believed they had succeeded in eradicating the rust forever. Your kind were no longer needed, as far as the Archivists were concerned."

I thought about my race's history with humans. I could guess what happened. "The humans didn't just thank us, did they?"

"After their supposed triumph, the humans set about undoing what they had done—they set about the task of trying to erase the new, temporary world they had created, so they might restore the old one. This archive was created for that purpose, as was one other, so the past's knowledge could be restored. Their creations, the dragons, who then numbered in the tens of thousands and were led by their magic-wielding ember kin, resisted. That possibility was anticipated. The humans released a pre-designed virus that had been created at the same time as the dragons—a disease to which dragons were uniquely vulnerable. It decimated the new creatures of this world, as it had been intended. However, like most human creations, it wasn't perfect. A small portion of the dragon population, including several ember dragons, somehow survived."

"So we fought the humans. My kind versus the humans." I looked at Harlan. "Is this why some humans hate us so much?"

Oracle answered. "The war was terrible. The ember dragons in particular had been created to wield magic. To the surprise of their creators, these dragons were more adept at controlling magic than ever anticipated. They could manipulate the new framework of the magical world that had been created. With the humans' old knowledge and power now useless, the creation forges no longer operative, the remaining humans were no match for their creations. This was the true war. It raged twice as many years as the fight against the rust."

Dread enveloped me. "How...how did that happen? The humans would've been careful with their virus and with their magic. They would've been so careful to make sure their creations didn't turn on them once again."

Oracle dipped her head again. "Your instincts are excellent. There is no definitive data that reveals how any dragon survived the virus. It should've been impossible. They were literally created to die. Additionally, even if the virus failed, dragons were created to be infertile, to mature quickly, and to die within five years, when their creators expected the war to be long over. But that didn't happen. However, an ember dragon kindly allowed me to examine her in exchange for access to this archive, so I do have some additional information on this matter."

An ember dragon. It had to have been my mother. "It was the rust, wasn't it? The rust helped dragons mutate. Helped us survive."

"That is a distinct possibility, although I do not understand how. The enemy of my enemy is my friend. It is an old proverb in human literature. The rust may have come to the same conclusion."

"Which side won the war—human or dragon?"

"There are almost no records within the archive of that time. The facts suggest that neither side won, as both humans and dragons currently exist. However, it was during this time that the created-moon, Rima, was shattered, which may have been the rust's ultimate objective all along—to destroy the new power that was its greatest threat."

I shivered, a terrible shiver. I'd never been so cold. "Rima? From the sky?"

"Rima was created by humans."

It seemed impossible. "How...why create something like that?"

"Rima was how the Archivists changed the world. Its purpose was to harness energy from the sun and channel it to the world below. It makes some things not work, and replaces it with a new reality. You might say, it is the source of all magic." Oracle paused. "Apologies, I am missing pieces. I also have no direct information as to which side damaged it. However, the result was the catastrophe that came to be known as the Cataclysm. It altered the environment on the planet far more than ever intended, swallowing many of the lands, including the island known as Farlight. Rima's destruction also stripped the mightiest of the ember dragons of much of their power, which may have been the intent all along. With Rima damaged, balefire faded from the world. But Rima survived, and still functions. With neither their old devices nor their new magic available to them, humanity scattered, falling from their former glory. Dragons, too, had been decimated by the virus, and only a few ember dragons remained. Each of the lands of this world went its own way. That is the world of today. A world that is too weak to resist the rust. It has been patient. Now it returns."

"After so many centuries, where did it come from?" I asked.

"That information is not available to me."

"Do you have a guess?"

"It is not within my nature to guess. I can eliminate possibilities. The first scenario that I project to be highly unlikely is that the rust continued to exist anywhere obvious on the surface of this world. The humans and dragons were very thorough. The dragons' sole task, as well as that of other creatures, was to hunt and eradicate that taint. The nature of a balefire reaction is that it will continue to destroy until the ordered substance which it attacks is gone. It is unlikely the rust simply was missed."

"So where did the rust hide?"

"The logical explanation is it hid somewhere that humans never imagined. A place dragons could not find. Somehow, it found a place to deceive both the creators and the dragons."

"Where?"

"Again, there is no definitive information."

"Anyway, you were made when these Archivists made the other dragons?"

"Yes, humans made me in a creation forge. I am the last of their original creations, and the last of my kind." She sounded both proud and mournful. "My creators knew they were going to destroy the old world, but hoped that destruction would not last forever. They collected as much knowledge as they could and placed it here. Their old devices for recording information would be destroyed in the new world to come. They gathered books, but even the millions of volumes they collected and the cubes they placed here would not be enough to re-create what had been lost. No one would be able to absorb so much information. So they made me. A librarian. A teacher. Now, I am Oracle."

"But your creators never came back for you."

"No, they did not. This place was forgotten for centuries. But eventually, the humans of Illium found it. They had no knowledge of the world that preceded this one, and no interest in re-creating it; even if I could've helped them with that, I would not. A few humans came to dwell here, bringing in more books, which was the medium they were comfortable with. They re-copied the old, preserving the records. Even new knowledge was added—including knowledge of the force you call magic. For example, information about the power of the artificers of Illium, who could move the ground itself, and perform other acts of power, all came here. My nature is to gather an understanding of all things, so this was acceptable."

"So, you have all the knowledge that remains of the old world and some of the new one. You must still know so much." My vision faded, but I pushed on. I needed more from this Oracle. "You can help us save this world."

"I will not live forever. No creature lives forever. In fact, I will not live much longer. Soon, this place, too, will be gone. The Archivists have failed." I thought I detected a whiff of regret from the old dragon.

"You mean the rust will destroy this place? It has not so far."

"It invaded the archive years ago. There was a fight, which was inevitably lost. But at first the hollowings, as you call them, did not destroy. They searched, although their method of doing so was unlike those of humans or dragons. They were looking for something, a greater understanding of this world. Perhaps even of magic. They were quite interested in such power in their strange way."

That sounded ominous. "Did they find what they wanted?"

"I do not have that information. But, approximately one year ago, the situation changed. The hollowings departed. The rust pushed through, contaminating everything. Spreading everywhere."

"But you have managed to keep them from this island, this place."

"Yes, until you came."

Uh-oh. The chill came again. Tremors racked my body. "Me?"

"You are infected. You brought the infection of the rust to the Core. That is why the ghastray tried to kill you." She sounded only mildly resentful.

The cold. The terrible cold. "I. Am. Infected?"

"I can smell the rust on you. It must have touched you."

I thought furiously. The terrible truth hit me quickly. I knew when it had happened. Harlan had jumped on my back as we fled the rust's trap in the cavern above. I'd lost altitude, dipping too close to the ground, close to the mounds of rust. Some must've scraped my chest. I looked down at myself.

The rust was all over me.

THIRTY-THREE

"I've destroyed everything."

The guilt within me was almost as terrible as the rust on me. This great archive, which had stood for hundreds of years, would meet its final end because of me. The knowledge that could've possibly saved the world would be lost. Because of me.

"It was inevitable," Oracle said, still without apparent emotion. "I estimated that my own death would have otherwise occurred within eleven years in any case, even if the rust hadn't found a way across the boundary before then. Eleven years is very little time relative to the span I have lived."

"This place was the last hope for finding the answers we need," I said, my tongue thick with despair as my body failed. It was as if all of me was leaking away. "If not here, then no place. The world is doomed. The rust will spread everywhere."

"I don't have the information necessary to prove or disprove your statement. No being knows the future. However, you are correct that the rust enveloping the world seems a distinct probability."

I stared down at myself. I could barely stand the sight of my own putrid scales. "How long until I become a hollowing?"

"Based on my observations of the humans that dwelled here and became infected, once approximately forty percent of your exterior surface area is covered, your own life force is extinguished and replaced with...whatever it is the rust replaces it with. However, my sample is small and based entirely on humans. Dragons may react differently. You may have a bit more time, or less time, but not much. It spreads quite fast."

I wasn't going to become a hollowing. "You can't do anything?"

"Beyond what I have told you about balefire, the information of how to destroy the rust is not in this archive. At least not anymore."

I looked at Harlan. "Then I must die. I will not become a hollowing."

He looked stricken as I spoke the words. I hardly felt happy about the situation, myself. "It is not over," Harlan said through clenched teeth. He spun toward Oracle.

"Bayloo's mother came here. She spent years here."

"The other ember dragon? Yes, she wished to understand the rust. She even learned to read the human books, believing that might have held some hidden knowledge that I was unaware of. Not the case, of course."

"She believed there was a way to stop the rust. She left Ni-Yota and went to Rolm for a reason. She must've been searching for something," Harlan insisted.

"The dragon did not share her theory or her plan," Oracle said. "But she did leave here believing there was a way to stop the rust, even if she did not share it with me."

If my mother had hope, then it could be stopped. Even as my own death loomed, that thought stirred something within me. The answer was in Rolm. I didn't want to die. I had too much to do. Oracle didn't know how to get the rust off, or wouldn't tell me. All the knowledge of this place was useless in this moment. I just needed the blight off me.

The foulness of the rust was worse than the pain. I forced myself to stare at my tainted scales. Even as I stared at the ugly crimson moss clinging to me, it grew. Or maybe I imagined the horror. Its presence was a weight, like a huge block of ice compacted into a miniscule space, pushing at me. I wasn't sure whether the rust would envelop me or crack my scales first, but one or the other seemed dauntingly certain. My hearts raced with each other in a competition for which could pump fastest.

I raised the claws of one foreleg. I needed to scrape the rust off of me.

"Bayloo, don't."

I heard Harlan as one hears birds chirping in the distance on a new morning. I paid the sounds no mind. I extended a claw. The rust had grown as I dithered. It had to come off.

A pain almost as terrible as that of the rust startled me, both for its sharpness and its location. I realized someone had dug a blade into my flesh, prying into the narrow gap between two of the scales on my hind leg. To my shock, it was Harlan holding the blade. My blood surged.

"Clear your head, Bayloo. If you touch the rust with your flesh, even your claw, it will certainly spread there." Harlan held his dagger in front of my eye. "You are still conscious because it is on your scales only, for now. That won't last."

My claws trembled, aching to get the plague off of me. "It cannot remain."

"I'm coming. I'll use my blade to scrap it." To Oracle, Harlan asked, "Will this work?"

The strange dragon hesitated—a first. "I do not know. There is no record of someone trying to scrape the rust off a dragon's scales with a dagger. I doubt it will be successful, based on the resilience of the rust, however."

Harlan nodded as if Oracle had said something useful. "Just keep steady."

I lowered myself to the ground, rolling over to lie on my side. Harlan quickly positioned himself beside me and went to work like a swordsman carving up his enemy, wielding the dagger as ably as I might use my own tail. I watched as though my life depended on his efforts, because it did.

The rust resisted. The blade hit it, but it didn't budge. It didn't come off. It was no petty fungus to be scraped away. Harlan clenched his jaw. "This may hurt."

He pressed harder, digging the blade into my scales, attempting to slice off the layer of my armor that had been afflicted by the blight. I wouldn't have thought a human blade capable of such a thing, but Harlan's little dagger pressed through my scales. It probably hurt as he had warned, but the freezing cold of the rust numbed any other sensation. Harlan peeled off a piece of my chest scale, then another, and a third. Sweat dripped down his forehead. My legs trembled, but not from fear, although I was afraid. Something else was happening. Harlan worked ably and quickly, but the rust was quicker—it had spread to a foreleg and the edge of my neck. This wasn't going to work. Harlan probably realized it as well. He tried to cut quicker. I heard his heart beating ever faster.

"Harlan, it cannot…"

"Shut up, Bayloo."

He kept working. His hands moved as fast as any human I had ever seen; even my old ryder, Brindisi, would've been impressed. He moved so intently, he didn't notice the danger to himself, but I did. "It spreads, Harlan. See your blade."

He ignored me.

I was going to die. I wasn't going to let Harlan die in a vain effort to save me. I wiggled my body. Harlan wasn't expecting that. Instinct made him pause, if only a moment. Our eyes met. Dragons communicate most effectively that way. Harlan was no dragon, but I saw what was within him: Fury. Desperation. Sorrow.

"Drop your blade. There is no point in you dying as well."

Finally, Harlan gazed at the ruin of my chest, then at his blade. The rust had spread over the metal. It was already crawling down the tip along the sharp edge toward the hilt and his hand.

"This dagger was Darrien steel. Unbreakable." Harlan said it with contempt. But still, he didn't drop the blade. Instead, he gazed at my chest. I did as well. My time grew short. I shivered again.

"This is where my journey ends, Harlan Dor. But it need not be the end for you. Drop the blade and climb onto my back. I'll return you to the surface, at least."

Harlan clenched his jaw in frustration. He didn't move for several heartbeats. Then his eyes found me. He looked upward. "Perhaps there is something outside that may aid you." He said the words, but he must've known there was no hope. Even if such a miracle existed, I had no time to find it.

"Let us go now," I told him wearily. "While I might still have the strength to carry you safely from this place. You will be at the edge of the world, stranded, but perhaps fate may deal more kindly with you than I. You have a knack for the sea. There may be a ship about, for humans once traveled to and from this place. A hidden moorage. A way for you to return to your sea. You must carry the knowledge we have gained from this place. Travel to Rolm. There is a ryder there; her name is Bethy Rann. If she is alive, tell her this tale, and she may aid you."

Harlan stared at me as if I were mad. Perhaps I was.

Cold racked my body. A fate worse than death awaited me. I didn't want that. I had one final escape to make. "You say you always have a second dagger, do you not?"

Harlan didn't move.

"I need you to make sure I never become a hollowing. Do you understand?"

Harlan didn't blink for several long moments. Then his eyes changed. He dropped the tainted dagger. "You idiotic dragon. Let's get out of here while we can." Harlan scrambled onto me. It was not a moment too soon. My limbs numbed. "Fly, Bayloo. Back out. Get out of here while you still can."

Stretching my wings was an agony worse than any wound, but I did it. It might be my last flight. I wasn't going to fall. At the very least, I was going to get my companion out of this rust-infested place where I brought him. Although I wouldn't be able to get him back to Ni-Yota, much less back to his home and his wife, as we'd once planned. It seemed a distant promise, although it hadn't been made very long ago. With my jaws clenched, I forced my wings to move.

At first, they didn't. They felt as if they were carved of stone, a costume piece attached to me rather than a part of me. I forced myself to remember the sensation of flight. I tried again. The muscles in my chest trembled, but I finally lifted off the ground. I didn't look back. I couldn't bear to see what I had done. Knowledge more precious than any single life, lost forever.

I struggled to keep my course steady, heading back up through the portals, past the great caverns of spires and books. I wobbled, but Harlan held fast to me. I made it back to the great passage through which I'd entered. I could've walked on the ground the rest of the way, but I was a dragon—I wanted the remainder of my life to be in the air.

I flew Harlan through the last tunnel, punching into the open sky with a burst of speed. It hurt, but it was worth it. The wind greeted me. The light shone on my scales, driving the chill from my bones, if only for a brief, precious moment. I banked around the mountain, intending to deposit Harlan on the narrow shore of the Silla Peak. The tide had risen while we'd been inside. The salty waves crashed against the white mountain. As places to die went, it wasn't that bad.

I set down on the rocks, so close to the water that the waves splashed onto my claws. "You have that second dagger?"

"I have it, my friend, but it won't—"

I had no more time for platitudes or sentiments. The rust covered the entirety of my chest. "Just get off my back, careful not to touch me. Your blade is too short to reach my hearts, so you must thrust it up inside of my mouth. Stab upwards. It must be a mortal wound, the blood—"

"Bayloo, shut up."

"If the rust claims me, if I become—"

Harlan kicked me. It didn't really hurt, but it surprised me. "I said shut up. You aren't going to die unless you can't bring yourself to stop jabbering. I didn't know dragons were so fond of spouting nonsense."

A wave of dizziness swept through me. I was confused. Was this Harlan's final jest?

He got to his feet while still on my back, then jumped, landing in the shallow water at the edge of the peak. "Open your eyes, Bayloo. The answer is right in front of us. The blight spreads across land. Across mountains, rock, even steel. Anything solid. But not the sea. It reached Silla only because of the land bridge, and only with great difficulty."

It was true, but I still didn't get it. My mind wandered. I saw at least two Harlans.

"The seawater, Bayloo!" He was nearly screaming. "Remember what Oracle told us: the ancient humans poisoned the water against the rust. It can't survive in the sea. Dive into the water, my friend. Swim for your life!"

HERE CONCLUDES BOOK 3. If you enjoyed these pages, I once again humbly ask that you leave a review on Amazon. Bayloo's journey of magic and mystery continues in Book 4 of The Remembered War, *A Dragon's Burden*, available on Amazon. If you haven't already gotten your free copy of *A Drugon's Doom* by signing up for my mailing list, you should do so now at www.robertvanenovels.com. Once again, thank you for coming along on this quest with me.

Get A Dragon's Burden HERE

Made in United States
Troutdale, OR
08/13/2024

21985511R00155